books by
Peter De Vries

forever panting

forever panting

by Peter DeVries

little, brown and company

boston toronto

T 05/73

The author is grateful to Alfred A. Knopf, Inc., for permission to
quote from "Sunday Morning" by Wallace Stevens from *The
Collected Poems of Wallace Stevens.* Copyright 1923; renewed
1951 by Wallace Stevens.

Library of Congress Cataloging in Publication Data

De Vries, Peter.
　　Forever panting.

　　I.　Title.
PZ3.D4998Fo　　　　813'.5'2　　　　72-10989
ISBN 0-316-18187-0

*Published simultaneously in Canada
by Little, Brown & Company (Canada) Limited*

PRINTED IN THE UNITED STATES OF AMERICA

More happy love! more happy, happy love!
For ever warm and still to be enjoyed,
For ever panting, and for ever young.
　　　　　—Keats,
　　　　　　　"Ode on a Grecian Urn"

part one

part one

one

Or look at it this way. Psychoanalysis is a permanent fad. A vogue here to stay because it tells an old story in a new way. I mean the traditional conflict between flesh and spirit, as viewed by the Christianity now supposedly outmoded, isn't likely to ease up because we have scrapped the notion of sin and now speak instead of the ego and superego between them riding herd on something called the id. It's the same keg of nails any way you open it. "Id" isn't just another big word, either. Far from it. It's a good solid term for a solid fact, man's creature half. I even have a name for my own id, whom I see as a rather hairy party inhabiting me as a lodger a house, a primitive of rudimentary appetites for the satisfaction of which he clamors day and night. I call him Blodgett.

Theological concepts of the soul-body Siamese twin-ship are valid, and also helpful are the man-beast figments of mythology — up to a point. The "spirit" is guilty of evils often worse than the bestial variants it presumably bridles, while, alternatively, the animal within us may be a decent sort, to be "trusted," say, with women the ego might abuse. A better image for this whole duality might be two men handcuffed to each other in a railroad diner, neither of whom is readily identifiable as the detective or the prisoner. In fact it was from just such a pair that I got the name for my own personal id. What I at first, watching from a nearby table, took to be the detective turned out actually not to be him at all but the crook, doing his damnedest, on one last ride up the river to Ossining, to be mistaken for the dick, putting on airs as he tucked away his final public lunch, or glancing nonchalantly out the window at the passing scenery.

I wasn't straightened out until I heard the other snap at him, "Two pieces of pie is enough, Blodgett." Blodgett. I immediately seized on the name for my id, the satyr half of me, embodiment of the pleasure principle, of the often unaccountable urges of the unconscious (such as the instinctive adoption of this very moniker for itself), that gross but also cunning Doppelgänger to whom I remain manacled for life, as much his prisoner as he mine, till the end of the Journey, when we reach that bourn from which no traveller returns, or glue factory.

Blodgett, then, overeats and oversleeps. He drinks too much. For Blodgett I wait with a patient smile till he has guzzled his visual fill of girls undressing on the beach, lowering my eyes again to my book (a biography of Berlioz) when they have at last wriggled free of their dresses and robes and disposed their buttered limbs upon the hot sands, or run squealing into the sea. Blodgett is a coward and a sloth. He lolls with his head back on a crowded bus pretending to be asleep, thus excused from focus on a bony hand known to be grasping the strap above him, that of a poor old woman shifting, in the other, a brown sack of groceries. He twitches his foot in his shoe to recover the sense of an aching blister there, reminds himself that he is dog-tired after a hard day's work and must get up early tomorrow . . . A lurch of the bus swings the standees like a row of suspended beeves, the old soul all but landing in his lap, her wrinkled cornucopia threatening to empty its contents on his head: a can of Dinty Moore beefstew, say, a six-pack of Schlitz, a tin of Ajax with which to scour up after so meagre an evening meal. One rises and yields his seat with a doff of his hat. One's better nature revealing itself at last? No, Blodgett again, executing his gallant gesture for the benefit of a dimpled Corybant of twenty or so, whose smile is his rotten, sensual reward.

One thing about your id, of course, is that he has never heard of psychoanalysis — of himself. Blodgett doesn't know from personae. Dem are jawbreakers fa Chrissakes, gimme a break, willya? And as for self-alienation, the new wrinkle, you know, people out of touch with themselves, or parts of themselves, modern, duh, fragmentation, one thing and another? Knock it *off* fa Chrissakes, his head hoits. He's not out of touch with this, that or the other, he's just not gettin' enough lately. Simple. "The withness of the body," said Alfred North Whitehead, likewise a stranger to Blodgett. That means not only the official lusts and itches of the flesh but its other passions as well: greed: anger: hatred:

even violence, senseless or otherwise. Blodgett is the beast that sleeps in all of us (dozing lightly in some) .

You have your own Blodgett. You know him of old. He wants that last chop. He begrudges the guest the end of the wine you graciously empty into the guest's glass. For his part we would never dine, but only eat. He belongs to the Gashouse Gang, who waylaid you on your way to the liberry, where for all of him the books would be walls of dummy spines, swinging open to reveal stores of bourbon and Scotch. If genuine volumes, he wants only to know where the porno is stashed.

Now he has really torn it, or threatens to. I can scarcely believe it even as I set it down, but Blodgett — we strike straight to the heart of our story — Blodgett has taken a shine to his mother-in-law. I mean my God! Oh, not his real one, that we might put past even him, but rather his wife's aunt, who raised her when orphaned at the age of six, now staying with us for a bit. Still, it is an untimely maggot, as a wayward whim is termed in one definition, capable of eating its way into the vitals of a household, according to another. Classic mythology has its legends for incest; whether there are any embodying this pretty convolution on an in-law basis I don't know. Perhaps, the ancient world having been so uncannily comprehensive in its roster of archetypes.

I first began to suspect what was going on one morning when I was taking a bath. Blodgett was lolling in the tub, luxuriating mindlessly among the warm suds, that voluptuous evocation of the amniotic womb, our first waterbed, when, hearing my mother-in-law astir in the breakfast alcove below, I suddenly remembered I'd dreamt about her during the night. The dream itself teasingly escaped me, for the time being. I could recall a dream from which I'd awakened toward morning shouting anti-government slogans. Perhaps the two had something to do with one another; psychologists tell us that in any given night we work on the same psychic problem, in this case possibly that of a man's natural sexual anarchy rebelling under tribal restraints, as embodied in this or that regional or temporal "administration." I free-associated in hopes of clarifying this tenuous connective thread. The White House, my own lower-case white house here in Connecticut, the Oval Room in Washington again, egg-shaped, the inscrutable and plenipotentiary Mother Yolk (oh, good God!), the plenipenitentiary institution of marriage . . . The dream continued to evade such heavy-footed intellectual sleuthing, like the soap in the tub slipping free of my diving fist, yet unmistakably hovering just beyond the grasp of recollection, by steady application perhaps to be coaxed into full recall, like the village of Combray from the crumb of madeleine dipped in lime tea . . .

It was as I walked into the breakfast alcove where she was sitting over her second cup of coffee that the dream sprang completely back into my head.

You yourself are doubtless familiar with the way in which people are subtly altered when we have dreamt about them — especially those of the other sex. Some powerful alchemy operating in the deeps of slumber leaves them changed for varying periods of time in our waking state, as though what we have imagined actually happened — the more chimerical, the more vividly "real." Cardinal to this phenomenon is the illusion of intimacy we retain in regard to the dreamee, whether inimical, or, as in the case of my mother-in-law, amorous. It was a strange woman bathed in a distinctly erotic light the sight of whom, sitting there in the ruffed orange dressing gown worn in the dream, brought back, as she looked up smiling from the morning *Times*, every last detail of the dream itself.

The house was on fire, but instead of telephoning the fire department I was reporting the conflagration by mail. Or we were. Together. It was with the sense of utmost urgency natural to the occasion that, I seated with pencil and paper at this very table, she standing over me, we collaborated on a draft which would not disgrace us as an example of epistolary English, however much in haste it must be framed. The letter sealed at last, its flap pounded fast with my fist, we were then seen charging down the street by Buick to the nearest post office, I in my pajamas, she in her nightgown and robe, clinging to my neck as we rounded turns with the insane speed of fire engines themselves.

Passing her now on my way to the kitchen in what for want of a better term we call real life, I drew a deep breath, so as deliberately to inhale her perfume. Blodgett again. While I myself resumed the burden of interpretive association. House warming, like a house afire, burning passion, no hurry to put it out, hot stuff still at her age, some resemblance to an old flame . . . ?

"That's a nice peignoir. I've always liked it."

"Oh, thanks, Stew."

A humming in one's head, like that made by automobile tires shooting over a steel-grate bridge. Still and again more Blodgett — Barney Blodgett? — for whom I squeezed some orange juice in hopes of keeping him quiet while one's cerebral centers were given half a chance, carrying it over to the table where two soft-boiled eggs and a baking tin of good steaming cornbread awaited one — handiwork of the other dream principal. She was pouring one some coffee from a silver pot she had given us, flotsam of a wrecked marriage of her own, securing the lid with a crimson-nailed finger. I drank back the cold orange juice, a taste enjoyed with special gusto by Blodgett though I was amused by his wonderfully fraudulent pinky lifted in midair — an attempt to be mistaken for me as clumsy as those of the prisoner to be confused with the dick escorting him up to stir on the Penn Central for God knows what bungled heist.

She was laughing. Half an octave of loin-tickling tintinnabulation. "Then that's what a peignoir is," she said, fluttering out an end of the skirt. "I was never sure."

"That's right, Aunt Ginger," I said, pinning small hope on the absurd vocative as a counter-stimulant. One had climbed out of his very bath in need of a cold shower. She was a ripe, handsomely hewn woman of forty-something, only ten years my senior who am that much her daughter Dolly's senior. One was in the middle. Leaving the elementary, alimentary Blodgett far behind, really giving him the slip, I set my drained glass down with a smack and sang out:

"Complacencies of the peignoir, and late coffee and oranges in a sunny chair, and the green something of a cockatoo upon a rug mingle to something . . . mingle to dissipate the holy hush of ancient sacrifice."

"Come again?"

"Wallace Stevens."

"Who he?"

"Poet. Who was also an insurance executive. Right up here in Hartford." I jerked a thumb upstate, looking at those white teeth in a rage who could only, like all men, grit his own at the sexual stimuli by which we are remorselessly bombarded. It's a state of affairs I think of as Gnashville. We live there on a public street, a train, at the office. Tongues of flame, licking the . . . mother-in-law's tongue . . . Merciful God!

"Yes. Well, poetry has got to be snow that began in the gloaming, or either the French storming Ratisbon, for old Ginger."

"Nonsense," one said, though seizing on the "or either" solecism as an ardor-dampener. As an anti-aphrodisiac don't you know. One was going to need a lot of them in the days ahead if this was the way the wind stood! Also performing that office was her report of an evening spent at a Pinter play, nearly the whole of which she had sat wondering what in God's name had happened to the prompter. Here the memory of one's wife's response was also of substantial help as anti-aphrodisiac. "Mother. Those are pregnant. Pauses. They are not. Actors. Forgetting. Their lines." Oh, indubitably that provided an aptly timed mental cold shower, what? That douses a bloke's errant yen, eh? One would need plenty of those before we were out of the woods.

"It was the Hartford Accident and Indemnity. Can't you just see him spinning those exquisite nuances among the fire insurance policies?"

"No."

"Dictated some of it to his secretary, so they say."

"It doesn't sound typewritten. What you just recited. It sounds handwritten."

She was one of those women who manage to be both dizzy and intelligent. The scatterbrained woman is not the worst company in the world, if it's brains she is scattering. When I said I considered "Sunday Morning," the opening lines of which I had just been spouting, a modern landmark scarcely second to "The Love Song of J. Alfred Prufrock," she said she had never read any of Prufrock's stuff either, but intended to, having heard a lot about him. Swell. Wayward fires being quenched now? Oh, quite. Mess of clinkers in a minute, leaving a chap to get on with the work of the world. Everything proceeding as hoped, *her* pinky going up with the coffee cup, local women's club, meets on alternate Tuesdays to hear papers on the poetry of Alfred Prufrock and the novels of Humphrey Clinker.

"It's the name *of* a poem, by Eliot," one says, and instantly feels a twinge of compassion *in one's very loins.* You mean Blodgett cashes in on one's *spiritual* side? You got it, Mac, as we'll all damn jolly well see.

She gave her characteristic burst of self-deploring laughter, revolving a finger at her temple in happy acknowledgment of a screw loose as she declared that living under this roof was like a perpetual free extension course. The bracing note of goofiness was also emphasized by a momentary enlargement of blue-gray eyes already great enough, as she stared across the table at me while awaiting some reciprocal response of my own. When I obliged with a comparable burst of Eliot, she took off on a lecture of her own about the moderns as she had found them. "Everybody famous is obscure," she stated soberly — then, hearing what she'd said, gave again her "goofy" laugh.

She did on the whole quite well in a household admittedly arcane as measured against her two marriages, one ended in death, the other liquidated in

Nevada. Always a little wary of one, the bolt of laughter nervously in readiness. "Marriage is a give and take," I had said one night when I'd had too much to drink, then begun to eat my necktie with my eyes crossed to rule out any implication that my wits were wandering. At the party in question, where she'd been present, there had been a long and pedantic discussion of German wines other than the Moselle on which I'd gotten three sheets, and after hearing names like Graacher Himmelreich, Piesporter Michelsberg and Maximum Grunhauser Von Schubert bursting in air, very little less to my consternation than to hers, I threw in that I had recently tasted an excellent Liebestod '69. She had remembered it, and tried to get some for my birthday. Lamb. At that point her daughter had stepped in and said I was "carrying this sort of thing too far." I had pointed out that her mother had been an innocent bystander; it was the snobbery of others I had undertaken to prick (one woman there had been upstaging us because she had been mugged on Montparnasse) and it had never occurred to me that anyone would take seriously what I had said, except for the grim silence with which it had been greeted by the attendant connoisseurs. In the end one resolved the dilemma by saying she had misunderstood; what one had said was Liebfraumilch, as best one had been able with by then probably slithering speech. Three bottles of that arrived at the house in due course.

A man sometimes spikes his fancies for women who populate his daydreams with other daydreams that are "sequel" antidotes; for example those that conjure up the spectre of conversation at breakfast, as the price of the night's revels — like the hell to which one consents in a pact with the devil. And perhaps lunch and dinner as well, an eternity of such meals the payment. I now spun cautionary scenarios in which she and I must sit discussing the poetry of Prufrock over a bottle of vintage Liebestod, of which there was no variant in the cellar; she jabbering from strength to strength with the superior verbal stamina of women, oneself a defeated hulk at last, no longer caring, his brain rotted, his will sapped, his strength gone.

There was one bug in this stratagem. The delinquent fantasies (requiring the damper) were often as not quickened *at* breakfast. This was food for thought all right enough, what? God save this house.

"There may not be a straight line in all the cosmos. Space itself is curved, you know."

My auxiliary relative having expressed such gratitude for the privilege of living among people from whom she could learn, I gave unstintingly of myself, in this case explaining why water runs down a drain clockwise on one side the equator, counterclockwise the other. "It's something to do with the contrary magnetic pulls of the North and South Poles. Could I have a little more coffee?"

"That's not true."

We all of us look ten years older when differed with. An inadvertent gander at oneself in a lurking wall mirror confirmed this hypothesis. Also our scalps may twitch when contradicted, as you may have noticed on the part of us actors using this technique to register a reaction at being balked (among lesser craftsmen, accompanied by an involuntary movement of the ears). Watch for this at the movies.

"That whole thing is a fallacy," continued my pupil. "Water runs the same everywhere. The difference is just in the way we're looking at it. Our *down*, as we watch our bathwater draining away, is people in Melbourne, Australia's *up*. But the water is running the same way. Know how?"

A noncommittal grunt as one extends his cup to be refilled, the cup emitting a nervous cackle against the trembling saucer. "Grrmblk," one's throat says, clearing itself.

"Contrary to the rotation of the earth."

"Shun of the earth," one chimes in in the nick of time, womanwise. The cup cackles, though perhaps a shade less unstably, as one sets it down before oneself. One's dumbbell mother-in-law continues.

"Do you understand what I'm driving at?"

"Well . . . " I bent to retrieve a napkin fallen to the floor.

"Here. Let me show you."

Hauling her chair around to mine, for we were again at morning meat, though this time fully clothed and not in the dishabille in which we'd plunged down the di Chirico street to post the letter reporting the fire, and seating herself beside me, she began to draw some complicated diagrams on a sheet of paper. Circles of arrows flowing in countervailing horizontal orbits (think of a wheel and its rim turning in opposite directions) represented the rotation of the earth and that of vorticizing drainwater (the latter of course simply an illusion created by the former), while arrows pointing up and down (through the wheel's hub) indicated the lines of vision of hypothetical bathers in the Northern and Southern Hemispheres respectively, watching their bathwater run off. "What spins clockwise to one will appear as counterclockwise to the other. But it's really all the same."

"Where did you get all this?"

"Bill Truepenny. My first husband. Dolly's real stepfather."

"Where did he get it?"

"Brazilian coffee planter." Going down the drain also was a concept hitherto held by one as gospel truth, invoked by the sound of the speaker at her own ablutions overhead, a Monet nude materializing above and slightly to the left of one, not half an hour ago, stored up as grist for table-talk when at last she would descend. "They got into an argument over it just like ours here, and the planter, Bill was visiting him there on business, explained it all to him. People never get this straight. There was a movie about it with Clark Gable once." She chewed the rag. "He finally got it, but not until his own head had been spinning quite a while itself. I was on the verge of cutting out paper dolls, and I don't have a mind like a steel trap, till suddenly it all became clear. Know how?"

"I have no idea."

"Lie down."

"I may have to."

"No, I mean here. On the floor. We're going to move you 'down under.' Off you go to Melbourne, Stew, to become this bather there. No, wait. First north, standing up. Get up."

I rose from my chair and watched her cross the room in peach-colored slacks and a roughly matching velours jacket, all but envying chaps whose mothers-in-law conform to the archetypal ogre begrudged house room when threatening a brief visit along lines laid down by humorous folklore. She returned with a round black ashtray, with which she continued the elucidation.

"The earth rotates like so, right? Water like so, the other way." She slowly revolved the ashtray in her two hands in what was, to us looking down at it with our heads together, a clockwise fashion. "You've got that? O.K. Now then. Down you go to Melbourne. Stretch out flat on your back so that you're looking *up* at what I'll keep turning *exactly the same way.*"

A man answering my description lay down between his mother-in-law's legs, with which she straddled him as much for convenience as to insure the accuracy of the demonstration. A foot thus solidly planted on either side one's chest, she asked, continuing her maneuvers and peering down at one past the ashtray, "Now which way does it seem to be going?"

"Counterclockwise."

"You see?"

"Ah, yes. I see it all now. I see everything. I grasp it all of a sudden as one grasps something hitherto needlessly, and fruitlessly, wrestled with in the belief that it was complicated, when all the while it was utterly simple, hitting you as a sort of apocalypse," I said, hoping all this was not too abstruse for the poor woman.

"Well, I wouldn't know the geometrical term for it. You're better versed in all that than I am. But it is simple. So there you are."

"Keep turning it. Just double-checking something. It *is* clockwise to you topside there, in Connecticut?"

"Oh, yes."

"And to me the reverse down here in Melbourne, sure enough. I'll be damned. Don't go away."

"So anyway, that's it. Now you've got it."

"Wait. One more thing. It just now occurs to me — an interesting point I think you'll agree — how does water behave *at the equator?*"

"Oh, I never think of that."

"Brazilian planter never brought it up, eh?"

"I suppose . . . Let's see. I suppose in any case you're not absolutely on a level with it, as a bather I mean, but still north or south of it, if only six feet."

"Ah, yes, I suppose that's it. Tell me, have you ever been below the equator? I mean personally?"

"No."

"Neither have I."

"I've always wanted to go."

"Me too."

"Good morning. Well, what are you two doing?"

"Good morning, Dolly. I was explaining to your mother this business of water seeming to drain in opposite directions here and the other side of the world. You remember we were discussing it at the Wusdatts' the other night. Come lie down here and we'll show you."

"No, thanks." Dolly stood smiling down at me, her arms folded. "Well! *You* certainly talked in your sleep last night."

"Oh?" I rolled over onto my knees, them climbed to my feet. "Anything . . . ?"

"Nothing I could make out clearly, but you sure went at it, even for you. Something about the ego and the id."

"I can explain everything," said your correspondent with a laugh of relief, "but some other time. Let your mother run through this other business once more for the benefit of late comers. Would you" — I closed my eyes and took a turn on two wheels — "Mother Ginger?"

Shudders of horror went through everyone, killing that experiment aborning.

The hydraulic lesson mastered, the problem was forgotten. Then at some point in that day, I was suddenly in doubt as to which way drainwater *does* in fact run here topside, and there was half an hour or more of collective hanging over tubs and wash basins and even the kitchen sink, watching — with no real progress toward a solution. The whole thing had got to be re-examined. Sometimes it seemed to go one way, sometimes the other, occasionally just straight down, blaach, couldn't get a performance out of it nohow, responding to no law but that of gravity. Sometimes one of us thought it went down clockwise, another that it took the alternate method of self-disposal, or I should say *the* other, because Dolly soon tired of experimentation, lacking the spirit of scientific enquiry that left her mother and me kneeling, together at last, beside the tub in her bathroom. So it shouldn't be a total loss I prayed for strength. Because Blodgett again sank to the occasion, revelling in the blisses of scented proximity.

Now, within the main flow, as you probably know, tiny individual waterspouts will often form, and trying to discern the direction of their dizzy spin during the few seconds of their existence as they vanished under our eyes was crazy-making. Such materializing miniature twisters drift lazily one way or another within the larger maelstrom, if any, while themselves whirling at insane speeds, like tornadoes racking Kansas, or a man's blood, where, similarly, anarchy prevails and havoc is wreaked in obedience to binding laws, what? Would one watch in paralytic horror Blodgett throwing the pass one had in fancy often imagined? One might go suddenly and completely to hell. The potential was there.

"Get some Worcestershire sauce."

"How do you mean?"

"That's how we finally settled it. Bill and I. I remember now. Or ink. Anything to discolor the water as it goes down. The way you stain a laboratory slide."

"I'll be right back."

Dragging Blodgett by the hair, I tramped down the stairs into the kitchen. Rummaging unsuccessfully among the condiments for the Worcestershire, and finding an ink bottle in the library to be empty, I settled for some Angostura bitters obtainable at the bar.

"It won't be long now, as the monkey said when he backed his tail into the lawn mower."

That she too might be wearying of research was evidenced by her having taken advantage of my few minutes' absence by changing into the black leotard in which she did the daily round of exercises that kept her in such commendable fettle, her figure something a woman half her age — in other words, a girl — could have taken pride in. So sheathed, she knelt once again beside me at the tub, in which your correspondent drew the fresh modicum of water necessary to the experiment, his senses reeling. She pushed the plunger beneath the taps that raised the drain plug, over which I held the opened bottle of bitters in readiness. "There's an eddy! Quick, get it," she said. I shook out several drops into the spiral, through which they were instantly sucked out of sight in a definitely counterclockwise direction.

"There, that settles it," she said, springing lightly to her feet and giving the shoulders of her leotard a hitch.

"Let's just double-check the basin. Remember I had the impression it was the other way there."

She laughed. "The spirit of research has certainly got a hold of you. It's bound to be the same if the rotation of the earth is what does it. Law of cause and effect."

"That's been scrapped, haven't you heard? Eddington and that crowd. The universe is unpredictable. Chance. The *I Ching* you like to throw yourself. Even Jung gave that his blessing."

She had by now, shaking her head, run a basin of water, over which we again watchfully hung. An instantly appearing vortex whirled the bitters away in an unmistakably clockwise direction. The reverse of their behavior in the tub. She looked at me open-mouthed.

"Well, I'll be damned," she said.

"We'll all be damned," I thought to myself as I made for the bar, there to put the bitters to more urgent purpose in a stiff old-fashioned, gulped at before its own whirlpools, clattered up with the muddler, had quite subsided, unlike those still roiling one's misbegotten guts. Sipping it more leisurely, I moved to the bottom of the stairs. I listened intently a moment. Audible only was the faint tattoo of Dolly's typewriter from the distant back room where she wrote her plays. This was presently mingled with the rhythmic thump and thud of calisthenics one should have been at oneself, as one's equatorial middle reproachfully attested.

That night Dolly and I made love as though we were an endangered species, and, oh, how gratefully one sinks into that sweet membraneous vortex of which the descent into sleep then seems the soft continuance, till

the bliss and the peace together are one funneling
whirlpool through whose vanishing point one is sucked
at last into the black, blind, blessed drain of Night.

"The id was born in a barn." Now one was explaining *that* to *both* women. We were at dinner. "The id
was born in a barn. The ego says, 'Were you born in a
barn?' A slightly higher level, you see. Highest of all is
the superego, who says he was born in a barn, yes, on a
clear winter's night in which sheepherders traipsed
down from the surrounding hillsides, to the accompaniment of overhead music, to do homage, like the three
others, famed for their sagacity, who arrived on camel-
back, bearing gifts."

"Oh, *I* see. Sort of lower, middle and upper class,"
said the mother-in-law.

"Well, they're degrees of refinement, or rarefaction,
yes. From the undifferentiated impulses coming steadily from the id, to the ego and superego as ceaselessly
sorting them out according to principles of morality
and conscience which, at their highest level, are capable of being mythologized into religions. Like I say."

Dolly spoke up.

"But isn't the conscience supposed to be partly
'unconscious'? Which is where the id has its being.
Doesn't this thing we call the conscience have one foot
in each department, the conscious and the unconscious? Isn't that what the psychoanalysts claim?"

"I'll check into it," I said with a twinge of married
vexation, rotten Blodgett at the same time running an
eye, not to say mental finger, over the other woman's
sunkissed shoulder and down along her ripe bare arm.
Oh, *natürlich.* Oh I shouldn't be too hard on him. He
was restless, bored in a seminar into which he had

inadvertently blundered, totally oblivious to the rack and strain of the, duh, dichotomized sensibility — mine alone to endure! "It isn't as though they're layers in a cake, even one standing on its side to get rid of the 'higher and lower' idea, but ingredients in a psychic batter in which identities have merged while remaining operative as vital forces. Are there any other questions?"

"No, really, it's a hell of a nice conceit, that about the barn, Stew. I may even steal it for my play. That scene, you know, where Blicksome is trying to explain some fine point of psychology to this dumb broad who can't understand what she's actually exemplifying in her conduct? Blicksome lectures away as he stumbles about the bedroom peeling off his clothes. The woman is a patient of his. You remember my Dr. Blicksome the gynecologist? Has all the spoilt suburban women?"

"The miscarriage trade."

"Wow! Can I have that too?"

"Heppy seffy," I said, employing a locution that was one of her mother's more reliable ardor-dampeners. Ma herself spoke up.

"So what are the id, the ego, and the superego?"

"I have no idea."

We left it that way, or would have were it not for other elements ceaselessly vexing our home waters. Forces far more ungovernable than Blodgett's crude turmoils were at work here. These could be contained — indeed quite handily were, as you have seen. But temptations often more insidious than those that assail the flesh address themselves to the ego, and that being the arena into which the struggle was now to be carried, we see me next as my official self, one Stewart Smackenfelt, who, even his ego threatening to capitulate, might have to fall back in the end on his very superego — that one who as you know must keep on the ego the same snaffle the ego keeps on the id. I visualize mine as vividly as I can Blodgett, though without any name. I think of him as a sort of Peter O'Toole type. Just the last word in civilized cool; always a bit of all right; with that easy persuasion born of a conscience clear as consommé. Reedy, handsome, given to pinstripes, sky-blue eyes. A shrewd sideliner while yet in the thick of the human scrimmage. Him you might have heard at a recent party summing up a conversation having, by chance, to do precisely with this whole problem of the Apollonian control required over Dionysian man. It was very recently indeed, when the wringer through which all our household was still to be put had only just stopped its predestined grinding. Splash of brandy in hand, a lean leg slung loosely over the arm of his chair, he remarked with his slashing smile: "In the end, you know, I suppose we can only say of domesticity what Churchill said of democracy. That it's the worst system in the world, except for all the others that have been tried."

two

Smackenfelt's sanity hung by a single thread: the belief that he was Edwin Booth. Unsupported by this delusion he would have gone quite mad, and even with it was at best precariously balanced; often violent.

Naturally his being Edwin Booth gave him access to many another identity as well. Rosmersholm, Willy Loman, Marchbanks, Lord Illington were only a few of the characters, not that he had played onstage, necessarily, but among which he all the more freely shuttled in everyday life. Nor need he stick to his own sex. In the croaking contralto in which he had done Lady Teazle in college years, he would sometimes order groceries over the telephone; as Huncamunca, plead for fuel oil in the bitter weather. He did a peevishly cerebral, existentially offhand Hamlet very much of our time indeed, articulating the soliloquies with an urbanely implied *Weltschmerz* as he plowed the remote corners of the house in the laudanum hours. If the classical and the naturalistic represent the two basic schools of acting — chewing the scenery as against throwing your lines away — Smackenfelt could — now get this — Stewart Smackenfelt could *throw* chewing the scenery *away*. Wallace Stevens' self-disclaiming rhetoric was another example, Dali's mock floridity still another, of this devilishly suave, insanely difficult art. In real life, being married, he was of course the Socrates each man plays to the Xantippe of his choice, for it is a fact universally acknowledged that a husband is the most ridiculous thing on earth, except for a bachelor.

Now he was marking time as a priest in a piece of schnitzel nearing the end of its Broadway run, finding relaxation in the impersonations he polished up for the amusement of friends at parties, as well as to hone his craft on. He awoke suddenly toward dawn of a Sunday morning late in August absolutely certain that he must add Boris Karloff to a "suite" of impressions he was working up, in which he recited "Ulalume" as each of several stars would do it. His nerves were a can of worms, but he was keyed to exhilaration pitch with the need to get up and audibly try what he could mentally hear with astonishing clarity, there in the bed whose sheets looked as though they had been caught in an electric fan.

Gingerly removing himself limb by limb from his oblivious wife, like half a nail puzzle autonomously extricating itself from the other half, he put on his robe, stole along the passage toward his mother-in-law's room and down the dark stairs, chuckling haggardly. His bare feet had memorized the staircase enough to avoid without conscious thought the steps

that creaked, as feet will, giving him the sure touch of
the spider, who is never entangled in his own web
because he knows, and therefore treads only on, those
strands free of the adhesive fatal to callers, who do
not. Thus with the glues of flattery and rancor do we
trap friends and foes in a cunningly doctored gossamer
of our own weaving. The madman is finally enmeshed
in his handiwork, thrashing to his destruction in
that silken heap of the mind because he has lost track of
the system. Smackenfelt trod softly, adroitly, with infi-
nite inaudible cunning, till he had reached the parlor,
where, switching on a light, he began pealing out the
famous hokum as Boris Karloff might:

> *"The skies they were ashen and sobah*
> *The leaves they were withering and sere . . . "*

He shook his head in disbelief. Karloff to the life. By
God, he was ready for an audition with the Kopykats,
the dazzling troupe of mimics who swept everything
before them on television. The bit certainly went
straight into his parlor repertory. The upcoming Wusdatts' bash being an anniversary, he would be expected
to do a turn there. His "The Boy Stood on the Burning
Dock" (there was a ship strike, not a soul aboard) had
gone down quite well. He growled out another snatch
of the claptrap:

> *"It was down by the dank tarn of Auber,*
> *In the ghoul-haunted woodland of Weir . . . "*

As he strode about, going from strength to strength
with the new number, his appreciation expressed in

further haggard incredulous chuckles, he heard his wife's voice overhead:

"If you're going to walk around the house in the middle of the night doing imitations of Sydney Greenstreet, at least go down in the basement where no one can hear you."

He marched into the vestibule, where, looking up, he could see her leaning over the bannister, her face mashed with sleep, her hair hanging in disheveled strands.

"Of who?"

"Sydney Greenstreet."

"I see."

She smiled encouragingly. "There's no mistaking it. But I mean . . . And my mother . . ." With rather too much craft of her own, she jerked her head in the direction of the bedroom, where, judging by the hollow whisper to which her voice had dropped, the woman would be lying stricken with at least three fatal diseases, of none of which she was aware but any one of which could carry her off by morning.

"Hold it."

This could not be let pass. An example must be made, retribution exacted. His eyeballs disappearing dangerously upward into his skull, he stalked to the foot of the stairs like a monster unmistakably the product of a demented scientist messing about in his laboratory with secrets best kept from mortal men, something begotten of a successfully cajoled bolt of lightning upon the body of an infernal machine. For extra measure, he turned the lids of his eyes up until they were hideous pink glops. Finally, so that there could really be absolutely no doubt — no excuse for the sort of thing he had just been subjected to — he graduated the lisp. Yes, perhaps it could do with a little more of that, for Karloff.

> *"The fkies they were ashen and fobah,*
> *The leaves they were withering and feah,*
> *It waf night in the lonefome Octobeh,*
> *Of my moft . . . immemorial . . . yeah."*

But she was gone, padding back to bed trailing muttered repetitions of her plea that he bear in mind others were trying to get a little shuteye around here.

But that was dead now. She had murdered shuteye.

He marched downcellar precisely as bade, leaving the upstairs in darkness and settling with a generous brandy in a sprung lawn chair in a corner of the basement between the furnace and a row of packing boxes that bore signs of slowly sea-changing into a man's retreat, or "den." Supplementing the chair into which he sank were a piecrust table, a magazine rack principally stuffed with back copies of *Variety* and *Show Business*, a standing ashtray retained as a souvenir of college days, and a bridge lamp recourse to which was scarcely needed in the blinding light from a naked bulb dangling from a cord overhead. The chair, one of the folding canvas kind, had been brought in for repairs never so far forthcoming, so that it sagged dangerously under an occupant of any weight. In fact his bottom was within an inch of resting on the cement floor.

Suddenly famished, he crept back upstairs and fixed himself a Blodgett, as he called the sandwiches improvised in Dionysian fits of appetite from odds and ends in the icebox. He had in the course of this nocturne donned a small tweed cap, of oatmeal weave and garnished with a half-belt behind, found to be ideally suited to training a tumbledown forelock (not unlike the conductor Leonard Bernstein's) which the epicene director said would be right for Father Plight, the priest he was playing in the piece of schnitzel in town, a tormented cleric of at once rumpled and fastidious temperament. Now, as he hurled meats and cheeses every which way into the poppyseed roll, he suddenly plucked the cap off and scaled it across the kitchen. Like a Frisbee, it circled in a wide arc toward the stove, where it landed upside down in a kettle of beans set out to soak overnight, for the morrow's soup. Indifferent to its trajectory after leaving his hand, he seized a water pistol from a table — one used for dousing flareups in outdoor charcoal broiling — and blew his brains out. "Jesus Christ, but Sydney Greenstreet." Again snapping off lights in his wake, he made his way back down to the basement with the sandwich and a can of cold beer.

Seated once again in the lawn chair, he reviewed the drawbacks of matrimony as an institution. Biting hungrily into the Blodgett and gulping the ravishingly icy beer, he felt his spirits rise a little. The incident must be put in perspective. He must forgive her. He gave his Sydney Greenstreet chuckle — a double note very much from the belly, "Hm-hm," the mouth closed and its corners of course turned downward. Sinister rather than maniacal, quite in character with the gaze with which he now raked the opposite wall.

Smackenfelt had once read for a part in a television picture about a cunning German scientist who had, in 1945 when the jig was clearly up, quick-frozen three hundred handpicked Nazi officers in keeping with a conspiracy hatched in Berlin, the cream of the German army, for thawing and release at a time that seemed propitious for another try at world dominion. He had painstakingly groomed himself for the role with a script the producer had let him take home, so that by the time first rehearsal was called his diction was flawless. He had spent the intervening ten days polishing his jawohls and his achtungs, hideously gargling all the gutturals as he strode about the house with a monocle screwed into one eye and clicking his heels to a fare-thee-well. Then when he got to the studio he learned he was not to play the scientist at all but one of the three hundred stiffs to be put on ice for the kraut apocalypse. There was only one quick shot of Smackenfelt, already freeze-dried, being slid out of sight in a glass drawer in the specially built mausoleum where the elite meat was to be stashed until Resurrection Day.

"You were great," his wife reported to him on his return from the kitchen, for he had stepped out for a beer and missed himself on the tube.

"You couldn't see me breathe?"

"Not a bit. You always watch for that, you know, when somebody's playing dead. It's hard to do. You were swell. Look good in uniform, too."

In principle, Smackenfelt had remained the wizard of the laboratory. He alone knew where the stiffs were kept. A score of the Junkers were bricked up here in this very basement, behind walls he could see from where he sat wolfing the Blodgett, laughing maniacally now and again, "Mmbahaha," some forty or fifty in an abandoned ice house on the edge of town which the Party had secretly purchased from a local traitor named Hoffman, the First Selectman yet,

"Mmbahaha," the rest systematically disposed about town in the coolers of butchers also sympathetically in cahoots mit der Vaderland, "Oh, mmbahaha . . . Oh, dot's briceless."

More than relenting, he smiled affectionately now at Dolly's booboo on the stair, remembering, with the amused tenderness the recollection always evoked, the first thing he had ever heard about his wife-to-be. "She's a dingaling, but awful cute," Cordial Schenck, their matchmaking mutual friend, had said, in arranging the blind date destined to land him here, staring at a wall lined with bricked-up Nazis. And there were more at home like her, what was more, the mother's belief that a mendicant was a liar being a mere sample of her ability to tap hitherto unsuspected resources in the English language. She said, "John Jock Rousseau." And a dish into the bargain! While one courted the daughter, wouldn't Blodgett already then secretly have liked to whack off a slice of the mother. Not so baroque by today's standards, such a troika would have been either; that already permissive yesterday had been only a few years short of the finally emancipated today when anything goes. One had in the end been a brick, though, plumping for nothing but marriage. With the sexual freedom prevailing, Dolly had told him right out that she was a virgin, making no bones about it, though prepared to waive ceremony with the first man who suited her down to the ground, as Stew Smackenfelt indubitably did. An incident in the restaurant to which they'd repaired for a sandwich after a movie had shown him, straight off on that blind date, to be the ticket.

The four had shoved along to The Piccalilli Pot for a thick hamburger and some lip from this rude waiter. A

dispute had arisen between him and Dolly over something Smackenfelt didn't clearly understand, her half
of it having been waged while squeezing his hand hard
against her flank under the table, a highly distracting
element in itself. Since the evening's first sight of her
walking toward him with her hips swaying like a bell,
her breasts under her silk blouse going "Quelk . . .
quelk," he'd been a seething vat of hormones. When
the waiter scurried away, after some rejoinder for
which apparently he should have been horsewhipped
to hear the others tell it, Dolly stuck her tongue out at
him, while still pressing Smackenfelt's hand. On his
other side, Cordial's friend, a Persian-born importer of
eastern stuffs named Bah, turned and gave Smackenfelt a look which asked why he wasn't going after
the beggar to demand an apology. Wasn't one a man?
Well, the fact was that under all this sexual excitement
one's Johnson was up; so that proving one was a man
had really better wait a moment till one was in a less
virile state. Rising to one's feet just now would have
scared up more embarrassment than, huffing off with
the secret fairly bursting out of one's toolbox, one
could manage to resolve.

This Bah had been rather a dose. Throughout the
few moments of time stalled for, by means of hanky-
panky with the napkin, inarticulate threats growled
while truculently assessing the kitchen doorway
through which the offender had vanished, Smackenfelt
was aware of Bah continuing to give him the "Four
Feathers" routine via the ripe-olive eyes steadily fixing
him under the bushy brows. His Johnson problem at
last settled, Smackenfelt rose and marched toward the
kitchen door, his fists clenched for the mouse he really
wanted to hang on this Bah (who in addition to the no

doubt inherited import business had some connection with the Stock Exchange, where characters like that made a hundred thousand a year and tips) .

Smackenfelt's reduction to idiocy was completed by his stopping on a dime at the kitchen door, on a corollary of this whole chivalrous principle according to which it would have debased his lady's cause further by being carried into the scullery regions of this eatery. So he stationed himself resolutely before its flapping portals to await the miscreant's return. ·He rehearsed a few possible openers. "Look, Mac, I don't know what it was you said, but I'll thank you to take it back . . . Civil tongue . . ." Half the diners were by now closely watching this attempt to avoid a scene. At the end of three or four minutes the lout still hadn't emerged. Peering on tiptoe through a pane in the upper part of the door, one caught a glimpse of him more or less hiding between a stove and a refrigerator. He had obviously sensed the spirit of Smackenfelt's pursuit, and was worriedly consulting with another servitor, who obviously persuaded him to take his chances by coming out, which he did, pale and full of apologies. Which Smackenfelt duly transmitted to his injured lady. "He says he knows now dat he shouldn't oughta said dat," he reported, delighting Dolly as much with his mimicry as with all the knightly bustle. She was in raptures over his impersonations, which she said were "absolutely true, right on the button every time." Within a week he had a handsome cabinet-size photograph of her, signed "With Love." A "portrait study," it showed her seated with her elbows on a tabletop — now get this — her palms together and her cheek inclined to the back of one hand, wearing an expression of aristocratically musing detachment. Thus had the photographer caught the essence of a dingaling who stuck her tongue out at people, to say nothing of stretching her mouth with a finger hooked into either corner while articulating spiced pig Latinisms such as "Uckfay ooyay, otherbray."

Smiling to himself at all this, forgiving her of course, he dozed off in the chair toward dawn.

He awoke with a start to find Dolly standing there, the dripping cap in her hand.

"No wonder you've got insomnia. All you ever do is sleep."

He gave her his Barrymore leer, as though accusing her of trafficking in paradox when she should be up in the kitchen fixing his breakfast. But that was where she had found the cap, evidently in the soup, which was where her discovering it now squarely landed him. He had been a fool not to have followed its orbit after having given it its freedom. In a twinkling she had recovered the advantage, as martyr. He was now the offender, she the injured, the exact reverse of their positions at last encounter. She had snatched the grievance from him by means he had himself provided.

She now emphasized the insecurity of his position by stepping over and slapping the wet cap against the side of the storage bin. Quite vehemently, again and again, mesmerizing his stare. "Hmfwarmpf, hmfwarmpf" went the soggy garment against the planks in remorseless succession.

"My mother sets beans out to soak, to make your favorite soup. And this is what you do. This is the thanks she gets."

"I know."

It were best to admit unworthiness in this area,

rather than brazen out some show of self-justification.
He flung out a hand, a wordless gesture subtly communicating guilt but also urging mature acceptance of the
absurd, the idea that a touch of surrealism in everyday
life — say a bit of motoring apparel discovered one
morning in a kettle of legumes — may be precisely
what one needs to start off another round of existence
so remorselessly humdrum, so bottomlessly, irreduci-
bly, plain out-and-out goddam uckingfay —

"She makes you grape ketchup. Of which you hadn't
even *heard* till she came to live with you. Now a
favorite of yours."

Another canard. It was his favorite condiment in the
sense that "Home on the Range" had been Roosevelt's
favorite song: he couldn't stand it. Thanks to some
misunderstanding, the result perhaps of having murmured an indicated compliment on first tasting the
oddity, an example of culinary mixed media, he found
it on his table as perpetually as the chief executive
heard the ballad played over the radio or on special
occasions honoring him. Free of it only in the death
mourned in final, numbing deluges of its banal
rhythms.

This was not the moment to protest, however, or
touch on the parallel with F.D.R.

"I didn't realize what I was doing." As though one
had hacked one's relatives to bits and left the parts
evenly distributed among lockers rented in the major
metropolitan railway terminals!

"Of course you realized what you were doing."

"I did not. You don't think for a minute I'd throw
my cap into it on purpose, do you? I flung it across the
kitchen and didn't look to see where it landed. I'm
sorry it landed in the soup of your mother — who's not

the one gelding husbands around here. I mean Sydney Greenstreet!"

"You don't imagine I thought for a minute that's who you were doing? You really ought to be better able to take a joke than that, Stew."

"Still, it's a kind of crack that hits a man where he lives — his profession."

"Well, I'm sorry. Come have some breakfast. I'll just leave this here. I think it can go into the washing machine. And we won't tell Mother about the soup. Much less throw it out. We'll simply eat it."

She beat the cap a few more whacks against the storage bin for good measure, preparatory to setting it down on top of the washing machine. She started back upstairs. He brought her up short on the bottom step, as smartly as if he had lassoed her across the intervening distance.

"Who was it?"

"What?"

"Who was it, if not Sydney Greenstreet? That I was doing."

She bent to pick up a magazine off the floor and throw it onto a pile of waste paper, pausing a moment to tidy the stack. She cleared her throat somewhat hoarsely.

"Charles Laughton."

Rolling his head in the negative on the back of the lawn chair, his lips compressed in a tight smile and his eyes closed, he soundlessly but elaborately articulated the word "No." Pantomimed it rather than said it: "Nooo."

"Basil Rathbone."

"Nooo," again inaudibly articulated while he burrowed well down in his grievance, possession of which

had now been fully recovered, like a momentarily fum-
bled football. The tide was again running in his favor.
It was now doubtful who was punishing whom. So his
imitations all sounded alike, did they? Had this unify-
ing thread, so to speak? This pattern marking them the
work of one man, the artist's signature as it were?
Well, that cross she would bear with him. That she
herself knew she must pay for her booboo on the stair,
as the criminal knows he must pay for his crime, that
she would not go hence till she had paid the last
farthing, was clear.

"Could you do a little more?"

"I'm afraid that's out of the question."

"Edward G. Robinson? Tallulah Bankhead? You
sure know how to hurt a guy!"

It could be any one: send thy knife-blade home!
Hardly knowing herself whether she was twisting it in
his vitals or her own, or pleading with him to join her
in a burlesque of his sensitivity over an issue not in the
least entailing his actual professional skills, she plowed
blindly ahead with her end of the farce into which
they had blundered.

"Charles Boyer? Charles Ruggles? Jimmy Stewart?"
Standing on one dainty foot, the other cocked for
stamping, she called across the cold cellar, going for
broke, "Peter Lorre!"

"Good girl! And Peter Gurney and Peter Davy and
Dan'l Whidder and Harry Hawke and Old Uncle Tom
Cobleigh and aaall!" he sang at the top of his voice,
"And Uncle Tom Cobleigh and all!"

His spirits were soaring dangerously, with the exhilarating rewards of failure, the almost voluptuous exac-
tions of concern by which we see to it that our lot is
shared. A mate must under this arrangement be in part

a Simon of Cyrene, conveniently on hand to shoulder one's cross for one, at least partway up the long road to Golgotha (the roles of course subject to reversal at any time, that much was only fair) .

"You crazy bastard," she said, smiling as she blinked away a tear or two, a detail not automatically to be given face value since her ability to produce them whenever required onstage had been not the least of her values as an actress. She'd been in a piece requiring that very knack at the time they'd met, in fact; the blind date having occurred in Boston, where the company she was in was about to open *Quail Hash*, hoping for mixed reviews. (They'd been uniformly bad on the road so far.) She stood there shaking her head, as though unable to believe her luck. "So play your little game. Don't tell me. But come have some breakfast. Spontini will be here soon to apologize, and you know what that takes out of everybody. What the devil were you fighting about last night?"

He couldn't recall, either that or much else of the party he'd looked in on, after ducking out of the theatre at the end of the first act. His brief stint as Father Plight was over by then, and he didn't give a damn whether his absence from the curtain calls was noticed or not.

"So come on," she said, now in fact disappearing up the stair. "You've had your little joke."

Women are always saving their husbands' faces, as though they are lengths of twine to be kept for some future use, perhaps not at the moment visualized.

three

"These doubts are mine infirmities!" I sang at the top
of my voice. The old hymn had suddenly soared into
my mind from nowhere as I bathed. Well, from the
organ of the old Dutch Reformed church in Chicago,
actually. There are times when breakfast seems the one
thing worth getting up for, until you can climb back
into the sack again and awaken dreaming of hot
muffins and ham and eggs once more. Everything between downhill. The group on the train, the bunch at
the office, people incidentally encountered in the
course of the day? Forget it. And yet people seem glad
to see one another. They get together. Rum bunch,
people.

How good it was to feel bad, to wallow in one's
melancholy. Old Flaubert knew that. Said something
about it. And there was Mahler sitting at the piano
running off for the conductor what-was-his-name, Otto

Klemperer, a little private preview of the immedicable sorrows of *Das Lied von der Erde*, saying to Otto as he tickled the old ivories, "What do you think? Will people do away with themselves when they hear it?" Having the time of his life of course. Oh, *natürlich*.

One's euphoria scattered at the sight of the bathroom scale. My pact with myself to weigh in once a week was absolute: Sunday morning the appointed hour. And Blodgett had been scarfing it up like Laughton in *Henry VIII*. I postponed the reckoning by watching the black cat, Mordecai. Clearly in league with the devil, the animal stepped onto the scale itself, to see what it weighed! Oh, it pretended to be merely watching the numerals rolling under that bulging glass eye, a toy to swipe at with its paw, but I knew it had purchased human powers by a covenant with Satan, and could read. Smackenfelt reeled back against the wall in horror, as with stricken eyes upraised he made the sign of the Cross to exorcise the demon, breathing a prayer for deliverance from the beast that had laid a spell upon this house, lot and garage, the succubus despatched from Hell to commit unholy intercourse with our Smackenfelt as he slept, not only draining away his creative powers but making all dietetic sacrifices of non-effect. Stuff like that there. At the same time glancing into the mirror to see how he was doing with the rhetorical bit. Had to keep your hand in with that tradition, who knew when he mightn't get a call from one of the Stratfords? "How much dost weigh?" he chatted with Mordecai, as one chatting with a malign agent it were wise to remain on the good side of. " 'Sblood," he whispered in an aside to the audience, cocking a hand to his mouth, "he knows I know 'tis vain to put him out o'doors o' nights, who can slip back in through the very keyhole." Then back to Mordecai. "Wouldst sabotage all my self-denials then, my lout? By jinxes, spells and hexes various, contrive to see that Blodgett further fleshes these upholstered bones, hah? Out, Beelzebub!" I gave the beast a kick, oh, just brushed him off the scale with my foot, really, after peering down to see what *he* tipped the scales at. Twelve pounds. "Putting it on yourself, eh?" I Rex Harrisoned it. I shooed the animal into the bedroom, closed the bathroom door, and stepped gingerly onto the scale. I stared straight ahead at the tile wall a moment. Then slowly lowered my eyes to take the reading.

Two hundred and nineteen pounds. Christ, I had gained four since the previous Sunday! Something diabolical *was* lousing me up, for note that in that interval I had consumed absolutely very few starches and sugars, holding Blodgett to proteins though lusting for flapjacks and sausages. Of course all that booze added up.

I shaved and, as one disillusioned with animals returning again to live among people, give them another whirl, I crept down the stairs, making the now rigidly stylized descent: I glanced into the wall mirror to make sure my eyes were still like truffles, overshot the second and third steps, paused to murmur a word of encouragement to the rubber plant languishing on the landing, apparently traumatized at having been sent C.O.D., avoided stairs eleven and thirteen, checked the floating villagers in the Chagall print to see if there had been any loss of levitation since last viewed, and stopped cold on the bottom step, cocking an ear. There were too many voices coming from the breakfast nook.

"But Aunt Dolly, whoy?"

Birdie Truepenny. Wife's cousin, few years junior to her twenty-four. Aunt probably some courtesy designation, or even a joke from childhood. Working for her master's in psychology at nearby university, doing thesis on obesity, emotional causes of. 'Sblood, had she come to pick my brains again? Though at ten o'clock I was once more ravenous, my stomach was at the same time upset. There were prolonged rumblings down in there, like pocketed poolballs traveling along the runways into the rack. Man's home his castle no doubt, but there were times when one felt more like a page in it than the reigning cheese, at best a court supernumerary slipping along passages and pausing behind doors to catch if possible some scrap of conspiracy bearing on oneself.

"Usedn't he to take yoga?" asked my mother-in-law, who was trying to get the hang of correct English despite all efforts to discourage this insane program.

"Another passing fancy," Dolly murmured. "We all have them. Like smoking a pipe. I smoked one myself for a while. Have some more cornbread, Birdie."

"Oh, thanks." Had the girl been asked to breakfast, or taken on faith the standing invitation to drop in, telephoning ahead first? "Um, it's not as though Uncle Fats were uptight about it. He's not in the least sensitive on the subject. In fact he's one of the sanest men I know."

He could visualize Birdie as she talked, working the pink little muckle mouth, licking her lips in that charming manner of hers.

"I didn't ask him, of course, I'd never do that. *He* said for me to feel perfectly free to ask him anything — explore any, um, causative aspects. The fact is he can be quite a gas on the subject, always making allowances for humor as a protective mechanism and understand that too. Again up to a point."

An associative gear now clicked into place in what I had thought was my mind. The thesis was to be a study of a selected *case* of obesity. The subject's weight problem would be scrutinized in depth, as they say, for clues to its emotional origins, with special attention to any personality conflicts, adverse formative experiences, or friction in the home situation for which appeasement might be sought in recourse to foodstuffs. She had laughingly hinted she'd "adore to" use me for a guinea pig — my own term in the idiotically tossed off offer that she "help herself," probably when she had her pink legs crossed. I remembered all that now. Christ!

"I mean he even volunteered," Birdie repetitiously made quite clear to them now, "and it's not as though he were a Sad Sack or anything. I would never dream of it then. I mean he's personable. The kind of man a woman would find, um, palatable? Don't you think so, Aunt Ginger?"

"Oh, def."

Considerately, one waited for a less sticky point in the "conversation" at which to enter. They had been lowering their voices. More normal tones ushered in a change of subject. My mother-in-law was off on a thesis of her own, that this is the worst nourished country in the world despite its being the most overfed. She was a health crusader, diligent reader of labels, and the scourge of merchants stocking detrimentally doctored or otherwise blameworthy provisions. Smackenfelt was poised to make his entrance on this neutral note when

Birdie appeared suddenly again deep in a discourse on the roots of gluttony.

"Heavy eating is the same as heavy drinking. Whoy? They're both escapes."

"I only knew one alcoholic," said my mother-in-law. "An uncle. Know what made him stop drinking? Converted. Fact. He accepted Christ as his savior in a tent near Cedar Rapids, and from that day forward he never touched another drop. Fact. It's mysterious — and yet is it?" She often conferred an element of profundity, or at any rate resonance, on what she had just said by pausing in mid-utterance and calling it into question, thus shedding grave doubts on its validity.

"No, it's not mysterious," Smackenfelt silently shouted from the depths of auditory voyeurism to which he had sunk in his own house by force of circumstance. "He was 'tipsy from salvation's bottle,' as Dylan Thomas put it. Proving what the Marxists have always insisted about religion being the opiate of the people." He started toward the breakfast room, prepared to give them all short shrift on this line of thought, when his advance was again checked by a fresh tack of Birdie's.

"Well, would you believe it can do the same for overeaters? I know a case of a woman who absy gorged herself on everything she could lay her hands on. She was absy gross. Three hundred pounds or more. She'd eat two or three chickens at a sitting, a pie, a couple of quarts of ice cream. It was positively Gargantuan. Then one day she found Christ and lost two hundred pounds. Slimmed right down. Like one of those 'after' pictures in the ads?"

"Your Uncle Stew has lost six hundred pounds."

"*What?*"

"Not all at once. Over the years. All told. Now ten, now twelve or fifteen. Gaining them all back again, of course, then losing them, many times over. It adds up to in the neighborhood of six hundred, he says. It's one of his jokes. Cushioning the subject with a little humor?"

"Oh, sure."

There was a pause, during which Birdie might be visualized jotting a notation to that effect in a notebook. Cushioning his padding with a little humor. Dolly rattled whatever section of the by now disembowelled Sunday *Times* she was intermittently engrossed in.

"Funny we should be talking about this. Here's an article on religion curing drug addicts, in the magazine section. Junky after junky testifying to the power of Christ in making him kick the habit. Remember we saw a television documentary on the same subject, Mother? Several addicts gave testimonials. Just like the way they used to do on street corners."

"They're back *on* street corners. There are religious revivals going on all around us right this minute. Oh, not this early in the day on Sunday, but you know what I mean. But those things are valuable for some people. It has meaning for the individual."

Smackenfelt, another dart forward aborted, rolled his eyes in supplication that no such fate befall a member of his household. "Please, God, don't let anybody get religion around here. It would be the last straw, Thou knowst it." He was forever praying, these days, that "cups" of one kind and another would "pass from him," in the manner derived from Gethsemane. Mentally kneeling right there, as in the Garden, he besought heaven as head of the house that this latest cup too would pass from him: namely the Jesus bag.

"This is absy marvelous cornbread. Would you give me the recipe, Aunt Ginger?"

Smackenfelt took a few more steps forward in his bathrobe and slippers, and, giving himself a fidget, briskly entered the breakfast room.

"Hello, hello, hello! Well, Birdie!"

There was a bright babble of greetings in the key established by Smackenfelt himself. When it had subsided, Dolly folded her section of the newspaper shut and rested her elbows on it. "So!" she said meaninglessly.

"Well, Birdie," he said, batting eyes that, so far from resembling truffles, glittered, according to the mirror again unintentionally run foul of there, with an almost morbidly metallic brightness, like blown fuses in which pennies have been inserted to make them operative, at least for the time being. "What brings you here on a day when the fkies are ashen and fobah, though the leaves are far from withering and feah?"

His gaze penetrated them successively, coming significantly to rest on Dolly. Notice that she was not quite yet off the hook, the account not quite yet closed. Her mother instantly sensed what was required of her, too. Veteran of two marriages of her own, she understood the triumphs and the ordeals of the game in which she had been dealt a hand, of sorts, when she came to join them under this roof. She realized that she was to "guess."

"I know that. 'Ulalume.' "

"No, no, Mother. Whom he's imitating. As *who* would do *what* he's doing. Give her a few more lines,

Stew." Dolly threw the whole burden wearily onto her mother. She had buckled under the weight of the Cross, a Simon of Cyrene whose knees had turned to rubber halfway up the slope to Calvary. While Smackenfelt heartily obliged, she sat with her head bowed on a hand, like someone in a game of charades illustrating the Sickness Unto Death.

> *"It waf night in the lonefome Octobeh*
> *Of my moft . . . immemorial . . . yeah."*

They watched with bated breath as Ma "thought." Her fingertips spread across her lower teeth, she screwed her face up and rolled her eyes toward the far wall. Dolly could be physically felt to be seething with suspense. This was all or nothing. Would they live or die? Would the marriage last or founder on this rock? The very house seemed to teeter on the brink of a precipice, like the cabin in *The Gold Rush*. This union could not survive the implication that Smackenfelt stank. If he did, he would pull the whole temple down with him, like Samson. And there it was.

The thinker dismantled her pose.

"Boris Karloff."

Laying a hand on his mother-in-law's shoulder as he passed behind her on his way to the sideboard, he felt a pang of desire it would have been idle to pin on Blodgett; indeed churlish. He acknowledged it as his own, and as just that, desire; not merely lust, to be so recognized, stamped, and filed away. The worm had bored its way into the ego. The house indeed trembled in the balance!

"Go to the head of the class, Ginger." Dishing himself up some sausages and scrambled eggs from the tureens that were also gifts of the good woman from her stores of hereditary silver, he sensed Dolly's glow of relief: their marriage had been reprieved. Face had been saved all around, though it had been a near thing.

"Well, Birdie, to what do we owe the pleasure of this visit? Come to ply your nefarious trade?" Her he would let off the hook too — amnesty for all! "I seem to remember volunteering as one of your guinea pigs. Do we begin rummaging about in me old innards this morning?" He would want to cut his throat tomorrow, but no matter; today must be let blossom and glimmer as best it might. "When do we start poking and picking about in this mental potpie?"

"Well, I just took up your invite to drop in for brunch some Sunday, but if you want to rap now that you've slimmed down some, why, swell, Unc. You really look great, Unc." Birdie smiled vindicatedly at the others. "You see how loose he is on the subject? I mean anybody who'd so freely leave a magazine like that lying around isn't uptight in the least." She indicated a *TV Guide* on a nearby table, the cover of which featured an article entitled "What the Stars Do about Flab."

"Oh, that's not his, that's mine," Ginger laughed. "He's not the only one fighting the Battle of the Bulge, you know." She patted her own irreproachable middle, snug in a pair of cherry-colored shantung slacks Smackenfelt could not remember having seen before. He was almost as distressed by this constant notice of her wardrobe as of what it encased, the shapely product of those calisthenics enacted behind doors so scrupulously closed at hours so sacrosanct as to be imagined some kind of Eleusinian mystery. Her almost pedantic attention to what one should eat and how it must have grown completed, in fact, the fanciful sense of her as a Demeter-in-residence.

"The wish to be attractive is a physical hunger, like that for food," Birdie lectured. "We *desire* to be desired. So that whether in the end we curb our gluttony or not isn't so much the discipline question of mind over body, but which of our desires wins out — our appetite, or our wish to be appetizing. Does that seem valid? Am I laying too much on you?"

All eyes were fixed on Smackenfelt, as the one to whom the question had principally been put. Returning from the buffet with a mounded plate, he had poked a succulent stub of sausage into his mouth. He raised a finger aloft as he chewed and swallowed, to indicate that comment was imminent.

"Have you ever read Auden's essay on Narcissism? He makes the point that Narcissus needn't have been a beautiful youth at all, or anything to write home about in the least. He falls in love with his reflection not because it's beautiful, but because it's *his*. He may as easily have been a humpback, or a middle-aged man doting on his pot, as a handsome youth."

"Really? I must look that up." Birdie dug a notebook from a huge carpetbag on the floor beside her chair. She was dressed in the playing-grownup manner of the young people just then. Numberless looped ropes of beads hung to the waist of a green velvet dress with leg-of-mutton sleeves and the waist up under the armpits — very possibly plucked from her mother's closet, or rummaged out of her grandmother's trunk. Strands of hair hanging loose to her shoulders added to the impression of a girl gotten up to play Ophelia, after making her way to the theatre in winds of gale force.

One expected her to rise and, babbling dementedly, strew flowers about, instead of systematically noting a point made in an essay. She bore no family resemblance to either of the other women. A tilted upper lip so perfectly repeated the line of her duckbill nose as to make almost for caricature, though of a kind beguiling rather than not, especially when she smiled, and the lip further protruded itself, drawing away from her teeth.

Her pencil flew on as Smackenfelt told a story of how, as a boy of ten selling magazine subscriptions door to door, he had glanced into the front window of a house he was soliciting and seen a Santa Claus beating his wife with the belt of his uniform. His speculation was that, having for years needed to stuff himself with a pillow in order to play Santa in local department stores or at children's parties, the man now suddenly found himself in middle life no longer requiring the padding, and was taking it out on the woman. In the course of this ramble, fabricated as a personal reminiscence though squarely based on fact as the related memory of a friend, he became aware that the phone had rung and that from an extension in the adjacent kitchen Dolly was conducting a conversation the other half of which was all too deducible, even before she hung up and returned to report it.

"That was Poodle Slater. The usual to-do about Spontini. He's full of morning-after regrets over what he called you last night in his cups. *You* get his hangovers."

"You don't mean he's coming to apologize again?"

"Afraid so. But he wanted to check with Poodle first about what exactly he called you. He thinks Poodle overheard, but Poodle says not. What did he call you?"

Smackenfelt shook his head, polishing off a mouthful of johnny-cake. "I can't remember. I was three sheets myself. Christ, these morning-after rituals are more wear and tear than the fights."

"He's a pseudo-masochist, this Spontini," Ginger explained, nodding knowledgably to Birdie.

"Oh, Mother, good God. Not pseudo. *Sado.*" Dolly sat in the same head-in-hands manner as when she'd explained that the protracted blanks in the Pinter dialogue were intentional elements in the artistic fabric and not a prompter asleep on the job. Hunched over his plate, your chuckling protagonist listened. "Sado-masochist."

"That probably says it better. Anyway, he's a case. They all are around here."

"Hostility is often a device for concealing its reverse," Dolly said.

"No, it isn't," Smackenfelt said.

"So that when you tell me this Spontini is always fighting with men to whom he then inevitably comes to apologize . . ." She shook her head ominously. "I mean it's almost a variation of kissing and making up."

Ginger nodded, informedly pondering this judgment. "You mean he could be AM-FM."

"Oh, Jesus, Mother." In dealing with motherisms especially hard to bear, Dolly drew on one of her mother's own most expressive mannerisms. Shutting her eyes, she put her hand to her face, like a claw, and sat a moment as if rallying her forces for contention with something threatening to shatter her last reserves. They were a theatrical family. "Mother, it's AC-DC. Not AM-FM."

Dolly looked to Smackenfelt for support in her wish to be free of this immediate relative; indeed was trying to pin on him a subtle campaign to get her out of the house and back home to Philadelphia where she belonged. "I mean a husband shouldn't be expected to put up with a mother-in-law. I mean that's not fair to him." But he wasn't buying very heavy. He was a Dutchman, a breed not noted for their need of privacy; on the contrary, rather famous for their ability to co-exist in sardine-tin density. They were geniuses at rubbing along. The privacy of his bedroom was all Stew needed. For the rest, he was glad to have a woman around who said AM-FM for AC-DC; called the hearse the Black Maria; and thought sodomite some kind of mineral. There was no doubt of this last. Where else could you get such free refreshment of the spirit?

"He sounds pretty kinky," Birdie was saying. "Theodore Reik in his chapter entitled 'Masochism in Modern Man' points up what Freud said, that masochism can't be understood apart from sadism . . ."

Tuning the women out, Smackenfelt mentally reviewed his long-standing feud with Spontini, beginning with their first encounter at a party in the course of which Smackenfelt had told Poodle Slater that Spontini's brother, a composer in the twelve-tone tradition, was "the Lawrence Welk of cacophony," which Poodle had lost no time in bustling over to repeat to Spontini. Stew and Zap Spontini had taken an instant dislike to one another. Each the other's Doctor Fell. There were almost inevitably words between them whenever they met, outbursts for his share of which the mercurial Latin would turn up the next morning filled with remorse. These scenes of self-immolation, with their attendant handclasps and spastic one-sided embraces, were indeed harder on our Smackenfelt than the ruckuses of which they were the product; endured at best in only partial comprehension, since an intervening night would have further blurred the memory of exchanges transacted in any case in an alcoholic fog. He now could literally not recall what had been the precipitating theme of last night's brouhaha. The details of their first meeting were clearer.

The Wusdatts gave a cocktail party, in the course of which someone mentioned Spontini's promotion at the agency for which he worked. When a guest asked what his new position was exactly, Smackenfelt jovially answered for him. "Oh, he's been made Vice-President in Charge of Subtractitives. You know — products containing-no. Without harmful such-and-suches." A glance from Dolly intended to warn him of the pitfalls besetting this line of humor in a roomful of advertising executives went unnoticed, as did the scowls of the agency chaps themselves. Feeling good, Smackenfelt developed his delightful little tittup. "He was kicked upstairs from Additives. The accounts for things that are now-with-improved-so-and-so . . ."

Then, let's see. There had been an incident arising out of preparations for a Fourth of July celebration on the local green. A tolerable amateur baritone, Zap had been tapped to sing "America the Beautiful," and Smackenfelt had hit on the idea of a pastiche of the verses striking an ecological blow. He would write it. First Zap would sing a stanza or two straight — No, he would rise, nod to the band to strike up, and belt out the paraphrase straight off, hitting them without preparation or warning with a scathing denunciation of all the pollutions presently defiling earth, sea and air of this now anything but beautiful realm.

Three days before the Fourth, Smackenfelt had his

parody ready. He bawled the lines over the telephone to Spontini in something of the exhilarated white heat in which they had been composed:

> *"Oh beautiful for specious skies*
> *For fields of tainted grain,*
> *Where everything in sight collects*
> *The fumes from car and plane.*
> *America, America!*
> *Whose youth are smoking tea,*
> *God crown her super-patriots*
> *From sea to slimy sea!"*

"Fats. Fats boy. We love you. But you're so full of hate, so full of hate you know . . ."

"You mean you're backing out?"

"Backing out. They'll run me out of town for Christ's sake! They'll tar and feather me, they'll revive the ducking stool, the stake — "

"I'd be billed as the author of the verses. There's another, let me just — "

"Sure, what have you got to lose? You're a free-lance actor with nothing to . . ."

Smackenfelt let him soak a moment in his own unintendedly pregnant pause — took a most skillfully timed beat on it. One that communicated very well Smackenfelt's own realization that Spontini really meant he had nothing to look forward to — not merely nothing to lose. Then he said, "If you mean you're afraid of getting blacklisted by some of your fat accounts who happen to be among the major polluters — "

"Are you calling me yellow?"

"No, just red, white and blue, Zap."

"Care to meet me somewhere and repeat that?"

"Oh, sure. Shall we say Dinty's Bar? That's about halfway between us."

"Fine. Behind Dinty's then in half an hour."

The rendezvous was overlooked only in the heat of the sharply resumed dispute.

"Look." This from Spontini, after a long, patient sigh. "It's the Fourth of *July*. A country wants to celebrate its *birthday*, its *past*, not without touching on things that are wrong with its present, that want correcting to be sure, but a–a blasphemous lampoon of itself for Christ's sweet sake! Plimsole, that history professor?, is giving the main address. I've read it, and I can tell you it's got plenty of barbs at the jingoists blind to our nation's ills. That in itself makes this just a little more than the traffic will bear. It's all very well for you to acknowledge authorship of this savage little burlesque, but it's me they'll clap in the cooler, and baby, not even Kunstler would touch the case. Now I know you don't like my stuff . . ."

A little confusion was jammed into Smackenfelt's brain here, racing at computer speed to a fuddled conclusion from the wrong data fed it. He thought Spontini meant by his "stuff" the canvases he turned out as a hobby. He painted puppy messes. Perhaps not merely as a hobby either; he might secretly hope, one day, to see his "stuff" exhibited here and there in at least a modest way. With reason, if so. The product of years of studious application to the purposes and techniques of his chosen vein, that of the currently revived, or "second generation," abstract expressionism, his work showed a growing mastery of the committed nuisance. But it presently developed that Spontini was referring not to his art but his professional output.

". . . why you refuse to be in them is your business,

Fats. All I can say is, if Hank Fonda will 'stoop,' as you consider it, to television commercials, if Cyril and José will do voice-overs for me, I fail to understand why someone in your position, and I say this intending no slur but in the utmost . . ."

Apart from the split sliver of time required to note that Spontini was being what his, Smackenfelt's, mother-in-law called "a sincere individual," that was when his computer sprang to rights. Spontini wasn't talking about his puppy messes at all, but the ordure extruded under his supervision in thirty-second intervals daily and nightly on the Box. To call this stuff "stuff" was the reverse of the modesty implied. It was pompous. Nay, it was megalomaniacal. He was a producer. As though women, even stars in their twilight, saying goodbye to stubborn stains, and *haute* catfood being consumed by kitty-cat connoisseurs, represented a body of work with a personal professional cachet. All bearing a stamp, noted in the trade, the Spontini touch — like the Lubitsch touch of yesteryear? While his computer gobbled down and digested the rectified input, Smackenfelt's indignation smoldered away at a much more subterranean level. This was bigger than the Fourth of July or Christmas or any other institutionalized botheration. Here we have an actor, himself, you understand, trained in the best studio, by an internationally esteemed Slavic director for whom his basic training had — now get this — had included the most adroitly executed pantomimic exercises as a flower, a fruit, then a vegetable — the class had once even easily guessed that he was being a stalk, first of green, then of bleached, asparagus — and there at the other end of the phone was a cretin in TV offering him a job as an ear of corn.

"I'll run through it once again," Spontini said, diverting attention from himself as the Fourth of July scaredy cat. He was running through it once again. He had the effrontery, the unmitigated gall. "It's for Corn Chippies, a sponsor that gives me pretty much artistic *carte blanche*. The character we want to build up will be a trademark figure systematically identified with the product, something like the Jolly Green Giant with peas. Because it won't be a one-shot by any means for the lucky guy who lands it, but a regular income, hopefully with terrific residuals if it catches on. He'll be half animation, half real. It's your face above a cartoon ear of corn, dressed in the hat and string tie of a Southerner — I've told you about that angle, haven't I?"

"Yes, but tell me again," said Smackenfelt, squeezing, from the orange of this crime, the last drop of outrage.

"The character will become known as the Colonel of Corn. Each plug he tells a corny joke or story, but everyone loves him because he serves the Corn Chippies we see him bite down on with a lusty crunch. That's where those beautiful big teeth of yours will come into their own, Fats."

"Why don't you get Maurice Evans?"

"He'd ask too much. And we want somebody unknown, who'll be identified only as the Colonel of Corn. Of course you'd have to read for the part, but I don't anticipate any serious competition. It's you exactly."

"Back of Dinty's then in half an hour?"

"And they say you can't play comedy."

"Who said that?"

"That idiot critic? About that Off-Broadway thing

where you played the robot filled with self-pity? Can't play comedy! By the time animation gets through with you, muffling that physog in husk leaves and cornsilk till you can't see anything of you but that Widmark grin —"

"I can make it in ten minutes."

"Ah, come on. Take a thing in the spirit in which it's meant. Well, what do you say?"

Smackenfelt sang him the second stanza.

> *"We copulate, we populate,*
> *Oh, God, it's all too late.*
> *Those alabaster cities now*
> *Are so much real estate!*
> *America, America,*
> *There's still the fruited plain*
> *Those eastern corporations buy*
> *And sell for private gain!"*

"Fats. Fella. Is there anything we can do?"

"I understand your position. Accounts like that insurance company that buys up all those Midwestern farms to run from New York office buildings. Such feeling for the soil. Which one is that again?"

"We all want to help, but what's your problem? Ah, Fats, Fats, Fats, what's your problem? A caper like this would be like devil worship in the Second Presbyterian Church, a gangbang in a nunnery —"

Ginger's voice broke into his revery.

"He's Italian, and Italians can be full of the old blarney. That can change in a twinkling though, and so you have people blowing hot and cold. But I like them a lot better than the French, where I've also been. Everybody loves France but who likes French-

men? They're buck-hungry. They're materialists. They
worship the almighty dollar." She looked around to see
how this rain of judgments was being received.

Well, moving counterclockwise from her own right,
there was her daughter. She was sitting with her head
bowed in her hands, so firmly in their grip that they
seemed like a vise she was trying to pull it out of. She
sighed heavily. Smackenfelt, next her, smiled. The
woman never missed. She was a find (apart from
roiling his loins in bing-cherry slacks). At length Dolly
successfully pulled her head out of the trap in which it
had got wedged, and glanced past Smackenfelt to
Birdie who, to complete the circle, was looking uncer-
tainly at her Aunt Ginger, in this case properly so
called. She seemed to be trying to think of something
appropriate to the occasion. What that might have
been was never learned, for as she cleared her throat to
speak the front doorbell rang.

"Cursing a blue streak," as his mother-in-law put
these things, Smackenfelt beat the table with both fists,
then softly hammered his head with them. "Goddamn
it all to hell, tell him I'm still in bed. Tell him I'm
dead. I just died. I've left for the Orient. Tell him
anything."

"You may as well get it over with," Dolly said, rising
to answer the door. "You'll only have it hanging over
your head. Besides," she added playfully, "Birdie's dying to meet Zap now. You couldn't not throw this
nugget to her."

The door was opened, and after an exchange of
greetings in subdued tones the penitent shuffled forward, mindful that his soiled brogans might somewhat
stain the floor. Smackenfelt turned in his chair with
enormous reluctance, as though it had required some

powerful, invisible winch to screw him even halfway around, before he could complete the maneuver on anything like his own and rise.

"Hello, Zap. Have some coffee."

Spontini shook his head. He did not deserve any. The good that he would he did not, and the evil that he would not that he did, and there was no soundness in his flesh, neither any health in his bones.

"The coffee's good here," Smackenfelt said, as though he were speaking of some wayside eatery to be heartily recommended, one frequented by the transcontinental trailer drivers. "No? Well, anyway, this is Mrs. Truepenny, Dolly's mother."

"Hello," she said. "I've heard a lot about you." She extended her hand, her smile like a pane of shatterproof glass. Truepenny had been her adored first husband's name, to which she had reverted after shedding her recent mate, the apparently dreadful Art Buckett, who was said to throw peanuts into the air and catch them in his mouth.

"And this is Birdie Truepenny, a niece of hers."

The greetings at last completed, Spontini said he might change his mind and take a little refreshment after all. "Living alone I never seem to get good coffee," he said, wedging himself into the circle on a chair slipped under him just in time, or so his nerveless condition made it seem.

"Oh, you're a bachelor?" Birdie inquired keenly.

"Well, I believe in non-binding marriages, like you young people there I think, and I've never . . ." Spontini gave a shudder of disgust, whether for the gruelling intimacies of the sexual bond as he had found and now remembered them, or for his own inadequacy in crystallizing even one of a supposedly countless succes-

sion of such relationships tentatively essayed, or, perhaps, for the memory of having become entangled only
with women too possessive for his taste. Certainly for
an erotic history deserving more than the bathos of
Ginger's brightly summarizing, "He's just never found
the right girl."

"I guess that's it," Spontini said, with another defeated shrug.

He seemed a wreck. His face was the color of modell-
ing clay. He wore tan chinos, an open red shirt, and a
tweed coat vulcanized at the elbows which had become a hallmark of these Sabbath penances. Perhaps
those appearances were a secular substitute for the
Catholic masses now these many years abjured. The
knowledge that he was known to have been at work on
a novel set in a mental institution, in which the visitors
could not be told from the inmates, conceivably added
to his aspect of sheepish guilt.

He was of medium height and size, one shoulder
giving the illusion that it was much broader than the
other, possibly the result of faulty tailoring. His dark
eyes, glittering with Latin vivacity the night before,
were now bloodshot and watery, giving his entire face
rather a brooding Slavic cast, as though overnight he
had undergone a change of ancestry; appropriate
enough in the light of these Dostoievskian self-
lacerations of his. His graying black hair poured thickly
out of his scalp, like smoke from a factory chimney,
bending abruptly to the right as though in a stiff wind.
The neat silver smelt of a mustache aptly graced a
perfect aquiline nose and full, fleshy upper lip. God
knew to what inner snazziness he had succumbed
when he first groomed his thick sideburns into exclamation marks, or what temptation of the chic world in

which they might presumably become a trademark. He was, in any case, occasionally mentioned in gossip columns as possessor of this punctuation-about-town. Thy mercy on Thy people, Lord.

"Fats, old boy," he began as he stirred cream and sugar into the coffee poured by Dolly.

"Excuse me. The drama section's missing from the *Times* and I want to see if it's fallen out on the doorstep."

Outside on the porch, breathing the cool air, Smackenfelt tried again to reconstruct the events of the night before. A murmur of conversation inside told him he could take a moment's respite, and, alone out there, he leaned against a post as jumbled scraps of the night's sequence began to collect themselves, if not into a unified whole, at least into more coherent fragments.

He had clearly been giving some of his impressions, for there were voices, linked by association with puzzled faces, "thinking" hard like Aunt Ginger, though with less success.

"John Wayne?"

"Gary Cooper?"

"Charles Bickford!"

They were midnight-muzzy, in second-brandy inattentions or fogs, else how explain these constructions of his Joel McCrea, so wide of the mark? He experienced the sensation common to such social occasions: the conviction that he could feel his teeth rot. Baring them in a patient grin he "recognized," from the floor, a Mrs. Gradgrind.

"Edward Arnold?"

Again he shook his head with shut eyes as he smilingly uttered an inaudible "Nooo." No, my dear, you too have failed the test as a Late Late Show buff.

That was how he was going to play it. It was they who
were falling flat on their faces, not he. They were
bombing, and there it was. Did she with her smile
presume to be articulating her share of a little bur-
geoning Saturday-night malice? The idea that Stew
Smackenfelt was so bad his parlor bits were trans-
formed into guessing games in which he stumped
them — just the most priceless gag of the season? Well,
he would consider the source, and let her have the
satire as a vent for grudges against the world they all
knew. She had a son who was sixteen and beginning to
think about boys. To say nothing of a husband whose
roving hands were no doubt an untiring effort to fight
the defect threatening to come to full bloom in the
offspring. "It's Spencer Tracy," has been *his* share of
the Smackenfelt-baiting. Charity was called for in
meeting the rancor of such types, as of the buster who
now piped up, "William Powell." Chester Blankenship.
He drank highballs with chewing gum in his mouth, he
lacked the sense not to wear blue suits with that
dandruff problem. Weren't his shoulders a winter
wonderland tonight. Next? As "the chair," Smackenfelt
sardonically "recognized," by mugging, an unidentified
card with a mouth like a knothole who said, "Slim
Somerville."

"Nooo." They were in full rout, no question about
that. Did they "give up"? Not quite yet. A woman with
a necktie raised her hand.

"Wheeler and Woolsey."

Aha! So the cockwallopers were out in force tonight,
the gelders from the women's emancipation losing no
opportunity to go snip-snip. Two, in addition to the
one with the wide cravat of a quite indefensible
green, none of them beautiful when angry, all busy

beating off men who aren't trying to get to them, don't
you know. But easy there. Charity, we said. "Neither to
weep nor to laugh, but to understand," as Spinoza
said. Part of the persecuted Portuguese Jewish crowd
given all that asylum in Amsterdam (from which the
Jews themselves then drove Spinoza). Her guess was
for the most part lost in a sudden flurry among an
adjoining group who were trying to haul Spontini bodily
off to the piano for some ragtime, a diversion under
cover of which Smackenfelt slipped back to his corner
chair, where he sat highball in hand. They would never know. That would be their reward. He would never
tell them it was Joel McCrea. They could go on guessing though night's candles were burnt out, and the
village cock had twice done salutation to the morn.

He became aware of Dolly watching him concerned-
ly from across the room. He took a copious gulp of his
drink, feeding her anxiety. The contingent dragging
Spontini to the piano momentarily cut off their view of
one another. Then he saw Dolly coming toward him.
She laid a hand on his knee and smiled, her face cocked
endearingly to one side in the ministering manner of
women everywhere. "Who was it? You can tell me." As
though they were speaking of something like the reports of recent tests for which one had been hospital-
ized, rumored to be positive for some degenerative
disease only the name of which remained to be revealed. She gave his leg an affectionate shake. "Who
was it?"

A squall of period syncopation, sudden and bone-
jarring, brought an abrupt end to the tender passage by
revealing that Spontini had been successsfully moved
to the piano where he would now for an indetermina-

ble spell hammer out vintage tunes in arrangements that made them often as not unrecognizable too, if it came to that.

Smackenfelt rose, patting Dolly's hand as he kissed her on the nose. "Spinoza." Then he was leaning negligently on the throbbing upright, an elbow on the folded-back top, smiling down at Spontini whose stylishly cut jacket of nubbed Italian silk lay folded beside him on the bench. His arms in their rolled shirt-sleeves worked like pistons, his shoulders wagging in the very evocation of an era — the prototype of the man who has fruitfully answered an advertisement for a course of home instruction guaranteed to make him the hit of parties.

"Which one is this?" Smackenfelt asked, charmingly.

"Which what?"

"Which tune? It's an old favorite, isn't it?"

Spontini's nostrils tautened as with lowered gaze he plunked on. The bent head and flaring nostrils were reminiscent of Smackenfelt's own moose-in-rut bit. Imagination supplied the detail of Spontini's pawing the ground preparatory to charging a rival.

"Look, just because people have trouble —" Spontini gave off, checking some retort that sprang to his lips. "It's 'Chattanooga Choo Choo.' "

"Of course."

Negotiating an intricate hot lick with his treble hand, Zap waved his free one to the buffet around which many were now crowding. When Smackenfelt made no move to go, he said: "I guess I don't know old movie stars any better than you do Dixieland tunes. Your impressions have gotten to be a sort of quiz for buffs, what? Nostalgic stuff."

"Yes. They were all has-beens."

"It's a fate that'll never befall you, old man," Spontini said, smiling suddenly upward.

Smackenfelt raised his eyebrows in grateful surprise. Giving Spontini's shoulder a squeeze, as if to say in turn, "Thanks, old bean," he made for the buffet. He must be nicer to Zap. He might even ask to see the latest of his puppy messes, which, God knew, was carrying friendship about as far as could be. Sunday painters were touchier about their work than professional artists — and more affectingly happy for compliments.

That was why he was surprised now, standing there on the porch, to have Zap turn up. What the devil was there to apologize for?

He put the question to Zap as they finally sat together in the living room, sipping coffee. The women conducted a discreet conversation in the breakfast nook, as a sort of polite screen of privacy thrown about the men in their act of reconciliation.

"I don't know what you're sorry about. As I remember it, we were talking about my having been doing a clutch of has-beens. Then you said something like, I don't remember exactly, 'It's something you'll never be.'"

Zap first nodded to confirm that résumé of the exchange, then shook his head in self-deploring evaluation. "I don't know how I could have said anything so nasty. I must have been in my cups."

"Nasty?" Smackenfelt's puzzled gaze fixed itself on a distant corner of the ceiling. "I don't get it. How do you mean?"

"You can't be on the skids without you're first on top. That general idea. And you, Fats, while not yet where you deserve to be, have nevertheless got the potential —"

Smackenfelt set his coffee mug down on a table in a manner illustrating the leisure with which the truth had dawned on him, yet also the deliberation with which he would now respond. "Why, you son of a bitch. What a nasty crack."

"It's what I'm trying to *tell* you. There was no *excuse* —"

"You don't have to tell me that!"

"So I've come to apologize. I couldn't let it go."

"The hell you have. You've come to make sure I got the point, which went by me for reasons I'll never know. It ate at you that your witticism missed. You've come to correct that, under the guise of apologizing. I'm going to hand you your head. This time I'm really going to hand you your head, Spontini. But not in here. There are ladies present. Shall we step outside? Excuse me while I get out of this bathrobe and into something else. I'll only be a minute."

His departure to do so recalling the only really serious criticism the Slavic director had ever levelled at him for an exercise at the workshop studio where he had trained, in this case an exit, with severance pay, from an imaginary office job from which he had just been fired.

"I didn't believe your elbows," Belchowski said.

four

The women watched from a side window as the men filed into the yard to square off. Smackenfelt had intended mainly that they separate themselves from the women's presence; when a glance over his shoulder revealed Birdie to be standing with her notebook still in hand, he decided that they should be removed from their view as well.

"Let's go over behind the garage."

"Right."

They picked their way across soggy ground past a jalopy that Smackenfelt had taken apart and put together again, not only successfully, but with several parts left over into the bargain. It had been the subject of some good-humored kidding in their circle, but now he could sense the enemy refining it into the charge that he was an automotive dolt, as well as a grievously deficient parlor whiz. The reflection dealt a serious setback to the conciliatory mood Zap had, in the past few moments, striven to recover.

"Those willows down by the stream there," he said. "They're quite beautiful."

"They have that exciting natural look."

"I know you don't like my stuff. Or anybody in advertising whatsoever. We're all swindlers."

As Smackenfelt, abstractly nodding agreement, surveyed the even muddier scene they had now reached behind the garage and out of sight of the spectators, for a spot dry enough to furnish a pair of combatants reasonable footing, Spontini continued his efforts toward a negotiated settlement.

"I know you have your rigid opinion as — and I use the term as an affectionate cliché — a stubborn Dutchman, and in a way it's your code, I respect that—" Spontini paused, to get a grip on his syntax. He decided a fresh sentence would be better. "While all that's true enough, it might surprise you to learn that some space salesmen have integrity. As much in their line as you in yours."

The designation for himself of space salesman revived an old fancy of Smackenfelt's: that of Spontini, swaddled in a rocket suit, all systems A-O.K., propelled by some kind of miracle fuel into the blue inane, trailing plumes of fiery exhaust and clutching a briefcase filled with plans for subdividing the outer reaches of the Milky Way, despite all efforts of the more discerning element to keep at least them out of the clutches of the developers.

"I came to apologize. Which is a form of taking back the statement. So this is really dirty pool. Holding a man to account for something he's retracted."

"You can do that later. You don't have to take back

the statement — I'm *giving* it back to you. And nobody peddling pots, tubes, cans and bottles of gunk for phobias they've themselves created is in any position to talk about dirty pool." Smackenfelt sprang gingerly *over* a dirty pool in his quest for more felicitous terrain. "To say nothing of that acting school whose advertisements you handle. You must realize what a racket they are. They'll take anybody."

"Then you should have no trouble getting in."

"Geronimo!"

The ejaculation was not only a warcry decently signalling his intention to strike, but also an allusion to the Apache chieftain as one who had at the last been baptized and received into the arms of the Dutch Reformed Church, believe it or not. He let fly with an intended haymaker that would have put Spontini to sleep had it connected. But the ground was especially luscious just there and he slipped and missed, losing his footing and more or less falling into Spontini's arms. Jerking back to avoid the swing had made Spontini lose his own balance, and so it was for mutual support that they stood, swaying, in an unsteady embrace, somewhat symmetrically buttressing one another.

"You take a hell of a lofty tone toward other people," Spontini panted in his ear. "Do you think you've earned the right?"

"I'm no goo peddler."

"I'll get you for that, Smackenfelt. Somewhere. Somehow. If it's the last thing I do."

They splashed inconclusively about in the muck, doing, for the moment at least, more damage to each other's trouser-legs than to their jaws and noses. The pavane continued.

"You're a bad actor."

"Just in what sense do you mean that?"

"Take your pick."

"All right I will — gunk vendor, junk hawker, poop peddler," Smackenfelt continued, readjusting his grip on the other's back. The fist fight threatened to become a wrestling match. He gazed upward, thinking. "Piddle purveyor."

"Keep it up."

"Slops salesman."

"One more, perhaps?"

"Manure merchant."

"That does it."

Spontini wrenched abruptly free of the embrace and swung with a short uppercut that took Smackenfelt off balance again. He recovered his footing and let Zap have one in the right eye. They were mixing it up in earnest when there were rapid footsteps across the driveway and Dolly was pulling them apart with no little vehemence of her own.

"If there's anything to be done with you two monkeys I'd like to know what it is. Stew has a matinee today, and you don't want him turning up with a couple of front teeth missing any more than we do. Now that's enough!"

It was this fear, understandably shared with her husband, that made her break his fights up at the first moment compatible with letting two men satisfy the requirements of whatever masculine "honor" might be presumed to be at stake, whether imagined or real. Zap scuttled at a threatening gesture from Dolly herself, muttering something neither of the others caught. He disappeared around a corner of the garage, slipping away like a footpad.

"He's sick," Smackenfelt said.
"So am I. Of both of you."

The episode had only briefly interrupted their family discussion of Spontini, about whom Birdie was able to offer more detailed insights now that she had glimpsed him first-hand. He was clearly a divided person, hung up on at least two of the seven stages of man as elucidated by the psychologist Erikson, and a candidate for impalement on God knew how many more of the others still awaiting a male only halfway through this earthly journey. Aunt Ginger was more concerned with an armistice than with analysis, and made no secret of how accommodation might be best attained.

"Just ignore him. Let his insults roll off your back, Stew. Consider the source."

"All right," said Smackenfelt to this refreshing counsel. He had quite forgotten poor Zap and was once more serenely packing in sausages and cornbread, closely watched by Birdie, herself mentally noting food as medicine taken by mouth for a spirit rent by conflict. Let her, he thought. We all have to make a living. Aunt Ginger rattled instructively on.

"A feud like this is an object lesson."

Having lost the attention of the others, she addressed her remarks to Mordecai, the cat, who had strolled in and settled his enormous black bulk on an unoccupied chair. "That it's as hard for people to get along man to man as man to woman. Shouldn't that prove that this sex-war business is exaggerated? Getting blown out of all proportion today?"

Stew rose to pour them all some more coffee. She paused to collect her thoughts, hoping this slight stir in their positions might somehow help her recover her human audience.

"I'll continue the sermon, this being Sunday morning. My text would be, 'A soft answer turneth away wrath.' That's what I'm preaching about, dearly beloved. It's good advice for marital relations as well as others in real life. *Don't* retaliate in kind when somebody's wounded you. That way you're way ahead of the game. That way you heap balls of fire on their head. What's the matter, Dolly?"

Dolly, elbows on table, had her head in the vise again. What she might have said when the struggle to extricate it was at last successful was never known, for the telephone rang again just then. It was Jerry Bock, Smackenfelt's agent.

He approached the phone without haste, postponing as long as possible the receipt of news Bock would not have delayed till a Sunday to transmit if it were good, since he would presumably have acquired it on a business day.

"Stew baby, how are you?" His resemblance to a beaver oppressed Smackenfelt almost more at moments like this than when face to face with him, since imagination exaggerated to the point of caricature the mouth held up to the transmitter, the teeth bared in a chimerical grin. "Well, the bit in *Bananaquit* fell through. They feel you're overqualified. The strength you'd bring to that five minutes would not only steal the act but throw the entire play off balance."

The best thing about the bit of inconsequential fluff into which he had thus narrowly missed being sucked, he told the ladies on hanging up, was the title — *Looking for a Bananaquit.* He entertained them with an explanation. A bananaquit was a small yellow-breasted bird, actually named in full the Bermuda bananaquit, classified by ornithologists as "accidental" in Florida. All right. Now. The comedy concerned an elderly couple displaced to a retirement village there, doomed to improve the heavy hours by watching for a glimpse of the bright visitor. "Wouldn't I be great in chin whiskers as the next-door codger tryin' to scare up some other dad-blasted hacks than peepin' through binoculars for a gol-danged bird? Such as mebbe coppin' a feel here and there?"

"Walter Brennan!"

Blodgett's reflex was that of something now dangerously near to going out of control. He not only reached a hand to Aunt Ginger's shoulder, but let it linger there, relishing the sensation almost deliberately invited to stoke the very desire that had sent it there. Smackenfelt withdrew it only when Dolly turned her gaze in that direction, smartly, as from a hot stove. "Sharp's a tack, bright's a dollar, and smart's a whip she is, I allus said," he continued, in the vein so quick-wittedly identified.

Her mother laughed. Then, hugging herself with a humorous shiver, she said, "Retirement villages. Brrr. Gives me the chills just to think of it. Before I come to that, though, I've got plenty more years alone in that Philadelphia condominium."

"Nonsense," he said. Resolutely avoiding Dolly's eye, which he knew to be sternly seeking his own in a warning glare, a reminder that the visit in question was being prolonged by a mother-in-law already endured over and above the call of duty, he finished spreading jelly on a last mouthful of cornbread. "You're not to think about going back there just yet. You're going to stay right here. But of course there are strings."

"What do you mean?"

"The first of the Concords are beginning to come in, and I see we're nearly out of grape ketchup. So how about it? I might even help you with this batch."

five

After all that bird's eye view of the id by the ego, a worm's eye view of the ego from the lowly level of the id might consist of Blodgett seeing His Nibs sitting in his favorite parlor chair, pleasantly glutted by that breakfast, listening to his two women from behind the *Times*. Spontini is gone, his mission of good will aborted or perhaps just postponed. Birdie is gone with her notebook and her impressions, together with a few specimens of Smackenfelt's doodles which Aunt Ginger tore from the telephone memo pad and furtively slipped her. She now says: "You can certainly pack it away, Stew, I mean you Dutch. A real hearty people. The breakfasts you get in Amsterdam! Cheese yet! At breakfast!"

Smackenfelt is immersed in a meteorological item predicting hurricanes of more than normal number and severity in the months ahead, and fears for the three hundred deep-frozen Nazi officers distributed about town, if a power failure puts out of commission for more than twelve hours the refrigeration units in which they are secretly ensconced. Walk-in coolers and one thing and another. Slowly they will thaw, then, numbly at first but with steadily growing recovery of their motor powers, the overall plan for another try at world domination intact in their re-animated memory centers, they will proceed to fan out across the countryside long, long before the time is ripe for another Hun takeover. He must personally see to it that electricity be first restored in the key areas, if necessary by planting agents in the major utility substations.

"And so sane."

"What?"

"The Dutch. They're so stable. Always known for that, your people. Live and let live. Sound in mind and body. You're — how can you sum it up — so *normal.*"

Smackenfelt nods, turning a page. "You'll find no dikes in Holland."

"... find ... no ...?"

"Mother, he's pulling your leg. A dike is a lesbian."

"Oh."

He's trying to keep his mother-in-law at arm's length, you have to give him that. Using these twits and sendups as reminder of how far off his wave length she is, how little his speed, it would be a shambles in a month. Deliberate anti-aphrodisiacs, all of them. He's making a real effort to summon himself back to the decency for which his folk are renowned, for which even now his mother-in-law is extolling them. But her hurt look at the dike rib only gives him a twinge of the compassion you feel in your very bowels, a pang of remorse that turns the fervor-dampeners into desire-provokers. The flames are fanned rather than put out.

Their big shtick is domesticity, these wooden shoes. Will the hearthside irony here be that this poor buster pushes domesticity as far as it will go, and then perhaps a fraction of an inch farther, in a triangle involving the mother-in-law? Christola!

"Yes," he chats, letting the paper drop and crossing his legs, "I remember how my grandfather used to tell the story about the time he shook hands with Teddy Roosevelt when Teddy spoke in Chicago. When his turn came in the queue, shuffling slowly forward to grasp the President's hand, he looked him slyly in the eye, one Dutchman to another, you see, and said: 'Stuyvesant, Knickerbocker, and Roosevelt!' And quick as a flash, all thirty-two of those teeth, Teddy shot back: '*Oranje Boven!*' The motto of the House of Orange. Hard to translate, but something like 'Three Cheers for Orange!' A great dynasty by any standards."

"And Teddy wasn't the only one the Dutch have given us. There's also F.D.R."

Dolly cleared her throat here. "F.D.R.," she said, "was about two-percent Dutch."

"It was all he needed," said Smackenfelt, and got behind his paper again, kind of the equivalent of flouncing out of the room, or saying "Touché!" Oh, all this sexual in-fighting! What a pain. Dolly isn't through teasing him.

"Stew gives us this song and dance about what his name means, but it can't possibly make any etymological sense, the way he tells it. *Smaak* means taste, *veld* field. How could a field taste? No, the name's been tampered with, over the generations. And for good reason. He's Jewish. Did you ever suspect that, Mother?"

"That's a lie! I will not have it!"

He rose and flung down his paper with a vehemence that made Mother pale. He snatched it up again and began to tear it to shreds, biting off scraps with his teeth and spitting them in every direction. At the peak of his insane frenzy he bolted into the adjacent smaller parlor, where he could be seen beating the table with both fists as he shouted, *"Ik ben een echt Hollander! Ik ben geen Jood! Ik ben een echt Hollander!"* He struck his head on the table, finally rolling on the floor and chewing on the fringes of a rug. It was the impersonation of Hitler, along with a cue taken from Dolly's smile, that made the other woman realize it was a sendup. She put a hand to her heart, rolling her eyes with a sigh of relief. He also occasionally enjoyed taking the reverse line, pretending he was Jewish in order to discomfit those overheard making anti-Semitic remarks. To which recalled fact his mother-in-law added a word of praise for his kindness to birds, remembering how he had nursed back to health a baby oriole fallen out of its nest. "Have you been here since *spring*, Mother? I didn't realize it was *that* long," said Dolly. Which her mother ignored, continuing, "He made little worms out of peanut butter and dropped them into that creature's mouth. Is he humanitarian or is he humanitarian?"

On this note she rose to clear away the breakfast rubble, leaving Dolly free to take Stew to task, in low tones and under cover of a distant rattle from the kitchen, for moral obligations of which, by way of contrast to the general encomium, he was falling short.

"Look, you ought to stop this sport with my mother."

"How do you mean?"

"All these things. First the Liebestod '69, then remarking behind your newspaper that they've discovered sodomite among the minerals on the moon, just to see how far you can push it, I suppose. Now this business about dikes. The poor woman can't help, well, what she is."

"Oh, it's only a game."

"Which you play to satisfy some wicked impulse in yourself."

"Thank you for these revealing glimpses of myself," he answered with a genial smile, "which otherwise I might not be vouchsafed." He gave her his Barrymore leer, slightly Mephistophelian in a consciously motheaten way, head cocked to one side and lowered, the better to discharge the satire directly upward from his eyeballs. Beneath her accusations lurked, without a doubt, her own guilt at wanting to be rid of the bloodguest whose part she was ostensibly taking. Oh, these actors! "Tell me more, do."

"Come now, Stew, you needn't be ironic. You know you can be a bit of a stinky pie."

He nodded to express agreement with this estimate, or at least register the receipt of it, as he glanced at the clock to remind himself of the three-o'clock Sunday matinee ahead of him in town, and the nine-o'clock performance after that. If she only knew for what he was trying to be his own wet blanket! He walked to the window and gazed out between the curtains into the street. Fresh rain had begun gently to pock the surfaces of pools already inches deep from days of intermittent downpour. A man wearing lederhosen went past the house on a bicycle, holding an open umbrella. He said what he had meant not to say. It slid out of its own accord, like an adder from hiding. "Maybe all this disguises your own guilt at wanting her to be off."

He heard her rise from her chair behind him, perfectly visualizing the deliberation with which she placed her hands on the corners of its arms and levitated herself to a standing position. "I shall never, never speak to you again."

He turned around, helplessly deploring his own conscious craft. "Let's don't, my dear," he said softly, borrowing the tone employed at a critical juncture in the rickety drama to which he must now repair, where in turn he utilized a lingering, musing smile drawn from Ralph Richardson's best vein, "let's don't be theatrical, shall we?"

With that she flounced out of the room.

The jolt of reality made him give a better performance, as Father Plight, than he had done since the start of his tenure in the run, three months before. The cast had all been "down," gone stale in a production for which the two-weeks closing notice had been posted, no doubt mercifully, on the bulletin board. Everybody said our Stew had certainly been "up" today. He left the theatre positively shimmering under their collective compliments, and the memory of the hand he had got on his exit from his one big scene, where no one could have failed to believe his elbows.

The total immersion in his character that had gained him these plaudits led to his still vividly retaining the sense of being Father Plight as he set out for the light supper he habitually took between an afternoon and evening performance. He wandered into an Automat still wearing the clerical garb. As he slowly consumed the crock of baked beans he fancied there, he became aware of a woman watching him from a table straight ahead, across two unoccupied ones. Her open cloth coat and drab blouse spoke of mean circumstances, a lifetime of feeling bargain goods in cheap department stores. Her tentative, almost furtive smile broadened in response to Smackenfelt's cordial glance. She rose and walked over.

"I sit down with you a minute, Father?"

"Of course."

She set down the cup of coffee and half a wedge of peach pie she had carried from her own table and eased herself into the chair opposite him. She took a bite and a rather audible gulp of these by way of establishing a sense of their breaking bread together, of "taking the evening meal," then, wiping her lips with a fresh napkin drawn from the dispenser here, said:

"Father, I have sinned."

"Well, look," he said, glancing worriedly about, "actually I'm not —"

"Oh, I wouldn't expect to make no confession right here or anything. I know you're not on duty. I just say that because I think maybe I deserve the problem that has been visited upon me, set smack in my lap, and that I have to talk to somebody about. Whose field it is. I mean if you have a minute. That O.K., Father?"

"Certainly, my child."

Smackenfelt again darted a look about the restaurant to make sure they were not being observed, or at least overheard. The only diners in their immediate vicinity were a thickset man in a filling-station attendant's uniform doing hearty justice to a drumstick, and a woman in a green tweed coat from a pocket of which protruded the head of a tiny dachshund. It was swung around so as to be more or less resting on her lap, giving her somewhat the appearance of a marsupial carrying her young in her pouch. His dinner companion had herself hesitated a moment in the course of this spot-check, screwing a troubled gaze into the vestiges of her pie. Then, appearing to pluck up her courage, she threw out her problem by clothing it in the guise of a universal question.

"Can a man leave his wife, I mean is he entitled to, because she won't let him" — here she herself cast a look about and lowered her voice — "you know, let him have his will of her?"

"That is a hard question to give a simple answer, my child," he told the woman, who couldn't have been ten years older than his own thirty-three. He was not so blind to the thin ice he had now permitted himself to be lured out onto as to offer any but the blandest and most widely applicable generalizations; at the same time struggling to remain within the terms of his characterization, on which he felt himself losing his grip. He lowered his own voice. Going about in costume, even for the briefest of bites between shows, was frowned on by Equity; the possibility that he might be "unfrocked," so to speak, was not to be dismissed, quite apart from the likelihood that his present behavior already constituted a felony, on a par with practicing medicine without a license. At the same time, the elements of danger — the possibility that this "evening meal" might be his Last Supper — heightened the intoxication he secretly experienced as he continued:

"These things are never one-sided, as you know yourself from having lived upon this earth of ours. Any shortcomings, wrongs — sins if you will — are mutual between two people, and flow between them as one." Thoughtfully munching a forkful of his own neglected and cooling beans gave him a moment in which to improve on these flabby profundities. "It takes two to tango," he continued, grateful for the cliché, "so the husband in this case must be in some way as guilty as the woman. We are all guilty, and judges are sinners as surely as evildoers have been wronged." There swam unbidden to his mind a memory of his own perverseness toward poor dear Aunt Ginger. Instances of this predated his having the hots for her, and so could not be justified as ardor-squelchers warning him that they were not one another's speed, that "that way lay madness." Often times he would baffle her with one of his homemade riddles. Why is a cruel judge like Marcel Proust? Because they both dish up unconscionably long sentences. She would laugh, but her face belying that she was really with it, could honestly be expected ever to have cracked Proust open. (But the "hurt look" is a mating cry.)

"God does not send us trials we cannot bear," he continued, with the exhilarating sense now of handling this precisely as Father Plight would, who had a delightful habit of rambling, of circling around from ambiguities to particulars. "Trials we cannot bear or challenges to which we are not equal, whether of the marital lot or any other. What we are assigned to bear is in a sense a measure of our stature. It might be said that we must earn the privilege of suffering — even that of damnation," he added, synthesizing a little Graham Greene. He drew a deep, delaying breath before delivering the tricky point. "You may have failed your husband or he you, but you may not deny him the pleasure of your body — within reason," he safely added, for whatever that might mean. "For God himself has ordained that the two — man and woman, you know — shall be one flesh."

The woman's attentions had not prevented her polishing off the remains of the peach pie during the course of this sermon. She washed down the last of it now with the gray dregs of her coffee. She shoved the dishes aside, wiping her mouth with the disintegrating paper napkin.

"It's ain't me I'm talking about. It's my daughter. I mean she dropped the question in my lap, see. I said can a man leave his wife for that, but actually it's the other way around. He thrun her out when she went on strike. It all comes to the same thing. He gave her the heave-ho. Now she's moved in with me."

"Ah! I think I'm beginning to see your problem," returned Father Plight with the ironic little twinkle in his eye.

The woman shook her head, not in demurrer at his note of cynicism, but in rueful reflection on the difficulties the reverberations of which had now reached her house.

"The scenes they had! See, he figured he could have his will of her whenever he wanted, like some men. You marry them and they pay your bills, so hence can pleasure theirself on you whenever they want. But that one of mine, huh! She's got a will of *her* own. When he tried to force hisself on her she'd pick up the phone and call the Police Department. 'Hello, Police Department? I want to report an attempted rape. The man? My husband.' 'But madam, it's not rape if it's your husband.' 'Oh, no? Look it up. The law's the law. And get someone down here and get this man off me, but fast!'"

In the course of this dramatic recapitulation the woman had raised her voice to a pitch that did, indeed, draw attention, not only from the nearby marsupial and gas-station attendant, but from diners in remote corners of the restaurant. Actual gestures, then pantomimes illustrative of a woman trying to fend off sexual attack, had begun to supplement her words as she acted out the scene.

" 'Get this man off my back, though it ain't exactly that part of me!' "

"Shh!" Smackenfelt said, stricken with fresh fears that he might indeed somehow be unmasked as a result of some fault in his handling of the scene the woman was creating (stealing, one might even say), booked for impersonating a priest, jailed for lack of bail money, miss the evening performance, kicked out of Equity —

" 'Get away! Stand back with that firehose nozzle. Just because you got one that's the envy of the gashouse gang —' "

"Please, Mrs. — ?"

"Wershba. 'Just because you're such hot stuff in one department don't make you the answer to a maiden's prayer, you know. I know my own marital rights —' "

"Lady, you've got to stop it," he whispered, his head lowered over the table, a hand to his brow. He seemed to be admonishing his beans. "Go to your own priest, see what he thinks. Get another opinion. I wash my hands of the case."

"I'm not Cat'lic."

"You're not Cat'lic?" Smackenfelt felt relieved, he could not have said why. Except that her being another fraud made him less a one, relatively speaking. Not that the fact made less precarious the pickle he had gotten himself into. He tried to wind this business up as speedily and unobtrusively as possible. "See your minister then. Better yet, get your daughter and her husband to see theirs. If they're not church-going people, then a marriage counselor. I'm not a psychologist, and would be acting under false pretenses if I gave you advice of that kind. These things can be ironed out. Now, you must excuse me. I must get back to the — to my parish."

"Where's that?"

"Other end of town."

"Too bad. I might join your church. You're nice. Kind of nice-looking too." With his nose in his own coffee mug he took in the woman's grin, rendered more beguiling than otherwise by a missing bicuspid. "Will you give me your blessing? I never had one of those."

"Certainly, my child." He made a hasty pass in the air to the accompaniment of a few murmured words, those of a benedictive Biblical text floating conveniently to mind from childhood, trusting to the woman's ignorance to safeguard him from exposure in a feature of the clerical office he had not been called upon occupationally to master.

"Thank you. You're the sort of person that makes you think priests should be allowed to marry. Do you think you will?"

"That's a hard question to answer. Now I must go," he said, rising. He was aware that the marsupial was definitely watching him now, with the steady unblinking gaze of her "young" itself, peering out over the top of its pouch.

"Will you pray for me?"

"Certainly, my child. Tonight. Who shall I say . . . ?"

"Mrs. Wershba."

"Ah, yes. And your daughter?"

"Mrs. Wollczienczieska."

"Ah, well. I'm Father Plight."

What he had experienced struck Smackenfelt as a theme for one of his and Dolly's home-front "bits" or "routines," the dramatic improvisations that had from the beginning been part of their domestic life together. He could not have foreseen that this twist in the road was the one destined to drive him an inch closer to that entanglement he was doing his best to resist.

Originally practice workouts for themselves as two actors and one playwright of varying, though scarcely ever recognizably ascending, fortunes, these rigmaroles made wherever they lived a kind of full-time studio. They also turned out to be psychodramas, not to say man-and-wife encounter groups of two, ventilating the problems and tensions of the married state—a secondary purpose that soon became the primary. No holds were barred and the sky was the limit. Anything could be told the other in the guise of the character assumed and in the heat of the situation posed — much like that of a motif accepted by actors onstage when thrown out to them by members of the audience. No restraint need be put on the emotion with which they laid about, for they were understood to be fencing with foils. Dolly herself had really given up acting for writing plays; none had so far been produced, but when their extemporaneous exchanges were on the boil she showed a keen sense of incident as well as a knack for the slashing phrase that might some day bear professional fruit at the typewriter.

Some of the identities adopted for their little mockups became permanent features of a marriage in which it was now difficult to tell real-life from play-acting (an increase of the mixture now held to be central to role-playing modern man). One such persona was Dolly's Swamp Tease. Smackenfelt, who had conceived it, directed her in it as well. He had even picked up a polka-dot dress in one of the second-hand shops in which he loved to rummage, which fitted Dolly a little too soon and was therefore perfect for the part. Barefoot, indeed otherwise naked, she wriggled and slithered on one haunch across the bedroom floor, retreating back out of reach as he lunged for her, darting behind the bed, emerging to inflame him once more before allowing herself, rash wanton, to be caught and possessed: primitive: feline: biting and scratching in her extremity. Welts down Smackenfelt's back, shreds of his skin under her nails, marked the hours when she need not be coaxed but slunk voluntarily forward in the Swamp Tease frock, by now itself in tatters. Smackenfelt did not much care for this scrimshaw work on his person for any length of time after the blind bouts of lust in which it had been born, but then. Sometimes she would tenderly sponge the results with warm water as he lay on his stomach, a Florence Nightingale dressing wounds she had herself inflicted, but not always. There was no guarantee of this soothing aftermath.

That was only one of many ideas worn thin by repetition, and he was glad to be able to bring home a fresh one after his encounter with the woman in the Automat.

"Now, this is the situation," he explained the next evening, a Monday when he had no performance. "I'm a hunky laborer and I want my nuts."

"That ought to be easy to work into the drawing room comedy I'm working on."

"This isn't for that. This is just for us — for hacks. So to try this on for size, I've come in the door, thrun my lunchbox aside, and intend to lay some pipe. Let's take it from there."

"Oh, I'm too tired." She was climbing into bed with a book.

"That's it! Great! You're dead on your feet, a woman claiming her right to a certain separateness, though as a Stella you wouldn't know what the hell that kind of talk was, and *I* don't get them fine distinctions at all. I'm a primitive," he continued, hunching his shoulders and letting his arms dangle to his knees as, naked, already steeped in the part, he lumbered like a gorilla to the bed on which she had settled stiffly back with the open novel on her chest, around which the covers had also been snugly drawn. "She's too tired. Pushin' buttons on dem labor-saving devices dat stupefy your soul all day? Dat got you tuckered? A man's got rights. You broads wit' dis liberation crap. Bunch of cockwallopers. And what's dis book?" He snatched it up and read the cover. "Flawbert. Who's dat?"

"I really am too tired," she said, twisting it from his grasp with a wan smile. "I'm not in the mood."

His part ran on then more or less as a monologue, regaling her. He shuffled and snuffled about the bedroom in his simian stoop (in more silken representations usable in her work in progress, his Ivy League slouch), beating his breast and baring his teeth as he rumbled in his all-purpose Eastern European accent, "Man got marital rights. Got nooky cominck to him end lonk day in mines. Go down shaft, come up shaft, day after day, man got rights have pleasure with his own shaft. Da! Do shaft job on you right now!"

Her elbows kept tightly clamped to her sides the covers he reached down to yank back, her eyes again fixed on the book. He grasped her arm, pulling it free.

"You're hurting me."

"Perhaps you're right."

He dropped the arm and turned away, though continuing to dilate on the possibilities inherent in the theme as stated, with its climactic potential for her: resisting priapic onset in no uncertain language, picking up the phone to call the police, or threaten to, all the elements of the scenario indelibly printed on his mind by the still haunting Mrs. Wershba. There was a side of him that enjoyed bracing immersion in vulgarity, though of a vicarious kind, and he was back in the swing of things the next day, the unlettered clod protesting his inalienable right to a nooner.

"I hate that expression," she answered, crisply.

"It's a bit coarse," he agreed, the first stage in a gradual ascent to more refined articulation of his sexual-drouth problem, a subject he found himself loth to relinquish, for some reason. Was he admitting to himself that it was more than a little autobiographical? Or subtly trying to accuse Dolly that it was? He felt his way around in assorted embodiments of the thwarted husband, settling finally into that of a hard-working executive whom more regular erotic releases would leave better fit for the grind of perpetual money-making. Drawing-room comedies were what Dolly tried to write anyway, not illuminations of the lower depths. She was a little more cooperative on being reminded of as much, though she didn't throw herself into things with as much zest as he—and she was chewing bubble gum a lot, an endearing habit that was beginning to nettle him no little. She could unobtrusively manage cuds of a size that sweetened not only her breath, but half the room. Gum helped her swear off cigarettes, and the consistency with which she chomped, snapped and blew wads of it nowadays indicated the need for serious appeasement that always went with concentration on a new work. She was off and galloping with something after a period of funk. That was good. All right then. Now.

"My dear," he began, one afternoon in their bedroom, taking up as an "educated" mate a subject that would have been far too prickly to handle were it not thus swaddled in make-believe, "you can't really call these prolonged silences of yours 'non-verbal communication.' I mean now that's really a bit thick."

"I don't want to talk about it."

"Thus we go round the same track. All right, we won't. I can think of something better. Come on to bed."

"Not today."

"I appeal to you."

"No you don't. Not any more."

Something about the elastic snap of the retort caught them both up short. There was a silence of a kind with an uneasy undercurrent. She tried to rout it by digging briskly for her notebook in the table at which she sat.

"I think I can use that."

"I think you just did."

She sat scribbling away at disproportionate length, both aware that, for one unguarded moment, she had not been fencing with foils. And the smile of ironic detachment he unsuccessfully forged made it equally plain that for the same instant he had dropped his mask. He stepped around to where he could see her face. Tears were rolling down her cheeks as she blew another bubble with the endlessly worried quid of gum. Again, real tears, or those of the actress who could cry on demand? Now with an effort to pick up the improvisation again, she said with histrionic excess, blinking away the tears with a smile to show it was all a game, "You men! You don't want a wife, most of you, nor a mistress either if it comes to that. Wives and mistresses alike spend too much time babying the bruised masculine spirit not to know that what a man really wants is — a mother!"

The only response to this was the "lost boy look," the fragile uncertainty underlying the air of worldly confidence but faultily concealing it, that she had found most beguiling in Stew Smackenfelt from the start, and that any woman worthy of the name must soon detect and want to clasp forever to her breast. Wearing this, then, he left the room (each seemed constantly to be exiting on strong lines delivered by the other), went down to the kitchen, where he threw together a voluminous Blodgett, which he took down another flight to eat in his basement retreat, behind the packing boxes.

He had finished the sandwich and was smoking a cigar over the Casting News in *Variety* when he heard footsteps slowly, apologetically, descending the cellar stair. His jaw tilted resolutely under the cigar clamped in his teeth, he hardened himself against any easy forgiveness, any quick pardon of the thrust on which he had been impaled. But when at last he agreed to raise his eyes from the *Variety*, in response to a timorously cleared throat, he saw that it wasn't Dolly's face deferentially poked around a corner of the packing cartons at all, but that of her mother.

"Stew? I come in?"

six

"Why did you stab yourself with a can opener that time?"

Aunt Ginger sat facing me close up on a camp stool she had drawn from a jumble of odds and ends in the storage bin against the side of which Dolly had slapped the cap that had regrettably sailed into the soup kettle, declining the lawn chair I moved to yield. She leaned toward me with the expression of one determined to have a heart-to-heart talk.

"Stewart? Why did you stab yourself with that can opener?" She gave my elbow a shake, as though to jiggle a reply out of me, as one prompts a bit of faulty machinery.

"It seemed a good idea at the time."

Why the woman had chosen a moment like this to ask a question like that, or asked it at all (save out of that sympathy that is often of a piece with their unimaginativeness in certain orders of good folk) your

Smackenfelt did not choose to explore. He remembered
the incident referred to with only partial clarity, and
no interest whatever. It had been brought on by a
mood another might guess at as lucidly as the principal could reconstruct: the sense of a long-standing
frustration of spirit that had prompted him, one night
in the lonesome October, when the skies were ashen
and sober, the leaves withering and sere, et cetera, to
jab his tum-tum with the pointed instrument alluded
to; choosing which, from an array of far sharper uten-
sils available in the kitchen drawer from which he had
snatched it, could be construed, now in résumé, as
much an act of self-preservation as its reverse. Right? A
"package" conniption, in the jargon of Spontini's trade.
Still, the puncture had required dressing and related
ministration from Dolly — performed in marked contrast to the stoicism with which she had stood with
folded arms a moment before and watched him lay
hands on himself. He wondered whether Birdie had a
notation on the episode for her thesis. He probably
owed her one, considering the preposterous project on
which he had encouraged her to embark. He might
also tell her about the time he had thrown a telephone
at somebody, another example of the "careful," or
qualified, violence of which he was becoming a master,
since the tethered instrument had of course never
reached its target, only fallen clattering to the floor.
Stuff like that there.

The milkmaid shifted a little on the stool and smiled
as she shook her head.

"Stabbing yourself with a can opener. That's not the
way."

"No, I know it."

Reluctant to plunge into the subject that had

brought her down, namely the marital row that had brought him here, she rose and examined the broken folding chair in which he sat. The tact with which she arbitrated quarrels was as remarkable as the uncanniness with which she sensed them. Vibrations of discord reached her through closed doors and from distant rooms, while the candor with which she offered her services as peacemaker was such as would long ago have got most mothers-in-law thrown out on their ear. It was a blend of walking on eggs and wading right in that never ceased to amaze the student-of-human-nature in one.

Dolly wanted to be rid of her, but not for "meddling;" in that role it amused one to think of her as a referee parting two adversaries in the ring, or, in less severe rivalries when something in the milder scale of a baseball metaphor sufficed, as a base or plate ump yelling "Foul!," "Safe!," "Fair!" or "Steeerike!"

She was now on all fours scrutinizing the trouble spot in the chair. It was split in one of the wooden crosspieces just at the joint. "I'd throw it out and get another one," she said, and sprang to her feet with a bright sigh, giving her plum-colored slacks a hitch, all signs that a transition was in the making. They were going to get down to brass tacks. Yet she seemed at the last instant to veer away from the subject of the wars — unless that wasn't what she had come down to be of service about at all. At last it was out. "I think I can help you take off some of that weight, Stew."

"Get this too, too solid flesh to melt?"

"You're all right but you need an editor. Look, why don't I just get my exercise manual and show you. I'll only be a sec."

As she ran upstairs to fetch it I could hear her meet

Dolly coming down from the bedroom floor. The two exchanged a word about provisions for dinner, then Dolly could be heard driving off to market in the car. I was hanging on by my teeth, more Gnashville. A town densely populated with all us frazzled egos. "When did the ego begin to stink?" asked Cyril Connolly, rhetorically of course.

"Here. Read this. I'll be back in half an hour or so, and then we can discuss the whole thing calmly."

The book with which I was again left alone was a large volume entitled *Taking Off*, which set forth a program guaranteed, if scrupulously followed, to reduce bodily measurements in areas one yearned to whittle down, the 'fat depots' (Oh, my God), for which specific disciplines were illustrated by pictures of trim young women enacting the calisthenics prescribed. These held one's interest briefly, to be routed by captioned descriptions of their rigors and the memory of an introduction calling for half to three-quarters of an hour of daily grind "without fail," together with a "rational diet" also to be rigidly adhered to. I laughed aloud at the notion of Blodgett being held to any such Spartan regimen. Poor Blodgett! It would be murder for him. The only faintly sybaritic note struck was: "Most of these exercises can be done lying on the floor, minimizing the danger of pulled ligaments and bad backs."

Letting the book fall into my lap, I woolgathered of sturdy ancestors who had reclaimed land from the sea and built dikes in feats of Herculean discipline, but had also given the world bedsheets. Soon back among the casting items in *Variety*, I saw that there was an audition call for the national tour of a play for which I had read in the first instance, and been turned down as overqualified. Each such rebuff made more sardonic the tone with which one would decline an Oscar, when the time came. In some versions accepting it, even more acidly. "We need not dismiss out of hand the 'mercuries of approbation,' as Emerson termed the self-appointed touchstones of merit," one would say, in white tie and tails, with an ironic smile for the thought that anyone there at one's feet had ever heard of Emerson, let alone read him. One would do the whole thing with one's high, dry, lop-chopped Walter Matthau, and so cool you could keep eggs fresh within a ten-foot radius around one. The headache induced by 'fat depots' slowly receded . . .

"Well? What do you think?" Aunt Ginger was back, starting me from my revery. I guiltily dropped *Variety* and picked up the manual.

"Sounds great. Will it really take an inch or two off your waist? And other fat depots?" The hideous little phrase had its hooks into me, despite everything.

"In a month, maybe three weeks. But you've *got to stay with it*, half an hour a day, rain or shine, no matter who's president. Do that and in thirty days we'll have you a comedian in baggy pants. I guarantee it."

Something in the "we" prompted me to shuffle back to a page on which it was pointed out that the exercises could largely be done on the floor, where my eye was also caught by: "Wives and husbands may do them together."

"It's going to be a kind of drag learning them from the descriptions."

"Oh, I'll show you. That'll cut corners."

Thus it was that I found myself lugging downstairs into the basement the wrestling mat on which my mother-in-law had been conducting her routines in her bedroom. Clad in the swimming trunks in which this move had been made, I stood on an overturned box while with a tape measure she took my dimensions and recorded them in a notebook, for comparison with one's sizes a month later to see how much progress had been made in slimming down. Like a kind tailor she forebore murmuring aloud proportions to be set down tangibly enough on paper. And each new suit of clothes was a moment of truth enough. That a few might now be taken in was the promise held out by the in-law kneeling there in her black leotard, pencil in her teeth and the notebook beside her on the floor as she girdled my parts and members in turn with the tape.

I began to be disturbed by something. I tingled with pleasure at these contacts. Worse than that, my excitement rose as she worked her way down from my chest and upper arms, to my waist, then steadily southward. I fixed my gaze straight ahead at the far wall, trying to set myself like flint against the now undeniable stimulations of her touch, her own abbreviated garb, and the fragrance drifting upward of mingled cologne and body powder, together with whatever unguents she may have applied to herself for these workouts. Talk about Gnashville! I ground my teeth as she drew the tape snugly around the upper part of my left thigh, helpless against inflammations with which I had not been embarrassed since a woman doctor had examined me for something in a hospital. I looked down at her firm legs and curving flanks swelling taut in the kneeling posture, half fearing some sign that she herself guessed my condition. In my animation, I was appalled. Truly sorry. Such an occurrence as threatened would be insupportable, reducing personal relations to a mess well-nigh impossible to tidy up. I tried to check myself with anti-aphrodisiac thoughts: an uncle who had recently died, leaving me nothing; Art Buckett, her recently discarded mate, throwing peanuts into the air and catching them in his mouth, as reported; possible gallstones, darkly hinted at by my physician; the spectre of unemployment a week hence — and not such a spectre either, a grim reality. Several rolls of wallpaper already purchased with no moneys in sight with which to hire a paperhanger. Oneself on a ladder getting at it with disastrous results, the ladder overturned and the paste-pot with it, oneself under a collapsing scroll with a foot in the pail . . .

That wallpaper was surely a counter-intoxicant? It was Aunt Ginger's taste. It had been an anniversary present, another of the countless things that we "needed" and she bought us under the guise of occasional commemorations, some trumped up, like the anniversary of my and Dolly's first date, or that of our having moved into the house, some openly ludicrous, like her "Fourth of July gift" of an electric broiler. A trail of such gratuities, easily afforded by Mother on money inherited from Bill Truepenny and wisely kept out of Art Buckett's clutches, marked her determination to pay her way as a lodger and then some. Once or twice when she had even coughed up the mortgage money for the house it seemed as though the young people were living with her rather than the other way around. Christmas would in all probability find her footing the bill for the paperhanger too. In fact, it had been all along clearly anticipated, and so letting the interior decorating be her "treat" had entailed from the start a kind of moral obligation to let her participate in the choice of paper. Not in so many words, simply by

letting her counsel prevail. Now the scenes-from-
Williamsburg rolls stood propped in a corner of the
dining room, soon to be unfurled like the battle-flag of
an alien taste. Why had Dolly yielded so readily to it,
from among flowered, striped and dotted semi-finals at
least a *little* less parochial? Could you detect a trace of
rubbing salt into one's own wounds, a Machiavellian
flick of perversity in Dolly's approving what might be
ammunition stored up for later use against me? I imagined the obligatory scene toward which we all slowly
rushed. "You wanted it just because it's so awful," I
could hear her say, "a daily reminder of what I make
you put up with. My family. Oh, God, the deviousness
of people!" I couldn't have agreed with her more,
though I would keep a firm snaffle on my own tongue.
I would watch with helpless affection the climax of the
scene as foreshadowed from the start: poor Dolly
clawing the paper from the wall with her bare fingers
as she exclaimed, "I won't have it! I won't be punished
any longer!" Sinking to her knees with shreds of
Williamsburg under her red talons (rather than fragments of my skin as in bouts of passion abed). I gave
my head a shake, as if physically to shake from my
brain the figments of this fantasy. But there was reality
sober enough in my recollection of her saying more
than once, "You'd like her to leave, wouldn't you,
Stew?" and my returning, all too honestly, "Not at all."
Yes, the precedent-setting, the ground-breaking, fron-
tier-forging truth, the plain unbelievable shrieking fact
was: I had the hots for my mother-in-law. I wanted to
go to bed with her.

I had once caught a glimpse of her naked, or as near
naked as made no matter, as I passed her slightly open
bedroom door. She was arrested in the charming sculp-

turesque mid-pose with which a woman slips an arm through the loop of a brassiere, and had glanced out as I did in. "Oh!" she'd gasped, kicking the door shut, yet not without a smile of searing coquetry. Not a reference was made to the incident, beyond the laughing shrug exchanged when we passed each other in the kitchen a few minutes later.

This woman was now at my feet in a leotard — or was it the thing called a tutu? — and, at the level where she was presently taking readings, my state must be inescapable. "Battle of the Bulge is good," she said, with a laugh. I lowered my eyes in horror; but the innocent creature had apparently only meant one's incipient pot, which she now took the liberty of poking with a forefinger. She laughed as she made a jotting in her notebook. I began to feel that the danger was passing. Calamity had been spared me in the case of the woman doctor, but it had been a near thing. The incident seemed to be repeating itself now, though it was if anything an even closer shave. A hair's-breadth now separated the moment when convulsion seemed inevitable, from that in which presently its threat abated with the tape measure's downward course, to the knees, the calves, finally, thank God, the ankles.

"There!" She shut the notebook and sprang to her feet, with the extra light bounce of which acrobats are fond. "We won't look at this again till a month from now, when we compare it with the new figures. Or figure." The brisk pedagogical tone with which she began instruction, quite as between teacher and pupil, completed the return to normality. All this while, I remained secretly amused at what was in store for Blodgett; indeed the clobbering he was about to get in the round of exertions, grim by his lazy lights, through which he was now to be put, in steeply escalating daily doses from which there was no prospect of his deriving carnal reward — in case he had that bee in his bonnet. The steaming intimacy of the gymnastic mat was not one he was going to convert to any fancy ends, of that I would make jolly well certain!

The first routine was the Opposite Arm and Leg Touch. Lying on her back on the mat, she touched her upraised left leg with her right hand, then vice versa, and back again. Easily demonstrated, quickly grasped. "We'll do this one thirty times," she said as I lay down beside her on the wrestling mat, will-less, in near despair. She switched on a portable phonograph, hauled down as optional paraphernalia, and together we kicked and swung in rhythm to the strains of "Yes, sir, that's my baby, no, sir, don't mean maybe."

"O.K! Ready and — *one*, two, three, four, *up*, down, up, down . . ."

Exercise is an unnatural act. The body loathes artificially imposed regimentation as profoundly as it exults in the unthinking muscular rhythms of walking, running, swimming, and of labor too, of felling trees and plowing fields and stalking game. Perhaps it is the mind that rejects clocked and tallied exertion; the entire organism in any case senses and shares the reluctance. Such business may even be unhealthy. Smackenfelt's resistance to the monotonously repeated calisthenics through which he, nevertheless, forced himself was of an unsalutary order. He detested these wretched rounds of gyrations, conducted on his back, most of them, but sometimes on his front, on this side then that, or seated, standing, even crawling on his misbegotten belly, that fat depot where he had once tried to run himself through — always heaving and snorting away beside the smoothly breathing fluidly flailing Tante Ginger. What a price Blodgett paid for the simple writhing propinquity of one whose ripe flesh there was no question of his being so much as let accidentally graze. Chaste revel! Celibate bacchanal! Let him rather puff and toil his share of the way toward that happy day a month hence when scale and tape measure alike would proclaim that we had at last and indeed mortified the flesh, who had been so long mortified by it. His taskmaster positively glowed at the end of the workouts, he by contrast slumped in the gray sweat suit, erotically deterrent enough in itself, decreed by the manual as best for the male purpose, glad that another round of hideous boredom and wretched slavery was over — and feeling that he could eat a horse.

My routines were graduated, ten for the first three days, a few more added on the fourth and fifth, and so on, everything previously introduced being retained till I had mastered the entire set of forty. Finished with my quota for a given day, I would sit by with a cigarette and a dietetic soft drink and watch Tante demonstrate what was next to be added to the repertory. Often then we would chat, background music not being a constant.

"What does *Schadenfreude* mean?" she asked, "bicycling" on her back.

"Why?"

"I've heard you use it several times lately, and then just came across it in a book, the way we do with a new word. What does it mean?"

"Malicious pleasure in the suffering of others. Why do you ask?"

"No reason at all. Just like I said. One of those

coincidences we have with words." The legs stopped pumping at their appointed count of fifty, and she settled lithely over on a haunch. "Now then. We're going to walk on our buttocks."

"Oh, no. I didn't see anything like that in the book."

"It's in the appendix called 'Six for Good Measure.' Spot exercises for reducing specific trouble spots. Abdomen and hiney are everybody's problem, and throwing you something out of right field now and then keeps away monotony. So come sit down on the mat here, like so, legs not quite straight out, bent a little, hands resting lightly on knees. Now we'll 'walk' on our tailums, ten 'steps' forward then ten backward. And we do this six times. If we start away at the end here we won't march off the mat. Maybe a little music for this one?" She snapped the phonograph on and set "Darktown Strutters Ball" going. "Here we go! *I'll* be down to *meetcha* in a *taxi* . . . Five, six, seven . . ."

This mat — where Blodgett continued to wrestle only with that part which, though perhaps not an angel, was determined to remain the better half — became presently the scene of certain workouts that struck me as peculiar for someone troubled principally with having got a bit thick in the flitch. So I consulted the book again to see what else I might be having thrown at me "out of right field." It developed that one of the disciplines, with dumbbells, was "for strengthening the pectoral muscles and firming the bust," and the other for "eliminating dowager's hump."

"Am I a buffalo, for Pete's sake?" I protested, "and what's all this about firming up in the pectoral department? I'm not aspiring to be a pinup for those beefcake magazines."

"Well, you have this kind of intellectual stoop, the

Harvard slouch we used to call it, not that you didn't go to Iowa State, but even apart from all that, the point is for straightening the spine as part of *toning the whole system.* You don't want to be this beautiful hard faun of a Pan below, and then above the belt this what's-his-name slob of a god you see sitting under a tree in ancient Greece with a mug in his hand, do you?"

"I guess you mean Silenus. The foster father of Bacchus. No, I don't."

"And so as for firming up the bust, have you done any jogging lately? I think you'll see what I mean, Stew. Or jump a rope."

Still in my sweat suit, I trotted a lap or two around the property, and saw what she meant. While not in the class of the girl who got two black eyes riding horseback without a brassiere, I could still feel the damned things flapping away for a fare-thee-well with each step. In fact I could *hear* them going clackety-clack in a most abysmal rhythm as I panted about the grounds. "My God," I breathed. Well might the stars concern themselves with what to do about flab. The subject was never again mentioned, nor did I ever again challenge my mentor's wisdom.

I kept my promise neither to step on the scale nor use the tape measure until the thirty-day trial period was up. Clothes tell their own story, though, and I had one suit in particular, a gray-green gabardine, that I despaired of ever again getting into, except for some low-comedy purpose such as a *tableaux vivant* series on old jokes of which this would illustrate "When they saw how tight his pants were they thought they'd split." Spotting it hanging there in the back of my closet, like a spectre mutely rebuking me, I struggled against the temptation to see whether the button and buttonhole of the trousers might now be brought within hailing distance of one another (confirming evidence conversely offered by some of my other pants that things were beginning to loosen up a little). Standing irresolutely behind my closed bedroom door, I could hear Dolly hammering away at her typewriter in a back room. Aunt Ginger, of whom this would be principally a betrayal, was reading in her own room. Suddenly I seized the suit, ripped the trousers off the hanger, and, trying not to cheat by sucking in my gut, climbed into them.

"My God," I gasped again, this time with delight. I could button them! Nor did the seat threaten to be rent from top to bottom, like the veil of the temple, when I bent over. A hasty experimental squat established that beyond all cavil. In an ecstasy, I decided to wear it to a party Dolly and I were going to that evening.

I popped into the hallway, to encounter Aunt Ginger bursting from her own room, waggling a book she'd been wading through.

"You talk about the agony of writing. Have you tried to *read* anything lately? This has no plot and no characters, is not *about* anything, only some vague abstract 'They,' and shifts from prose into poetry without a word of warning. That blank verse, what do you call it — ionic pentameter?"

Dolly shot from her workroom. "Mother —" She laughed.

She too was in a good mood, the new play going swimmingly, at least in terms of quantity of manuscript being amassed. How happy everyone was! What euphoria all around!

The Smackenfelts jabbered as they bathed and dressed, setting out for the Shaftoes' party in soaring spirits. They laughed as they scurried through a drizzle toward the car.

"Your mother thinks if I lose a lot of weight I'll get to be too big for my britches. That's exactly what she said, Dolly."

"She never misses."

"Then it's O.K. if she stays on for a bit?"

"If that's what you want."

"Because I need a little more time."

"I got a traffic ticket at this stop sign, for not coming to a full stop. What the cops call just a rolling stop."

It is after dinner at the Shaftoes', and the guests are trying to place the comedian your Smackenfelt is unmistakably taking off. Doing to a T with a little routine he has also worked up for their pleasure. They give every promise of falling flat on their faces again.

"A traffic ticket for not coming to a full stop at this intersection with a through street, ladies and gentlemen. So the next day I went by the same corner and stopped at the same sign, only this time I stopped *cold*. I mean a dead stop. Then I sat there and counted five to make sure, before starting up again. The same cop ran up with his ticket book out, and I says 'Now what have I done?' and he says, 'You're double-parked.' "

"Phil Silvers?"

"George Burns?"

"No, I think it sounds more like Henny Youngman. Yes, that's who he's doing, Henny Youngman."

They were bombing again, every last one. It was Zero Mostel, but they would rot in hell before he told them. He went on with the routine, gave them a little more. They were in this together, all of them, up to their rotten necks.

"An existentialist cop, you see. Man cannot win, a pawn in an irrational universe. So anyway, I went to this fortune teller with a crystal ball — I'm a seersucker, you know. A fool for clairvoyants? — this fortune teller who's also a theosophist. She believes in reincarnation. So she looked into her ball, and finally says, 'You're going to return to this earth as a turtle.' And I says, 'That'll be a snappy comeback.' "

"George Jessel," said Boots Pewbridge.

He gave his smiling headshake, his "Nooo" articulated with the inner serenity of all great performances. It wasn't now that if he stank — if, that is, his bits were subject to a spectrum of interpretations so broad as to accommodate all the above and God knew how many more yet to come — then they would all go down together. He wasn't rubbing salt into the common wound of their realization that he was so bad he had a following, like the terrible soprano, what was her name again, whose concerts were on that account sellouts, he wasn't riding the crest of a will to fail, or any of that. Not tonight. Tonight he plain didn't give a plugged damn. He was losing weight. In a euphoria such as he had rarely known he was wearing the gray-green gabardine into which six months ago he had abandoned all hope of ever again compressing himself. Even Birdie, who was here tonight, had commented, mournfully voicing the likelihood of having to give him up as her thesis subject — of which he would not hear. He took her by the hand, having had his sport, and led her into a corner where they might talk. Have another little interview, whether she had her notebook along or not.

"But Uncle Fats, you've already given me three earliest recollections."

"I'm only trying to help. You yourself say this earliest recollection thing isn't significant as a memory, but as a selective principle tipping us off to the personality. Well, that may vary with a change in trouble or fortune, and with it the incident fished up from the Sargasso Sea of the past. Now I definitely think it was watching the orange roll out of sight under my crib. Yes, that was it. That's as far back as I can go, or anybody. Don't let Salvador Dali put you on with his intra-uterine memories."

"Can I bank on this, Unc?"

"Absolutely."

"Let's go into now, then. You're slimming down beautifully because you're not overeating — but for what reason? An emotional need has been removed. Or replaced. But what?"

"No, darling, I think it's the other way around. I no longer have to seek comfort in food because I'm slimming down."

"But . . ."

"It's simple. I was stuffing myself because I was overweight. I ate because I was fat."

"Ah. Like the man in that play who drank to forget the ravages of alcohol."

"Go to the head of the class."

His euphoria scattered abruptly at the sight of something that now occurred.

Through a momentary gap in the clusters of guests wandering in and out of the smoky room, he had caught a glimpse of Dolly and Spontini holding hands. Or at least of Spontini holding hers. Dolly at the mo-

ment was saying something to the other of the two men
between whom she sat wedged on a small divan, so
that any "aggressive" in the act seemed rather to be
entirely Zap's. It may have meant nothing at all, no
more than such things ever did in the flushed and
jumbled camaraderie of a party boiling on past midnight. Smackenfelt, though, in one of the lightning
associations common to instants such as this, recalled
having accidentally clapped an eye on something of
the sort before. At the Wusdatts' once, the two had
marched in the processional to the buffet table with
their small fingers linked, like the twisted components
in those nail puzzles which can be extricated with only
the most delicately exact procedures — certainly not a
bust in the mush. That novelty-shop teaser was becoming an obsession with Smackenfelt, as a metaphor for
human entanglements of the sexual kind. That was
why he probably ought not exaggerate what he had
seen as evidence that somebody was trying to make
time with his wife, as they had said in Chicago and
possibly broader segments of the Middle West. He
would have dismissed it all from his mind but for
something else just then.

Zap, himself noting Smackenfelt's awareness of the
tableau of which he formed a part, impulsively removed his hand from Dolly's: a reflex that cost him the
betrayal of his guilt. To cover up, he pretended he had
raised both his hands in order to clap them, as a gesture of applause for the turn with which Smackenfelt
had, again, stumped them all.

To pooh-pooh what he had seen, assure himself that
his fears were groundless, Smackenfelt proceeded to
catch up feminine hands on his own. He even held
Milly Shaftoe's for some time, evidence that this sort of

thing went on constantly at parties and that a man was a fool to worry about it. They were part of a group in the adjoining library, from which she presently broke away to attend to a fresh social chore — namely the arrival of Poodle Slater.

That gadabout rarely spent an evening in one place, at least on a weekend. Hostesses didn't mind his party-hopping, since he flitted from one to the other carrying the pollen of gossip. Tonight the courier had a special tidbit. It was a crack Spontini had made about Smackenfelt's readings from Shakespeare at a local charity dinner. He regaled a group in the library with it, none of them aware that Smackenfelt was sitting nearby with his back to them, paging through a book he had plucked from the shelf.

"It's too rich." He paused to take a sip of his highball, while the others refreshed their memories or were filled in on the soliloquies declaimed, notably Cardinal Wolsey's wrenching, "Farewell, a long farewell to all my greatness."

"What did Zap say, Poodle?" one of his hearers prompted.

"He called it — it's too priceless. 'Funny without being vulgar.'"

Smackenfelt sprang to his feet, swivelling into view as the round of laughter filled the room. When it subsided, he shut the book with a report like a pistol shot. There was a collective gasp as he squeezed it back into its place on the shelf.

"Why, Stewart," Poodle said, giggling nervously. "I didn't realize —"

"Not at all. It was wonderful. I must go talk to Zap."

"Please, Stew — don't tell him I —"

"Have no fears, Poodle. This is one for the book."

He strode, smiling, into the main living room. He couldn't have been more delighted. He had Spontini by the scruff this time, all right. He threaded his way through the crowd, looking around for him. He found him still, or again, cozily perched on the couch with Dolly. Conversation in their group continued for a few minutes, then broke off when some of the guests became aware of Smackenfelt standing there with an unmistakable air of purpose.

"Zap, I heard what you said about my Shakespeare. 'Funny without being vulgar.' "

"Who said that?"

"Oscar Wilde. What he called Sir Beerbohm Tree's Hamlet, if I'm not mistaken, wasn't it?"

Spontini turned scarlet. "I meant who told you I said that?"

"What does it matter? The thing is, you've put me in very impressive company, and I'm grateful."

The blood now drained from Spontini's face, leaving it pale and mottled. His nostrils flared characteristically again in that resemblance to Smackenfelt's moose-in-rut bit. The others sat or stood in stunned silence. Spontini cleared his throat nervously, and at last spoke.

"It takes as much wit to remember a line at the right moment as to think of it."

"Wonderful! What the character in *The Scoundrel* answered, wasn't it, when overheard quoting somebody without giving credit? Who was it again? Nietzsche? Maybe it was Schopenhauer. We must ask somebody. Where are all the buffs? Let's get Bert Shaftoe, he'll remember. We've got to settle this. Hey, Bert!"

Spontini rose.

"We'll settle it outside, Smackenfelt. Shall we go?"

"Swell."

Three or four clutched at Spontini's arms, including Dolly, to restrain him. At the same time Smackenfelt felt his own elbows firmly grasped by peacemakers. There were outcries of, "Oh, my God, not again," and "When are you two going to knock it off?" and so on, as the combatants were forcibly hustled apart to separate ends of the room, and then, for the balance of the evening, of the house itself.

Dolly got Smackenfelt home soon after that. She drove the car, insisting he had drunk too much to take the wheel. He slumped against the door with a glowing cigar, apparently in the best of spirits.

"Women are always breaking up a good dogfight," he said cheerfully.

She laughed, herself quite recovered from the stern mood in which she had helped avert those hostilities.

"That was quite petty of him. Did Wilde really say that about Tree's Hamlet? You know your soliloquies went over with a bang. Everyone says so. So why do you take offense? Zap is — sick as we all are of the word — terribly insecure. Why must you always nail him to the barn door?"

"Me nail him. Love that girl."

Dolly drove in silence for some time. A good-humored silence in which, even in his haze, he sensed that she had something on her mind, something other than the thwarted fisticuffs.

"Zap thinks I have possibilities as a model."

"He's switching to representation?" Smackenfelt sat up, grinning amiably. "Nudes will certainly be an improvement on those cowchips he's been doing. Not that I'm any judge."

"He's having a show of those, you know. Man in Greenwich who's hung up on abstract expressionism is taking an interest in him. But I don't mean posing for him."

"What then?"

"TV commercials."

"What will you do, simply spray away unwanted hair?"

"Actually, he says I have a certain — you won't laugh?"

"Hardly!"

"A certain gamin quality."

"Saw it from the very start. First time I clapped an eye on you."

"Then why didn't you tell me?"

"I didn't want to make *you* laugh."

"Anyway that's what Zap thinks will come through. Might. This urchin note."

"Which we haven't really had struck since those first Italian films." He reached to squeeze her hand, which she overturned briefly to requite his caress before setting it back again on the steering wheel. "What will he do, rig you up in a ragamuffin sweater and a Jackie Coogan cap with the peak switched round to the side?"

"That might be a good idea. Can't you see me, thus photographed on a side street against the wall of a building from which the posters are peeling, holding out a cake of soap anybody can afford? First, of course, he'll have to give me a voice and screen test. Or would have if you hadn't bollixed it up."

Smackenfelt stirred upward again on the seat, this time genuinely amused. He nearly choked on his cigar, the stump of which he finally tossed out the window.

"Bollixed it up, I probably put it in the bag for you. Or locked it up, as they say in the trade. You don't have to be an amateur psychologist, or even have a woman's intuition, to know that anything he is doing *for* you he is doing *to* me. That would be a nifty package."

"Thank you."

"Oh, not that he isn't right. You'll be swell — as the stupe should have guessed long ago. I'm only talking about his motivation."

"Which would be news to Zap."

"He doesn't know anything about human nature, least of all his own. He wouldn't recognize it if it was under his nose. But you and I can see it, can't we? He'll make you a star, put your name in lights in a profession wherein I schlep along on two hundred a week, *when* I can get it. He wants to make a fool out of me. But by all means take a crack at it. We'll be out *on* the streets he'll make this bit about plucking you off of, if something doesn't happen soon."

"I agree with you, Stew. Main reason I'd do it would be for the money. Then we wouldn't be so dependent on my mother."

Regretting the cigar, a bootlegged Havana Bert Shaftoe had slipped him and which he had pitched away too soon, Smackenfelt gazed out the window at a stretch of woodlot they were passing. "Five will get you ten he'll be on the blower tomorrow setting up a date for this studio test. So much for my queering everything."

Smackenfelt was on his hands and knees on the floor of the garage, taking a hammer to a coconut. It was the next morning, Sunday, and he had a hangover. In fact a real katzenjammer, one of those tell-that-cat-to-stop-stamping-his-feet headaches. He had mixed himself a morning-after corrective of tomato juice and condiments, roughly a Virgin Mary, at which from time to time he penitentially sipped. He had the glass beside him on the floor of the garage.

He rolled the coconut about, trying to settle on a good position, or angle, at which to strike the definitive blow, like a diamond cutter with a rough stone. There was a TV commercial in which such a cutter managed this crucially delicate operation, apparently insanely suspense-making in its way, in the back seat of a Mercury, without turning the gem to powder, by way of demonstrating the car's smooth ride. Aunt Ginger wanted some shredded fresh coconut with which to top a fruit salad she was fixing for their lunch. He would have to prise chunks of the meat loose from the shell with a screwdriver or some such, which he supposed he ought first to sterilize, or at least thoroughly scrub. There was also the matter of trying to catch as much of the milk as possible. He had a mixing bowl on hand for that. He was thinking ahead to all these complex problems, the hammer poised in midair, when under the crook of his upraised arm he saw a pair of blue sneakers and the cuffs of some yellow duok trousers materialize soundlessly beside him.

"Have you got a minute, old man?"

"Hello, Zap."

"I've come to apologize," Spontini said, apologetically.

Assuming a sudden erect position, though on his knees, made Smackenfelt's head swim. He looked up slowly. Whether because of his condition, or because the facts were such, Spontini seemed to be swaying in arcs so large that one had the illusion his shoes must be nailed to the floor, as the only explanation for his not pitching forward on his face. Smackenfelt sighed heavily, then climbed reluctantly to his feet. As he did so, his eyes again mechanically swept the other's person for signs of sexual gratification in these self-immolations, the masochistic element now widely speculated on as present in the continual abasements of Spontini's, not only by such purveyors of explanation as Birdie and Ginger Truepenny, but almost anyone in local circles familiar with the rigmaroles at all. There was a school that held them to be civilized rarefications of the blood sacrifices conducted by primitive peoples, such as the Aztecs, the principal roles for which were said to have rewards as well as drawbacks. Zap's getup in general was an uneasy blend of Ship'n Shore and tennis garb.

"What I said about your Shakespeare was inexcusable. I've got to make it up to you."

"You will, Oscar, you will."

"Don't." Spontini closed his eyes and drew an endless breath, as though only by inflating his lungs to the bursting point could he acquire the strength to go on with this. "It wasn't as though I didn't appreciate certain aspects of what you did. Your gestures, for example, were superb."

Smackenfelt fueled himself with a similar respiratory intake. "Praising an actor for his gestures," he said, "is like recommending a seafood restaurant for its tartar sauce."

"Do you think this is quite the time for epigrams, Stew?"

Smackenfelt looked down at the Virgin Mary, the unsledged coconut, and the mixing bowl on the oily floor. He still had the hammer in his hand. He transferred his scrutiny from the coconut to Zap's skull, hefting the hammer slightly.

"I just wanted to get this off my chest and over with. It's too hot to hassle."

Smackenfelt stepped over to a thermometer hanging beside the garage door. "It's seventy-one. But then I suppose the humidity . . ." He walked back to the middle of the garage, picked up the glass with its repentant draught, and drank. He set the glass down on a bench.

"I think maybe you and I can bury the hatchet somehow on this committee we'll be working on, Fats."

"Which one is that?"

"For integrated housing? For the town? You're listed on the stationery. Or are you just letting them use your name?"

Smackenfelt's glance warned him not to be engaging in ironies for which he might be held further accountable. He then gave a sardonic snort and said, "Forget it, Zap. I forgive you. And maybe doing good works together will clear things up between us."

"Thanks, old man."

The ritual was over — except for the concluding handshake so much more trying than the hostilities it brought to an official close, followed by another of the *abbraccios* suffocating our poor Smackenfelt in smells of breakfast coffee, tobacco and cologne as Spontini, crushing him in the Latin bearhug, breathed into his ear that he wanted them to be friends. The Dutchman felt as though his entrails were going through a mangle.

"Want to come in a moment, Zap? I'll be right along after I crack this coconut."

"No! I don't want anybody else to . . ." What he

wished to spare others, or be spared, was not made clear, because his voice dribbled away in a mutter. Maybe he didn't want the women to see him looking the fright he certainly did. He turned and trotted away along the hedge toward his parked car, trailing promises of making it up to Smackenfelt by possibly "doing something for Dolly."

Smackenfelt shook his head as he watched him padding silently out of sight over the grass in the direction of the street, again like a thief making a getaway. He suddenly remembered an incident that could have been thought of as giving one an instructive glimpse into the tangled roots of sado-masochism — or whatever one might call this human duality that must have existed long before the clinical jargon that made it seem a product of modern man. No other word for it came to mind, though.

Smackenfelt had been riding the train into town. The coach had been one of those rattletraps the bankrupt railroad seemed to have gotten on loan from a museum run by transportation buffs. A truly vintage vehicle, with electric fans instead of air conditioning, and those wicker seats reminiscent of an era when men with celluloid collars and watch-chains spanning their vests went up to ladies travelling alone and asked whether they might be of service. Perhaps commercial "drummers" gallantly flicking cards into view, though on their way to some fresh skulduggery with a farmer's daughter. An arrow or two flying in an open window not inconceivable. This coach was dirty and foul-smelling as well as jammed. Smackenfelt was standing in the aisle next to a seat occupied on the outside by a plump, ruddy man one might easily picture as so dressed, and so behaving, in the foretime. He rose at one point to remove his coat, and, in so doing, inadvertently swung out his arm at an angle that caught Smackenfelt squarely on the nose, and with a force that made it start to bleed. Smackenfelt took out a handkerchief and held it in a wad against his face. The traveller could not have been more sorry. Smackenfelt told him to think nothing of it. "Please go back to your newspaper." But his nose didn't stop bleeding and it didn't stop bleeding. A scene built up, one of those things.

The man himself was by no means the only one who was by now thoroughly wretched. Passengers over an increasingly wide area of the car were drawn into the embarrassment. Then a curiously subtle thing happened. Our Smackenfelt began to enjoy their discomfort, as they perceptibly began to resent him as the one now at fault. Why didn't he move, or something? Why did he stand there and make them all suffer? That was what he sensed, grinning covertly behind his handkerchief. They actually started to glare at him. He twisted partially to the right and then the left, as though to demonstrate the impossibility of squeezing his way in either direction up the crowded aisle, though he hadn't the least intention of moving. He seemed positively to *enjoy* the pain thus turned back on both the man who had inflicted his on him, and the witnesses drawn unwillingly into its magnetic field. At one stage, as though they had all had enough, he looked at his handkerchief and murmured that the flow seemed to be abating — at least that the danger of a hemorrhage was averted.

"Hemorrhage!" the poor guy said, gulping.

That was when the others really did glower at him and rattle their magazines and newspapers in no uncertain manner. He was now the villain, there was no doubt about that.

At last he did, after a final glance at the handkerchief, pocket it, nodding and smiling at the offender, and letting the poor devils all off the hook. But the experience remained as an illuminating glimpse of the complicated dividends to be derived from personal pain as a method of Making Others Pay.

He had long ago finished bashing in the coconut by the time these reflections came to an end. He took everything inside to the kitchen, where he stood at the sink prying pieces of the meat loose from the shell with the hygienically boiled screwdriver. After that he shredded them with a cheese grater. His hangover gradually cleared, and by noontime he was quite keen for the fruit salad Ginger had prepared. It was topped with his gratings after being doused with kirsch. The bread they broke with it was one of those dark imported pumpernickels that are so much like chewing tobacco.

The two of them all but lunched alone. Ginger was about to call Dolly down from her study, where she had spent the morning writing, when there was a phone call for her. She had had an extension installed up there "so she wouldn't be disturbed when she was working," an absurdity Smackenfelt found as endearing as any. The gist of this non sequitur seemed to be that she could, without leaving the study, take calls for her which she would presumably not have foregone in any case, being a woman. She was a long time on the wire this time, so long that she paused midway to call down an instruction for them to start lunch without her.

They were nearly finished when at last she came

downstairs. Stew turned inquiringly, a quid of the chewing-tobacco-type pumpernickel in one cheek.

"That was Zap," she said. "He thinks he can set up the test for me about Wednesday. He has some copy ready already. And he loves your idea of the Jackie Coogan cap."

seven

Aunt Ginger settled the trousers on her lap and, with a sharp razor blade, deftly slit the seam along the seat from the waist down. He had lost fourteen pounds and three inches, and she was taking in his clothes.

Smackenfelt, pacing, glanced at the clock on the mantel. Eleven twenty and Dolly wasn't home yet, not having arrived on either of the two evening trains she could have caught even after "grabbing a bite" with Spontini.

"Bites" had been "grabbed" at such Manhattan holes-in-the-wall as L'Etoile, Romeo Salta's and Voisin, prior to studio night sessions on the street urchin at which she had presumably been working all day. Three pears sat on a table under a sunlamp: Ginger's method of ripening green fruit. He smiled to himself as he stewed: had he not always liked married life? He remembered a saying of his mother's. *"Zoals het klokje thuis tikt, tikt het nergens."* As the clock ticks at home, ticks it nowhere. In other words, home, sweet home. Of course the clock here was electric, and the second hand swam steadily on toward midnight around its inscrutable face. Perhaps a house had been a cozier place, better calculated to knit folk up for a lifetime, when clocks had tick-tocked audibly as its beating heart. He made a face at his own trite conceit, though again darting a look at the clock. Five minutes had passed in the course of all these ruminations. There was a train due in now, if on time.

The trousers were rearranged on the seamstress's lap in a crisp manner.

"I'd give her a piece of my mind."

"Oh, *would* you?"

He paced as the musician in a part for which he was reading, a protagonist impaled on the dilemma constituted by having an erring wife while in the throes of composing a symphony celebrating the new sexual freedom. Not a note of *The Erotica* was performed in the drama, but Smackenfelt could hear it plainly, drafting it in his head as an example of how thoroughly he prepared for a role. There was a short opening tutti of deliberately traditional, even bromidic, motifs, from whose thematic debris, symbolizing that of outmoded moral standards, rose a hymn to carnal joys. Iconoclastic twelve-tone variations suddenly drowned the hidebound diatonic-scale measures of the introduction, while a jubilant pounding on the kettle drums signalized the pulverization of Puritanic values. What seemed lingering twinges of conscience became squeals of pleasure as the flutes and piccolos emitting them succumbed at last to the general, all-healing bacchanal. "While the work in my opinion," he could see the critics saying in the papers the morning after its world premiere at Philharmonic Hall under the baton of Leonard Bernstein, "lacks the lovesick liquefactions of *Tristan* and the voluptuous, wallowing rhythms of the Venusberg score, I found it nevertheless a masterpiece of amorous musical literature, possibly in time to take rank with these symphonic mountain-tops. The audience also found the new Smackenfelt opus aptly aphrodisiac, judging from its tumultuous reception. People rose and embraced, flung their clothes off and marched out into the streets, where Philharmonic patrons and season subscribers promenaded naked, single ticket holders coupled openly in doorways and on the grass."

"There. See how these are now."

She turned her back modestly while he slipped into the altered pants under cover of the bathrobe he had on. Vowing again not to "cheat," he buttoned them without drawing in his middle.

"Wonderful! Oh, Ginger, thanks," he said, and threw his arms around her in gratitude.

Was this the embrace from which he feared he might not be able to extricate himself? It prolonged itself with the same bewildering amalgam of desire and apprehension with which it had been anticipated, or at least visualized. He merely held her in his grip, as though restraining Blodgett himself from further essayals. He did not seek her cheek, let alone her lipsticked mouth. They stood together, swaying slightly, like boxers in a clinch rather than lovers in a bearhug, philanderers real or potential. The four-nail novelty puzzle seemingly could not be solved. That cursed metaphor again! The infernally hooked parts were powerless to disengage themselves. Or was she struggling to free herself from a clutch all too guiltily his own? "It was your own discipline did it, Stew," she breathed into his ear, disclaiming credit for the sartorial victory. Yes, he could now feel her definitely writhing to free herself, while, alternatively, the scent of her perfume made his senses reel and crazed his brain. The puzzle remained fast, its parts inseparably locked.

No one could say what might have happened had there not been a footstep on the front porch just then and the sound of the door opening, dissolving the puzzle as though its members had become suddenly molten. They melted out of, rather than into, each other's arms. Smackenfelt ran to the vestibule, palming back his hair.

"Do you want to kill your mother? Do you realize what time it is?"

They all laughed together, there in the hall, as Dolly shook off her coat, with the little dance women perform when shucking off a garment. He took it from her to hang up.

"The scene needs a lot of work. A lot of work," she told the closet doorknob. "So we thought we'd go back to the studio after breaking for a bite of supper."

"And lunch?" he asked her shoulder, picking away a scrap of lint from there.

"Uh!" She rolled her eyes. "We didn't break till nearly two. This is worse than the stage. One take after another till I'll bet we did twenty. I blew them or something else went wrong. This is number five, and half a dozen more at least for the pilot series. I mean to show the sponsor. I'm dead. Why isn't everybody in bed?"

She lay down between clean sheets after a hot bath Smackenfelt drew for her.

"Where did you go for dinner?" he asked, hanging up her things.

"Oh, some Chinese place. Not very good, actually. For lunch he took me to his club."

He fabricated a little Coward now. "A club, my dear Lady Smackenfelt, whether it's one a man wields or joins, remains simply something to beat another man over the head with."

"Wonderful. You always did know your Shaw. Look, tomorrow I want to show you a sketch I've done."

"You're painting in there?" He pointed to her study across the hall.

"No, no, for a revue. That United Fund benefit Zap's agreed to produce. I wrote a number for it. I'd very much like your opinion, but not tonight."

She handed it to him shortly after noon, which was when she got up. He sat down to read it with the contradictory swirl of emotions attending any project of Dolly's that, successful, might somehow further disturb the already precarious balance of his marriage, to which a fresh threat was now posed by the mere fact of Dolly's and Zap's being thrown together in an enterprise conceivably a warmup for the major one of his Putting Her Name In Lights. He strove to choke down the churlish hope that nothing here, in these five typewritten pages, raised the spectre of a hometown triumph to be so shared — one from which he was to bear the further pain of exclusion as an actor who "couldn't play comedy" (unless so thoroughly hoked up as an ear of corn as to sink his own identity in the camouflage) . Certainly not light farce. He was overqualified.

He wiped his brow as he began to read, retaining the wadded handkerchief in his hand. He wet his lips.

The story was that of a young man unable to get a date owing to his unruly hair. A pomade commended to his attention by a friend corrected that grooming defect, and he got the girl. Married, he found he had headaches trying to foot the bills entailed by that state — until the right brand of aspirin plugged by an associate cleared them up. Freedom from nagging distress in the upper story enabled him to perform better at the office, where speedy promotion brought new worries leading to acid indigestion, which vanished so miraculously with the use of an effervescent urged on him by another sidekick that his efficiency again leaped to a point where he was kicked upstairs once more, this time to the main office in the East where the smog called for a leading brand of nasal mist. And so on. No improvement in his lot but bred a problem requiring more urgent self-medication, and vice versa, in a steady spiral leading to a pinnacle of corporate eminence where he was found, once again, with hair chronically rumpled from scratching it over a budget perennially strained by the standard of living finally attained in his upward march.

It was quite funny, so funny that Smackenfelt's face fell. He could not get his chops up. The payoff, showing the hapless hero hired by a top advertising agency, on conquest of dandruff, resolved to dish out the copy he had so long taken, offered a good blackout, while the title, "Diary of an Adman," gave the piece scope and meaning as a parody of Gogol's "Diary of a Madman." All in all, a gem by the little woman.

Can't get your chops up, Smacky? This would be Blodgett getting his own back at the ego by which he has been so long disdained and restrained. Wish you'd written it yourself, Smacky? What a put-down, and, brother, what a pool of blood you may be in. I mean the fact that Zap likes it even though it's a satire on his own profession must rock you, baby. And he won't let you play in it, letting you thereby, der, rehabilitate yourself at least a little, because he thinks as a comic actor you chew out loud. Remember? Pretending to differ with the critic who said you couldn't, but bringing the critic up anyway. But Dolly will play the wife, she'll be in it, and good too. Of course he'll direct her, so they'll pick up the marbles together. Yes, she's come a long way since those early short stories beginning, "Her drunken father's bloodshot eyes were like hemorrhoids," a looong way. She's got talent, your dingaling, maybe more — hold it, I'm not through — maybe more than you it'll turn out. How will you like them apples, apart from somebody's beating your time, hey? Hey you —

Smackenfelt gave his head a shake, as though to stop the sound of this taunting voice inside it, a new development, quite a switcheroo on the soliloquies and self-apostrophes that, as far as that went, occupied a great deal of his inner life. He had, in any case, something else to think about.

He was tumescent. He refused at first to believe the testimony of his senses, but it was true. There it was, as he found well enough to his astonishment when he had set the script aside, swelling up like a blowfish, like a snake that had devoured its prey (instead of been devoured!). My God, could this be the masochistic strain in modern man, a man so neurotic that — now get this — that his abasement is converted into sexual desire for her who has inflicted it? He had, on a few previous occasions, experienced something like it. Once or twice when beaten by Dolly at cards. Once on the tennis court when he had lost a match to her and had had to stride up to the net to congratulate her. But nothing like this. Not on anything like this scale. This was — what? An actually erotic manifestation referable, in part at least, to the concept of "surrender"? The surrender completed in that act of love in which one's very potency is indistinguishable from an impotent, self-hurling abandonment to the flesh and soul of the mate? He had perhaps momentarily tasted what is the woman's experience in this abandonment: conquered while conquering.

Only this, and not some poppycock about phallic counter-assertion, could explain a man's actual physical arousal, deep within his loins, at the impact carried by the first serious prospect that his wife might outstrip him.

When she came bounding down the stairs, some minutes later, to hear his opinion, he was lavish in his praise. "It's a jewel. It'll play like a house afire. I suppose you'll play the wife." He found himself, as he spoke, in the grip of an overpowering desire to possess her.

"Come to bed?"

"Oh, Stew, not now. I'm busy. I've got to do a little revising, Zap wants it tonight. We're having a meeting of the production committee at the Wusdatts' to see what material we've got. I'm glad you like it." She gave him a peck on the cheek and was gone up the stairs to her study.

You walk beside the water, Smackenfelt, wrapped in your fur greatcoat. The kind the British call an Immensikoff, or did. Your uncle passed on to you the little-known term along with the coveted bearskin, under whose weight you would playfully collapse as a little boy amusing his elders. A family joke at Christmas time. A fur cap, pulled well down over your ears against the first blasts of what looks like an early winter, completes your resemblance to some woodland biped seeking the shelter of the trees. It is for these you suddenly strike out, a growth of oaks screening Spontini's house from you, or you from him if he's by chance gazing from a window on this Saturday morning. Possibly a woodlot forming part of his own property. A hypotenuse cut through its rustling reaches fetches you out onto the municipal parking lot, in turn abutting on that of the drive-in bank. The girl at the window gives you the greeting for which you have described the wide arc around to it. "Good morning, Mr. Smackenfelt," through the microphone behind glass normally used for communicating with motorized depositors. You like this. To be conscious of being perhaps the only man on earth singled out, albeit by himself, to be given the time of day by a pretty girl through a loudspeaker, as ritual regularly honoring his passing on foot through a lane intended for cars, in order to receive it, occasionally even waiting in a queue of them to get it, is to be conscious of something delicious indeed. You like this a lot. Especially as flavored with the absurdity of your waiting in line for the blessing. Let her think what she will, even say it. "There's this crazy guy . . ."

Next on the order of your orbit is the awful diner.

There the reverse awaits you, though equally deliberately sought. Here absolute consistency of outrage is varied only by the form it might take on a given day. The mood of self-apostrophe falls suddenly away as you enter to gorge yourself on insult.

The thickset counterman who apparently owned the place shuffled in from the kitchen, wearing his customary expression of brute malice. Such parts of his arms as were exposed were completely covered with tattoos — possibly his entire frame was so garnished — and he wore a soiled bandanna around his neck. Clenched in his teeth was a short length of ignited rope girdled with a gold and crimson paper band bearing some heraldic crest, on which he chewed as much as puffed. The diner was otherwise empty. A radio was going. This alone was a nuisance giving fresh offense, of a sort on which Smackenfelt had often dwelt, particularly in the case of wallpaper hangers, linoleum floor layers and other artisans who either switch your own on or take one of theirs into the house and keep it going while at work. That this noise pollution is a completely gratuitous imposition is proved by their often as not whistling tunes other than those emanating from the station tuned in to. The counterman was doing so now. But things more savorably awful than that were to be encountered here, to be consumed *sur place* as well as stored up for later delectation with friends. Smackenfelt hung the Immensikoff on a wall peg, one certainly in danger of snapping under its weight. The cap beside it. He walked over and mounted a stool.

"What'll it be?"

"What's on hand today?"

"We're having a closeout on the beefstew."

"A closeout. What, exactly, is that?"

He knew very well. They were bargain prices on discontinued items such as are regularly featured in department stores and the like. But he had never heard of any such thing in a restaurant, even one that had such things as "sales" on hamburgers and macaroni and cheese, and where you could have all you could eat of the inedible. He wanted to hear more from the restaurateur himself.

"You know what a closeout is."

"You mean you're retiring beefstew from your menu — forever?"

"No — jist this pot."

"I'll just have some coffee today."

Stirring two pellets of saccharin into his coffee, Smackenfelt wondered whether this topped the slightly irregular Picassos on which he'd recently seen a sale in the art print section of a department store. "Seconds" they were also sometimes called. That was, so far, the prize in his collection of outrages. Only a truly great one could nose it out of first place. He would have to think about it.

The problems and nuances of refined and gracious living were driven out of his mind by other thoughts as a party of four customers entered, flapping their arms and blowing on their fingers, to wedge themselves noisily into a booth. Moodily stirring his coffee, he pictured a scene in which he was lying on his back, embracing a wife above to whom he said, "Think of the position this puts me in."

The sense of something more in the wind between Dolly and Zap than mere professional collaboration kept Smackenfelt more determinedly at his exercises than might otherwise have been the case, in the first flush of interim triumph over the flesh. The impulse to look to one's own palatability in the face of rivalry over what one had thought securely his own, and from a quarter hitherto not dreamt, expressed itself in a stricter attention to his diet as well as to the workouts, through a few of which he now puffed and grunted in

redoubled doses. From among those suggested in the
"For Extra Measure" appendix to the manual, he selected the series specially prescribed for abdomen and
backside, which he enacted "overtime" in the privacy
of his bedroom as well as jointly with his pleased mentor, downcellar on the wrestling mat. He particularly
went to town on the exercise called "walking on your
buttocks." He took many such strolls on his long-
suffering and belabored bottom behind the closed and
even locked door, doggedly stoking up his flagging will
with recollections of Charles Laughton as Rembrandt,
in the film of that name, railing at "you fat-rumped
Dutchmen." He used the epithet as a kind of rhythmic
chant as he rocked across the room, sometimes varying,
and extending, it by integrating it with the ditty with
which other immigrants' children had taunted him and
other first-generation Hollanders on the sidewalks of
Chicago:

> *Fat-rumped Dutchmen*
> *Belly full of straw,*
> *Can't saying nothing but*
> Ja, ja, ja.

These vividly remembered offenders had been mainly sloe-eyed Italians, urchins all, guttersnipes, street
Arabs, oh, yes, gamins if you will (they didn't have a
gamin quality, they were just gamins) , whose anony-
mous hordes were now resolved and centralized in that
predestinated surrogate, the local beret-topped Ferrari-
driving TV-producing Latin whose wiry form there
seemed not mountains enough of spaghetti to subvert —
whose image also lashed him through his paces as
though he were driven by the Furies themselves. Grit-

ting his teeth, he would imagine a hundred Spontinis intoning the ditty, varying it occasionally with another quatrain hooted at him then in those bygone Chicago days, now also of service in furnishing a cadence with which to rock from ham to ham across this Connecticut bedroom:

> There's ... the ... Amsterdam Dutch
> And the Rotterdam Dutch
> And the Potsdam Dutch
> And the other damn Dutch!

The bedroom floor, like the rest of the house, had the original wide oak floorboards, painted black and islanded only with occasional hooked rugs in order to show them off to advantage. On one of his sedentary journeys across its length, he picked up a sliver, quite a long one, which ran clear through the linen shorts he sometimes wore when alone, and well into his left haunch.

He tried to remove it himself, first by groping and fishing for it blindly with both hands, then in front of a full-length door mirror, screwing and twisting himself about in a variety of frantic positions, all unsuccessful. Finally he lay down on the bed with Dolly's hand mirror in one hand and a pair of her eyebrow tweezers in the other, picking away at the trouble. Also to no avail. All he did was inflame the injury, already painful enough. He dressed it as best he could by sticking a Band-Aid on it and tried to forget about it, trusting it would work its way out, as a splinter often will out of your finger, without producing a felon — or whatever it would be called in this case. He first sterilized the wound with a dollop of bourbon, fortifying himself with a nip as well.

That was toward noon. Three hours later found him limping about the house with increasing difficulty and discomfort. There was no alternative but to seek help. Where? A visit to his doctor was out. He couldn't fancy himself explaining to that ever-guffawing croaker how he had picked up the "foreign body," which was rapidly beginning to feel like a piece of the true Cross, much less to the nurse probably called in to assist, a girl with hair the color of ripe wheat and blue eyes like the round soft limpid globular *bongs* of a gently smitten dinner gong. "Been sliding down bannisters, have we? Mmbahaha." Alternatives were equally untenable. "I was doing some carpentry, you see," would evoke surrealist juxtapositions that would have to be further explained. For some reason he found more disturbing, he knew he would have been just as embarrassed telling Dolly. After some anguished indecision, he broke down and revealed his problem to Ginger. Her straightforward innocent amusement would be less jarring to his vanity than the suppressed smile he could predict on the part of her daughter. She was away at the time anyway. Ginger was painting a chest in the basement when he announced what had befallen him. She got up off her knees and wiped her hands with a wad of cloth soaked in turpentine.

"Come on upstairs," she said, leading the way. "I think there's some iodine in my medicine chest. If not, plenty of soap will do. I'll get at it with that."

"I've already soaked it with whiskey," he said, trailing her.

"A damn sight better use for it than you've been

putting it to. Everybody these days, I mean. Why, Stew, I told you to be careful only to do that one on the mat. Or at least a rug or linoleum floor. Well, we'll have it out in a jiffy."

He lay face down on his bed, stripped again to the shorts, hoisting up one leg of which gave the woman adequate access to the trouble.

"Wow! That is a long baby. And in too far for me to get a hold of with these tweezers. I'll have to fish for it. Let me just sterilize a needle. Don't go away, I'll be back in two shakes."

She shook her head as she went chuckling off to her sewing basket. She returned with a darning needle she had sterilized over a flame on the gas stove and then dipped in some rubbing alcohol for good measure. She resumed the surgery.

"This *is* a long son of a gun," she murmured, probing gently around the wound with the point of the darning needle. She was silent for some moments, intent on her work. Smackenfelt lay with his chin on his hands, trying to think things through. It seemed to him that the mother's ministrations were more tenderly solicitous than had been the daughter's, the time when he had pinked himself with the can opener in that fit of self-destruction (or self-preservation, again considering the utensil selected in the heat of the moment). But he admitted to himself that the reflection was a churlish one, prompted in any case by the circumstances of Dolly's absence. She would again be working overtime. Should he ask her mother out to dinner?

"What I've got to do is kind of *hook* the end of the splinter with the point of the needle . . . . Ah, there, I think I've got it snagged. Now to pull it out. Try to

relax. I don't think it'll hurt too much. O.K. Ready?
Bite on that bullet!"

"Right!"

"There we are." He winced as he felt the sliver being
drawn. It was nearly as long as the darning needle, he
saw when she held it triumphantly up. "Just a sec now,
let me give that a good wash with some soap and then
paint it with iodine."

The injury so treated, he dressed and went downstairs to join her in some afternoon tea.

Relieved and enormously grateful — to a degree in
which he felt himself again slightly unstable — he
amused her with some stories about the theatre, and
then, inevitably, a few imitations. These included an
actor he'd seen recently on an old Sherlock Holmes
movie run on television. Something else, however,
brought him constantly to mind.

Ginger Truepenny had a rather plump little round
mouth, of which the lips were habitually parted in a
circle when she listened to someone talk, particularly
to Smackenfelt as he expounded some fine point of
thought, or a nuance of the current time as embodied
in its ever-proliferating slang, on which he was an
authority. It had often reminded him of a poke-purse
of which the strings are drawn not quite closed — or of
Nigel Bruce. He entertained her with a bit now as they
sat in the breakfast nook, sipping their oolong flavored
with honey.

"Oh, I say, really my dear Holmes," he said, round-
ing his eyes out also, and tilting his head upward a
trifle, so that he looked down his nose. "You don't
really expect me to believe you deduced all that from a
spot of catsup on a chap's cuff."

"Don't tell me!" She snapped her fingers; smote herself; splayed a palm across her face, lowered with her eyes shut in concentration. "It's that man who played Doctor Watson."

"Really, old chap, you're pulling my leg."

"Nigel Bruce!"

Smackenfelt had intended merely to fling his arms aloft in a gesture of pleasure as he passed her chair on the way to the stove for the kettle of hot water. But they had a will of their own, those arms of Blodgett. He stooped to gather her in an embrace with the left, at the same time bestowing a gratified peck on her cheek, all with an exaggerated air of mock gallantry, or nothing to worry about. As he did so, she lifted her face with a flushed laugh, as though the "success" had been hers in guessing the subject of his imitation rather than his in having been on the beam. As a result, so he was always to tell himself later, he missed the cheek for which he had aimed and planted a hearty buss on the mouth.

The accident put an abrupt end to the courtly playfulness of manner as, incredibly, again refusing to believe the testimony of his senses, sinking to his knees as though sucked into a quagmire into which he had stumbled, he pressed his lips hotly to her own. At the same time, his right arm joined the other looped loosely still around her shoulder. She did not return his embrace — or withdraw her face. Her uneasy giggle became smothered in the continuing kiss. He broke it off shortly. He didn't get up, however, only drew back a moment to return her amusement with a smile, as though to recover thereby the sense of their being sportive and foolish, a pair of nuts rather than wrongdoers, before again seeking out the moist soft rosepetal flesh of that mouth in an impulse over which he had now simply no longer any control.

The term "non-binding marriage" swam idiotically into his mind, from the modish lexicon of the day. So did the expression "pucker up," from her more innocent time, and that really threatened, or rather promised, to put an end to all this with an involuntary explosion of laughter. A real ardor-squelcher, that "pucker up." Her hands went to his shoulders, which were already beginning to shake, as though she were going to force him gently but firmly off, then, after just a moment of hesitation, slid down along his back, until they were locked into an embrace. They seemed to have no wills of their own. Yes, that was undoubtedly it — they had no wills of their own. He was about to pant, "We're mad," when she nearly spoiled everything by gasping, "We're mad. Mad, do you hear." The cliché made him wince, but presently the passion that had engendered it swelled forward once again, sweeping them irresistibly along like twigs on a boiling stream.

She broke abruptly away. She turned in her chair.

"This is ridiculous."

"Of course. You're a very attractive woman. Very, very."

He rose and resumed the interrupted journey to the stove, returning with the kettle. She poured them fresh cups of tea from the pot, which he diluted to drinkable strength with the hot water he had gone originally to fetch.

"I'm not this way," he heard her say as he set the kettle back on the kitchen stove.

"I know that perfectly well. Neither am I. Neither is Dolly. That's why I don't understand it. I don't understand any of this."

"A person with ego — and you have it too, I mean the ego that goes with any professional or artistic drive — will respond to a man or woman, sexually I mean, who — well, gives them a boost. Respond in a way they wouldn't otherwise. She's *grateful* to Zap." She threw her arms out. "It's as simple as that. And that gratitude may make her fall in love with him. Or get infatuated with him. Or have an affair with him. Whatever it is. You know as well as I do something's cooking there. You also know I wouldn't dream of anything like this with you if things weren't the way they are between you and Dolly. Even now I'm ashamed."

"So am I. Up to a point."

"Up to what point?"

"If I thought there was anything between the two, and that's the way it was, period, I'd want to take you right upstairs and into bed."

"Oh, my God. I've got to get out of this house."

"Yes. We'll both go. Out to dinner somewhere this evening."

"Swell. Somewhere good. We've both stuck to our diets long enough now to deserve a lapse. Some place we can — what do you call it today, scarf it up?"

After dinner they took in a movie, one with a contemporary heroine of the sort whose readiness to pucker up is evidenced by her being seen thrashing about naked in bed with just anybody. There, having shared a box of popcorn, they sat in the dark, holding hands.

eight

"You've been seeing my mother."

Smackenfelt had had the sense of being watched from behind, as he sat reading the Casting News in *Variety*, down in his cellar fastness. He had heard Dolly descend the stairs several minutes before, then forgotten her while she rummaged in a storage chest for something never made clear. Then been arrested, in a sudden stillness, by the certainty of being fixed by a gaze striking the back of his head, like a dart from an invisible blowgun.

"I see her all the time, Dolly. Here, there, everywhere."

"You know what I mean. You've been taking her out. To dinner and so on."

"Well, a woman doesn't like to be cooking all the time. She likes to dine out now and again, take in a movie. You know?"

"Is there something between you?"

He could not help laughing at this. "Do you really think you're in a position to ask?"

"My God." She subsided on a chair, the three-legged stool Ginger had hauled from the bin the day she had first joined him downcellar, here where he went to lick his wounds. She gazed around, her eye coming to rest at last on the wrestling mat. "My God, all the while behind my back."

"It's like they say, the wife is the last to know," he then reassuringly chaffered.

"Oh, Stew, how could you!"

"Oh, for God's sake, can't you see I'm joking?"

"About a matter like this!" She threw her hands out and rolled her eyes upward, as though calling on unseen witnesses to judge her part.

He slapped the *Variety* down on the floor. "There *is* no matter, that's what I mean. If what you mean is having an affair. What need would we have to go to a movie with the house full of beds — and wrestling mats!"

"How do I know I can believe that?" she said, eyeing him sidewise, having twisted about on the camp stool at an angle accommodating this dramatic expression. "It all fits. Your never wanting her to leave — that's unnatural in a husband . . ."

"Is it? Lots of men like their mothers-in-law, I rather suspect. It's the daughters who can't stand their mothers. I never thought the mother-in-law was an ogre at all. I think it's a myth."

"I see." She looked at him narrowly. "I'm beginning to see what you mean. It's the wife who's the ogre."

"Oh, Jesus H. Christ!" He threw up his hands.

"The violence of your reaction only proves that's the

motive you're trying to hide. That's what you're trying to do to me. It's your vengeance. That's what you're saying to the world, with this affair. Or whatever it is. It's all aimed at me. Then that's the way it is." She rose and took a step away. "Then I'll take myself as freely left to my own devices."

"Now wait a minute, baby. Let's get causes and effects straight here, shall we? The sequence of events. You call my interest in your mother a reaction to your own little caper, which you then justify as a retaliation for mine. You can't have it both ways. You can't seize on something that comes *after* Zap — if it does — as justification for taking up with him. That kind of reasoning is like the kid who shot his parents and then asked for mercy on the ground that he was an orphan."

"How do you know I'm having an affair with Zap?"

"It wouldn't take a Sherlock Holmes to draw conclusions from the way you two were the night of your United Fund revue triumph, to say nothing of all those business overtimes in town."

"Maybe it's your imagination that's working overtime."

"I realize what you're doing seems perfectly natural to you, as stepping off into something new does to all of us, once we've gone over the line. Because we're doing what comes naturally. People rarely do what they don't want to. We may amaze each other, but we never surprise ourselves."

"Where did you learn that, at Mother's knee?"

"What do you see in him?" Stew asked, his tone suddenly softening to one of sincere enquiry. He was honestly curious. He would really like to know.

"He's doing the world for me. He's made me — Oh, but you think this identity stuff is all the bunk, I suppose."

"Not in the least. Go on."

"He's made me feel I'm somebody again, professionally, after being buried alive as a *Hausfrau*, I mean not that I resent that, or regret it. And not that anybody thinks a series of commercials is 'acting.' But it is putting us all on our feet again. You don't have to take a job, but can hold out for work in your own chosen profession."

"I quite understand that. You're grateful to him for giving you a leg up. As you might be to me if the roles were reversed. I mean if you'd had three or four years as a housewife to him, and then met me when you were stir-crazy and I could do something to spring you. I think a lot of modern women's trouble is simply cabin fever. I don't hold it against them. I understand all that. What I meant was, what do you see in him personally?"

"Zap has his own kind of appeal — like any man of course, or woman. He's really quite vulnerable under that aggressive husk of his. What are you laughing about?"

"Nothing." He thought it best not to remind her that it was precisely this "lost boy" reliance of his own of which she had, officially, tired. "What else is he, besides a frail reed and a tower of strength?"

"I see no need for you to be sarcastic. I've not quite forgotten your remark about his mixed motives in anything he does for me. That it's also something he's doing *to* you."

"You must take the remark in the spirit in which it was intended."

"What spirit was that?"

He shrugged. "I don't remember. I have no idea. I'm probably just doing my part to keep this conversational ball rolling. When do you suppose it will roll to a stop, or where?"

"I personally don't see there's anything more to say. If you're determined to do this to me. Make me look this way in the eyes of the world."

Smackenfelt had long ago learned that you can more easily pull a brick from a wall than you can dislodge from a woman's mind an idea that is emotionally necessary to her. It was a conviction from which absolutely nothing could sway him. Watching Dolly exit with what was almost a theatrical illustration of the concept of dignity, he called out in a voice charging them both with folly, "If nobody knows any better than this what the plu-perfect hell who's trying to do to whom, and why, then maybe we'd best call ·in Birdie!" And laughed so hard the long unmended chair finally collapsed beneath him with a loud crash. "Now maybe I'll *fix* this goddam thing!" he said, picking both himself and it up, then hurling the chair away so that it struck the furnace, completing its demolition. He stood, hands on hips, and watched her walk up the stairs, her ankles intermittently visible through its open boards. "I suppose now we'd best ask your aunt to leave. It's what you've always wanted."

"Not on your life! Not just yet. That would be a dead give-away to anybody who's seen you together, or heard. And I'd like this whole thing resolved under my eyes, if you please, not behind my back. We'll see what we see."

"Don't give people 'talking' a second thought," he said, suddenly reverting to the drawing-room comedy dialogue he had so often synthesized for her in the staged "quarrels" aimed jointly at supplying grist for her typewriter and emotional ventilation for their marriage. He found himself to be groping successfully toward an epigram. "That's the trouble with this permissive society, don't you see, Lady Smackenfelt. It no longer leaves us any scandal."

"Oh, baloney!"

The best marriage can suddenly go bad, like a Havana cigar or a vintage wine. Or a folding chair. What happened next may have resulted in whole or in part precisely from the reappearance of Birdie, who by coincidence turned up again two days later, to check up on the household after all in some measure in her care, or at least under her watchful eye. She was again delighted at the figure Unc cut, her sessions with him having been intended to be merely investigatory, never therapeutic.

Smackenfelt again talked to her freely about his childhood and early years, inventing as much as recalling. Often as not what came to mind concerned not himself but one or another of his playmates — in particular a boy so fat that what was true of him must be universally relevant to the weight problem. As Smackenfelt saw it, the literal truth of what data Birdie came away with made no difference, since the important thing was the thesis in which it would result. Names would be fictitious in any case. So he would chat away about repressive religious backgrounds driving one to the icebox, if not up the wall, bread-eating compulsions (of which he had read somewhere) and what not, while Birdie's pencil flew.

Of interesting psychological significance in itself might be the fact that when she left she forgot her notebook. She came back for it the next day, to find no one home. Aunt Ginger was shopping, the Smackenfelts out together on business somewhere. When no one answered the bell she tried the door. Luckily — or unluckily — it was unlocked. She slipped in and, after calling, "Anybody here?" and receiving no answer, darted into the side sun parlor where she had used the notebook. It wasn't on the table where she had presumably left it, neither on its glass top nor the utility undershelf where magazines and newspapers were stored. She was on her knees on the floor, rummaging through these to no avail, when she heard a car stop before the house. Hurrying to the window, she looked out and saw Dolly and Stew getting out, their faces set in rather grim expressions. Gripped by uncertainty, she looked wildly around the room, with the idea that she must find the notebook and be discovered with it in her hands when they entered, as proof of the reason for her having walked in with nobody about, imprudently she now saw. Her eye was caught by it lying on top of a bookcase. She snatched it up, and was about to start forward to greet the others when she heard words that made her freeze in her tracks. The two were obviously in the midst of a fine contention.

"— with just another woman might not matter," Dolly was saying, "but when it comes to hanky-panky with the wife's mother —"

"It's not hanky-panky, goddamn it!" he retorted, hotly for him. "And she's not your mother. She's your aunt!"

"It was the last thing you could do to me."

"Why is it being done 'to' you? I don't put that construction on your little lark."

Birdie felt she had heard far too much already —

certainly more than she could let them know she had, if the revelation could possibly be avoided. In panic she flew through the only doorway available to her outside the one the disputants were even now sailing through. It took her into the dining room — and there she was trapped. Blindly, she scurried behind a sideboard, or rather beside it, crouching down between it and a wall, trembling. There was only just space for her to wedge herself in. She prayed the two would go upstairs, back outside, anything but remain. But remain they did, and they kept at it hammer and tongs.

"Christ, let's not open that can of beans about the war between men and women," Dolly was saying. "Aren't you sick of hearing it yourself by now?"

"Not as sick as I am of waging it!"

It was here that disaster struck. Huddled down in her corner, Birdie had the notebook in her hand. Feeling that she absolutely must put her fingers in her ears in order to hear no more, she tucked the notebook under one arm. It was a large three-ring loose-leaf binder, quite heavy, and it dropped out of her clutch, falling to the floor with a thud.

"What was that?" Dolly said, in the main parlor where the forensics had been going forward. "My mother said she was going out. Mother?" When there was no answer, she walked to the doorway to the dining room. There the footsteps paused a moment, and resumed, more slowly, deliberately. Birdie cringed against the wall as far as she could. But something must have been visible — a protruding knee, an edge of her skirt. Or the notebook itself, lying on the floor. Dolly stood over the shivering girl.

"So. This is what you do, you little brat."

"I didn't mean anything, Aunt Dolly." She rose from

cover, picking the notebook up. "I only came to get this. I left it yesterday. The door was open, and I knew where to put my hands on it, so I figured it didn't matter. Then when I heard you two come in fighting like that I thought to spare both of us, I mean all of us . . ." She looked appealingly to Smackenfelt, who had now stepped to the doorway and stood there with a rather weird little smile on his face. He shook his head cryptically and went back into the living room to fix them all what might be taken to be much-needed drinks. He could hear the rumble of battle resume behind him, with the shift in one combatant.

"Here we give you the hospitality of our house, as much as tell you to make yourself at home here, cooperate with you on this — this silly project of yours, and this is the thanks we get."

It was the slur on her scholarly venture rather than the need to defend her presence that stung Birdie into response. She now quite found her tongue.

"It's not silly! You'd have to think that as a sheer defense mechanism."

"Oh, Gawd. Well, fat chance we had of escaping the jargon."

"I'd give anything to have avoided this accident, even at the expense of not having been given a glimpse of what has probably been Uncle Fats' trouble all along. You!"

"*What!*"

"Yes. That cheerful little earful I just caught would dispel any doubt."

"Now I must ask you to stop this balderdash right away," said Smackenfelt who had reappeared in the doorway with two drinks, which he offered to the others. They both ignored him, so he drank from one glass while holding the other in readiness in his hand as well. He leaned against the doorjamb with a mock detachment aimed at reassuring Dolly that what they heard was not to be taken seriously; the problem was one of restoring some measure of sanity to Birdie who was uttering it. "Or no. Go ahead. Let's get it all out of our systems, *then* we can get on to getting it straightened out again like civilized people. What say to that all around?" Not that there was much chance of sanity intervening to the extent of putting a stop to the catfight before it had run its course. The women ignored him, if they had heard.

"What do you mean?" Dolly asked this quivering cousin who insisted on thinking of her as an aunt. "Will you please explain what you're saying for the cheap seats?"

Smackenfelt smiled, crossing one foot over the other. It was a bit of slang Dolly had gotten from him, a coinage possibly put into general circulation by himself, for he had never heard it prior to its being dropped from his own lips, some several years back.

"You cut him down to size. Undermine his ego in little ways, so that he has to take refuge in food."

"Stop it, Birdie," Smackenfelt ordered. "This is ridiculous."

"Fat lot of good it'll do you to try to stop her. Go on, Birdie. How do I cut him down to size. In what little ways?"

"Well, using 'fat' all the time."

"In cooking?" Blank stare.

"No, talking. Always saying 'fat chance' and 'fat lot of good.' 'Fat part.' There's one that really hits him where he lives. All the fat parts he never gets. It's like all the 'noses' in those speeches in *Cyrano*."

Dolly took a step closer. "Listen, you little bitch. He's *lost* weight married to me. He's lost two hundred pounds at least. That's a conservative estimate. Have you got that in your profile?"

"Yes, and that he gains them all back, and more. Why? He seeks refuge in food. It's not for nothing they call you Hurricane Dolly!"

"Now, listen. Closely, because I'm only going to say it once. By the time I get through with you, they'll call you something a damn sight worse than Hurricane Birdie — Tubby! Because you're getting pretty hefty yourself, you little sow. Why is that? Thesis not going well, kid? Secret cookie eater? French-fry freak?"

"Oh, for God's sake, Dolly, let's knock it off, shall we?" said Smackenfelt, now reversing his former program by stepping forward physically to separate the two women. "I'll talk to her later when she's cooled down. Meanwhile, all this is just grist for her mill, don't you see? We've got to pull ourselves together anyway, your mother will be home from the store any minute."

"Yes, but you leave her out of this, do you understand?" Dolly now ordered Birdie. "Whatever you think you may have overheard when we came in a while ago."

That reminded Birdie of what, in the heat of the ensuing moments, she had forgotten. Her mouth opened in a gasp. "*Your* mother and — *him?* That's what you were talking about. I don't believe it!" And with that she turned and ran out the front door and down the steps to her car, in which she drove around aimlessly, crazily, fetching up at last in an Italian restaurant where Smackenfelt, having managed to follow her in his own car through every twist and turn of her bizarre course, sat down across from her in a corner booth, trying in a calm voice to smooth things over and make her forget what she had heard, while she gorged herself on a dinner of spaghetti and meatballs washed down with several glasses of Chianti, and topped off by a dish of spumone.

The Smackenfelts were eventually divorced. Dolly planned to marry Spontini while Smackenfelt became more or less engaged to Ginger.

"Then that's that," Dolly said, when it seemed all settled. "I'll only be remarrying, but you — you'll be making a statement to the world. I know that, Stew. 'A wife!' you'll be saying in effect. 'Even a mother-in-law is better than that!' That'll be your manifesto, your open letter to the world. That's what you'll be saying."

"No, that's not what I'll be saying. That's what you say I'll be saying. I'll be saying 'I do.' That's all."

These arguments all went better when they more or less ignored one another, as they did now. Each could then, without undue interruption from the other, articulately uphold his monologue, of the two that went forward, independent, yet somehow systematically entwined. They were like two satisfactorily orchestrated motifs, a kind of conversational fugue.

"The mother-in-law," Dolly continued, separately navigating the room, virtually talking to herself now as she tried her outrage on for size. "The final thrust of the knife going home, then the twist of the knife after it does, for good measure. The mother-in-law isn't the ogre. Not at all. No. It's the wife. That's the sandwich board you'll be publicly picketing me with. I got a lemon. Even the mother is better."

" 'I do,' " Smackenfelt mused on for his own part. "I'll be saying 'I do' for the second time — and I hope to God it won't be the last," he said, reaching out to give his Ginger's hand an affectionate pat.

part two

nine

Aunt Ginger proved to be all that a man could ask in a wife. Warm and affectionate; emotionally nimble at adapting herself to the moods of a mate himself pensive and rollicking by turns, without being herself mercurial; inherently sensible while lightening the hours with her own balmy humors, or the errant insights so stimulating to the more rarefied mind. Above all, indestructibly good-natured.

One night Smackenfelt stayed up quite late to polish his Churchill. His *Hiawatha*, as Winnie would do it, seemed to be going well. A few of the trickier corners had yet to be ground and bevelled down a bit, but on the whole it was Churchill to the life. Even in the oratorical cadence, that occasional upward tailing at the ends of periods which was just the opposite of the stylized "preekton," the preacher's tone, of the many Dutch Reformed ministers who had scourged his Chicago boyhood Sundays a quarter of a century and more ago.

Pacing the house articulating Longfellow's foolish rhythms in that grandiloquent growl that had once galvanized the free world, he rambled into the front vestibule, where he heard, then saw, Ginger standing at the top of the stairs, smiling sleepily down. He was keeping her awake with these expert mouthings, save for brief dozes from which each time his voice had fitfully startled her, being audible through the bedroom door she liked to keep open.

"Stew, it's all hours," she gently reproached, in fact was nice as pie about it, "and I like Wallace Beery too, we all remember him with affection, but I mean in the middle of the night . . ."

He reached into the closet and jammed a Homburg on his head, wheeling into view again with his hand held aloft in the V-for-Victory sign, the bulldog jaw thrust unmistakably forward. "We shall fight them on the beaches . . ."

But she was gone, trailing some kind afterthought about his needing his sleep too, leaving him to switch off the hall light and sit in the parlor for a bit, with a cigar freshly lighted and a brandy glass brimful enough to seem to be testing the law of surface tension, there to review the drawbacks of daily married life as against the trackless pleasures of the honeymoon.

They had spent theirs in New England, rambling by car from one Vermont and New Hampshire inn to another. "Come as you are," he'd said fondly from the bed, on which he lay stretched out as the Tempter, watching her undo, on the farthest edge of light filtering through the curtained window from an illuminated

shingle reading "Green Mountain Lodge," the draw-
strings of a garment he had never to the best of his
knowledge laid eyes on before, which she identified, as
she contended with it, laughing prettily, as a camisole.
He had heard of them. He had doubtless seen them in
wall prints portraying scenes of naughtiness or wicked-
ness in eras when morality still made such things possible, and which she charmingly evoked, there behind
the wingback chair which half concealed her. Looking
the word up in the dictionary, later, he was to learn it
had a variety of meanings, including that of straitjack-
et. That conjured a future possibility, even likelihood.
Indeed it was all settled: he would in due course go off
his head, all right enough. But not just yet. Tonight,
their nuptial night, it meant "a woman's ornamental
underbodice." Blodgett sprang out of bed as though
shot from a cannon, and on his knees made obeisance
to the naked result.

"My God," he whispered hoarsely. At last he was to
be appeased, at last, at last, and knowing on the razor-
edge realization of the moment that the long tantaliza-
tion to which he had been subjected would leave his
thirst the more rapturously slaked, he ran his ravenous
palms over curves as firm as the boulders dotting the
nearby mountainsides as he gasped, "My God, like a
young girl. You're lucky."

Smackenfelt sensed in a twinkling his *gaffe*, Blodgett's, and, standing over the two of them, the rejoinder
with which it would be met. A veritable *déjà vu*. It
pleased him to hear his Ginger retort, "No — you are."

That much was true. Then the four-nailed puzzle
whose image ever more deliriously haunted his mind
became eight-nailed as within locked limbs he seemed
to feel the marrow being drawn from every bone in his

body. Then they lay entangled in each other's sleep.
Then they sat in a daze eating a trencherman's breakfast in their room, smiling stupidly at one another as
they devoured slices of ham an inch thick. He would do
anything for her. He would look for parts again, and if
none came his way, for a job. He might become a
diction coach.

"How long do you want to stay here — Slim?" She
threw a fragment of hot biscuit at him.

"How long do you?"

"What about another day, if the weather stays nice,
then pick up sticks and head north. What are you
smiling about?"

"Nothing."

"I've said something wrong again. Oh, it's pull up
stakes."

"Not any more. From now on it'll be pick up sticks."

"No, you correct me. Women are notorious for getting expressions mixed up, and stories all wrong. I
know that. You call me on them, do you hear?"

"All right. But my heart won't be in it." He blew her
a kiss and returned to his ham and eggs.

"Was that vintage me? That last one?"

"Not by any means. You can do lots better."

It was in the lobby of the Boston hotel where this
connubial swath cut through New England came to a
close that a coincidence of a rather wry order occurred.

Smackenfelt had gone down for a cigar and a little
something to read, shortly before midnight, when he
became aware of a man on the other side of the swivel
rack at which he was browsing for a paperback, who
looked tantalizingly familiar. He had the unmistakable

feeling of wanting to place him without having to greet him. At first only part of the face was visible: half a pair of steel-rimmed spectacles between a set jaw and short-cropped iron-gray hair. The aspect was rather formidable, even grim. He looked like a man who was about to pronounce you man and wife. It was the memory of this as a first impression, whirling dimly out of the past, that made Stew finally tumble to his identity. It was Cyrus Bah, the Persian-born suitor of Dolly's family friend, Cordial Schenck, who had been Cordial's escort on the night of the matchmaking blind date for the Smackenfelts-to-be. Who later had between them agreed — it was one of his and Dolly's first domestic jokes — that the mercenary Bah had probably expected a finder's fee for the result. Equivalent aids to memory must have enabled Bah simultaneously to recognize the head peering at him around the edge of the reprints, where to an observer the two might have seemed in grim contention over which way to spin the revolving rack, squared off in combat to the death.

"Stewart Smackenfelt."

"Cyrus Bah," Stew said, feigning as much delight as the circumstances permitted, while the handshake to which he was now subjected brought another characteristic to mind. Bah had one of those grips, for some reason characteristic of lean and wiry men, that seem aimed at bringing the recipient to his knees, if not with a howl of pain, then at least with an acquiescent "Uncle." It was even worse than Spontini's spastic clutch endured in seizures of conciliatory remorse. (Spontini was now his son-in-law. He sometimes thought of that, and wanted to put his head back and howl.)

"What brings you to Boston?" Smackenfelt asked, pocketing his wrung extremity, as if to guard it from further harm.

"Breaking in a play. I don't know whether you knew it, but I've gone into producing — and directing — as a sort of relief from the business world. Like a lot of us."

"*Late Larks*. Is that your venture?"

"That's right. Not in shape yet, but may get there. Swell performances tonight, but needs rewriting. Author isn't the greatest on the barricades. Plenty of black coffee and hot baths seem to be his way of tightening up a scene. What brings you?"

"On a honeymoon, actually."

"I thought you and Dolly . . .?"

"We're divorced. I'm married to her mother now."

"Well. Congratulations."

That Bah received this news with no more visible response, indeed without batting an eye, struck Smackenfelt as indicating some kind of lack in the other's makeup, if not in the national psyche. Taking in stride the bulletin just handed him suggested a world of anesthetized emotions or impoverished standards, as though men went around marrying their mothers-in-law every day; at best one that had lost its capacity for wonder. Perhaps too many people were going to the moon and converting soybeans into clothing fabrics and construction materials. Such a union as he had just contracted seemed to Smackenfelt an anomaly with the elements of which one ought to be reasonably familiar at fairly close range to go any way toward comprehending; certainly not one to be loosely countenanced by a nearly total stranger, unacquainted with the details.

"How is Cordial?" he asked, then was immediately uncertain of his assumption that something had come

of *that*. But happily he had not put his foot into anything there.

"Fine. She's upstairs. Can you come have a
brandy?"

"Oh, Ginger's probably asleep. We're leaving early
in the morning, or we'd certainly catch *Late Larks*."

"Ginger of course she's called. I remember now her
name is Virginia. Couldn't think of it for the moment.
I've never met her, but Cora's spoken of her often."
Bah shot back a cuff to consult his wristwatch. "Today
is Tuesday." It would be a calendar watch, though the
gesture gave him a fleeting air of lunacy. "Matinee
tomorrow."

"That would make it much too late. We'll catch it in
New York. And let's keep in touch. Ginger often speaks
of Cordial. They were all old family friends, you know,
Bah."

He remembered now, sitting there in the parlor nursing his brandy, how *then*, on his honeymoon, he had
remembered being in Boston with Dolly on a tryout of
some play in which she'd had a part, shortly after
they'd been married. More or less still their own honeymoon. The role was that of a put-upon wife for
which she'd tried to keep her characterization fresh,
not to say give it depth and resonance, by improvisations in which he would be called upon to hector and
chivvy her in their hotel room, in terms of her onstage
husband. One of the first of their mockups.

"I'm yours to command. You've won. So get in that
bed, you bitch."

"Let me go, you animal."

"I'm putty in your hands I tell you. So get *down*
there, can't you. You slut with your apricot poodles."

"You're the most egotistical man I know."

"It's not my problem."

"You're common."

"You're preferred."

"Jesus." Laughing, Dolly collapsed on the bed, and with it the mockup. "Wait till the other girls get a load of you. But that Karloff in there was great. That lisp."

"Well, actually it was Bogart."

"They both have it. You slay me." She lay in quite helpless paroxysms, turning away from him, her face to the wall.

"What are you doing down there?" Ginger called.

"Mixing memory and desire."

"At this hour?"

He and Dolly had picked the rigmarole up again in the restaurant downstairs.

"Freud said at last he had no idea what the hell women want. Well, I know."

"What do women want? What do we want, women?"

"Something else."

"Meaning?"

"Tightmeyer. In your case. Your first Other Man."

"Then you've guessed."

"Can you really sleep with a man who parts his hair in the middle?"

"I consider that remark in bad taste."

"It's the old story. When we tire of domesticity, we go find somebody to play house with."

"You're a beast. And I'll sleep with whomever I want."

"At last I've made an honest woman of you."

"That went home. Oh, that went home!"
"Let's us do the same, shall we? Waiter, check."

"Please come to bed," he heard drowsily called again from overhead, and he turned out the lights and did. He may have been irrational, but he was not unreasonable. Mounting the staircase, his hand sliding ahead of him along the bannister, he felt a twinge of sympathy for Bah, whose maiden voyage on the treacherous seas of the theatre had ended in shipwreck, for *Late Larks* had folded out of town. Suddenly, then, he placed the title source. Something from Swinburne. "As when late larks give warning/ Of dying lights and dawning/ Night murmurs to the morning/ Lie still, O love, lie still,/ And half her . . . something something . . . And half her dark limbs cover/ The white limbs of her lover/ With amorous plumes that hover/And fervent lips that chill."

By the time he had finished undressing and brushing his teeth he had reconstructed most of the lyric.

"You heard me doing Wallace Beery down there?" he said as he slipped into bed beside Ginger, who was lying over on her side.

"In his own inimitable style." She reached behind her to bestow the reassuring pat with which she mumbled this, then dropped off into sound and conclusive sleep.

Gazing up at the dark ceiling with his hands laced under his head, Smackenfelt knew that he was a man with a problem.

He had in a handsome enough settlement quit-claimed over to Dolly his entire share in the house, which he and Ginger had then bought back from her with the sum realized from Ginger's sale of her cooperative apartment in Philadelphia, which she longed to leave for Connecticut anyway. It was too replete with memories of the "mistake" she had soon divorced, the deplorable Art Buckett seen (in another of Smackenfelt's inextinguishably obsessive images) as forever throwing peanuts into the air and catching them in his mouth, whom Smackenfelt foresaw no trouble in outshining, out of whose clutches she had thank God managed to keep what had been left her by the sterling Bill Truepenny with whom few, on the contrary, would bear comparison. But falling short of this touchstone of masculine merit wasn't Smackenfelt's problem. The problem was that, having married the woman who had come into these modest moneys, he might conceivably be suspected of having married *for* them. Such a thing had never remotely entered his head, but the thought of malicious speculation galled him. There was only one way to spike it. Get a job. Any kind, an office job if no roles were forthcoming, and he obtained no clients as a diction coach. Here he was at thirty-six, having fought, bit, scratched, kicked and clawed his way to the bottom. A Flunkenstein. If that was how it was, then that was how it was. But he would pull himself together and go to work rather than be accused of sexual parasitism on even the most miniscule scale.

Then there must be a détente with Spontini. That hatchet must really now be buried, once and for good, if only for the sake of the women, who, their own wounds healed and all the bitter words behind them and forgotten, wanted the four of them to see each other, at least once in a way. Continuing enmity was insupportable. He and Zap had had one confrontation since the remarriages, an accidental one. Crossing the town bridge from opposite ends, they had recognized one another's approach too late. It was a warm day, and Zap was carrying his coat over his shoulder hooked on two fingers, in the manner of hoboes and senatorial candidates (the latter seen in campaign posters against the Capitol Building, ready to roll up their sleeves and get on with the job) . He had veered with feigned abstraction for the one parapet while Stew had equally involuntarily made for the other, and there they had stood gazing out along the muddy river, pretending to be taking in the view. At length continuing on their separate ways. Such foolishness had to stop. A more mature way must be found, viable arrangements made. Dolly talked of their having dinner together, and that was now vaguely in the works.

All this having crystallized in his mind in the way of a firm resolve for the future, he turned over on his side and also went to sleep.

"*What* battered caravanserai?"

"Why, the one whose portals are alternate night and day, Ginger."

"Oh, yes. *The Rubaiyat.* I forgot." She looked up from her breakfast newspaper with a smiling curiosity, coffee cup in hand. "What brought that up?"

"Nothing." He returned to his own breakfast. She began absently to hum something, which turned out to be Cole Porter's "Night and Day." She was glad at any rate to find him talking again, having noted that in the past few days she "hadn't been able to get a word out of him edgewise." He said:

"I'm going to get a job."

"A part in a play? Oh, good. When did this develop?"

"No, I mean in an office. I've been to an employment agency and I think I've got something lined up."

"Oh, Stew, no. Don't do that. Keep trying the producers. Pound the pavements a while longer. Something will turn up."

"Probably it will. Meanwhile I thought I'd like to try this, at least as a stopgap."

"You're not a nine-to-five man."

"This is from ten to six," he said, giving an odd laugh. He went on: "It's the Rumsey Affiliates, in New York."

"A commuter!"

"For God's sake, how do you think I got to the theatre? Anyway, I've always been curious to see what it's like inside one of those conglomerates."

He soon found out. He had not been punching the clock very long at Rumsey — indeed it wasn't necessary to punch anything, one's entrances and exits being registered by a photo-electric eye — when he was seized with an uncontrollable need to fold, staple and mutilate. So soul-stifling did he find this computerized hell that he felt sorrier for the swarms of other wretches with whom he toiled in its sterile hives, numbed into resignation to a fate over which they had no choice, than for himself, who could leave any time he wished. These automatons would, at retirement, be as shredded as the tons of memos with which they bustled about; ants had more purpose, the ephemeral birds more future. Anyone released from this prison, by whatever means, would be better off selling sweets to children in the streets.

One Monday morning, two weeks from the day he'd started work, he darted from his cubicle and seized a poor devil rushing down the corridor in shirtsleeves, clutching a sheaf of papers.

"You're fired."

"Wha-what do you mean? Who are you?"

"Only doing my job. Your services are no longer required. We'll have to let you go."

"Bu-but hasn't my work been satisfactory?"

"Perfectly. It's not that at all. We're just cutting your job out. Go and be somebody."

"But I'm in Sales."

"Yes. We're eliminating that."

"All of it?"

"That's right."

The man was dumbfounded, speechless with astonishment for a moment. He recovered his senses enough to gulp, "What could be more important than Sales? The *Product*."

"Have you ever seen it?"

"Well, no, not actually, but —"

"Then how do you know it exists? How do you know you do? Or any of us? We're figments in the brain of —" He jerked his head to the great Upstairs. Darting glances up and down the corridor, he lowered his voice to a whisper. "From now on, we're going to manufacture something else."

"Something other than a *Product*, for God's sake?"

"That's right."

"What?"

"I'm not at liberty to say. But — this much I'll hint — it's a substitute for Matter. Incredible possibilities are being opened up for human happiness — if we work it right. Go! And" — once more an upward bob of the head — "you-know-Who-speed."

"Are we going to discontinue all products?"

"All." Beginning to be drunk with power, in addition to the idealistic fervor with which his first inspiration had been fired, Smackenfelt took the man's arm in a comradely fashion and led him down the hall at a leisurely stroll, pausing only to take the papers from his hand and chuck them into a trash container in passing. "The possibility of your coming back here, for a conceivably greater opportunity, hinges on your not having been let go, but quitting of your own volition. You dig? So if you simply go into Accounting and announce your intention to terminate your connection here, and would they have your severance pay ready by Friday please . . ."

Smackenfelt found it progressively easier to perform this act as he ironed out through usage his technique for executing it. From firing underlings he went on to giving higher-ups the sack. Neither was any more difficult than the other in the all-enveloping impersonality of this outfit. Or outfits, for it was a conglomerate on the most heinous scale. He would pick his victim — beneficiary he preferred to view the recipient of what was after all a favor — selected either on the instant or after long consideration, make a sudden sortie from his coop in the dark coat and bow tie assumed for the execution, and say, "Your services are no longer required," or its persuasive smiling equivalent. From a cipher, he ascended with dizzying speed to the status of big cheese. They took him from a silently respectful distance to be one, and he consummately acted the part. He even fired a vice-president. Such a veep would think nothing of the president's not giving him the axe personally, rather delegating it to a henchman, this agile hatchetman who popped from doorways to serve notice that you were being let out in the most recent shakeup. If the discharged veep ran into the president at a party or some such later, and the president said something like, "Sorry you chose to leave us So-and-so," why, So-and-so would think it all part of the face-saving hanky-panky. He might even get hired back on the spot.

At last, Smackenfelt braced himself to perform the one supreme feat of this chapter of his life, if not of his life itself, so far; its crowning achievement, the meaning of his existence: he was going to fire the Boss.

The bewildering maze of corporations and interlocking directorates now comprising the labyrinth in which he had himself very nearly vanished without a trace made it just barely possible. The Nibs ticketed for liquidation would not know but what the man addressing him, this portly figure in banker's gray and black bow tie, was the head of an even larger octopus in whose clutches this one at last had been devoured. Thus the Kafkaesque nightmare of accepted contemporary fact might barely, just barely, have brought within such reach the guarantee of its own extinction. With Stew Smackenfelt its destiny-appointed, flaming-sworded symbolic agent.

He spotted the Nibs alighting from his limousine one morning as he, Smackenfelt, was returning from his midmorning second breakfast. He was lounging against a pillar inside the glass doorway, nursing a toothpick. As the Fat Slob dismissed his chauffeur with some instruction and started in, Smackenfelt went out to greet him.

"Wagonknecht?"

"Yes."

"You're fired. Get your money."

Wagonknecht sank to his knees, pleading, his clasped hands one imploring fist. Not bloody likely!

"Who the hell are you? What the hell is this, some kind of joke? You some kook who got by Psych Screening over in Personnel? Get back to your desk, or whatever it is you do. We have no room for cards in this office," said the King of Print-outs, pushing past him through the door.

Thus he saw himself as the stapled, spindled and mutilated victim of his own Herculean effort to reverse Kafka. The try had failed, misfired at the ultimate level. He was himself discharged, for malversation of coffee break or some damned thing. The Boss had had him watched by an intramural toady who reported him to be spending upwards of an hour in the arcade cafe, instead of the approved eight minutes, and *swoosh* — a blow from the axe he had so briefly himself wielded.

Smackenfelt stole down the stairs to listen to Ginger and Dolly at tea below, making again his now more than ever ritualized descent: the glance into the oval mirror to make sure his eyes were still like truffles; avoidance of the steps that creaked, now five in number, still with the speed of the spider steering clear of those segments of his web that are mucilaginously doctored for the entanglement of prey; the check of the Chagall print to note any loss of levitation among the peasants floating at rooftop level; a murmured encouragement to the houseplant still languishing next to the umbrella stand, despite all such endearments. He paused in the hall to eavesdrop.

"How is Zap?"

"Fine. Stew?"

"Fine."

"In good spirits?"

"Yes. Well, actually I think he may be going through a religious spell of some kind. He's been looking for work again, you know, after getting canned, and he tells of the time during a recession when he was up against it the same way. He talks about a mysterious vision he had while hitchhiking through Pennsylvania, looking for work in the steel mills. Thumbing his way south from Scranton in a drizzle and not a soul would stop for him. Then something about slouching toward Bethlehem. Do you know anything about that?"

"No. I never heard anything about that. He never told me."

"It was Christmas Eve, and he was penniless and hungry."

"There were periods in his life that I don't know much about, of course. When he was trying to find himself. Jobs he took, anything he could get, to tide him over while he looked for parts. I don't think he held any of them very long. He once had an office job that he was fired from for using a can of sardines for a paperweight."

"A paperweight? How come?"

"He had snacks at his desk, to keep his energy up, and this was just a can of sardines he'd never gotten around to opening. The boss thought he was using it for a paperweight, and the sight of it lying there on a sheaf of inter-office memos was the last straw. He had a fit and fired him. Stew says his reaction was out of all proportion, something to behold. He sort of spun around with his hands in the air, letting out a howl of despair, and said to go get his money."

The women chatted away, while he ascended to Golgotha between ranks of the curious, staggering to his knees under the weight of the Cross of which this Simon of Cyrene at last relieved him. Together they mounted the fateful slope, while Aunt Ginger rose to rearrange some green fruit set out to ripen under the sunlamp.

". . . often think of the tea set we bought you when you were a little girl. Remember that little neighbor child, Amelia, you used to play with? I'll never forget the time you were downstairs together with the tea set and you came up to the kitchen to get you each a banana. You carried them down, peeled, one in each hand, and on the way you dropped one, and quick as a flash you said, 'Oh, I dropped Amelia's banana.' That was my girl."

"What about this religious period you say he's going through?"

"Well, then he goes around saying he's Thomas à Kempis, and yesterday he asked me if I was familiar with his Imitation of Christ. That's a joke, I gather."

"Yes, he's pulling your leg. Well, not if you realize it, I suppose. It's the title of a book. But I've heard him say he thinks Christ may have been a superb mimic, not just a satirist, really taking the scribes and Pharisees off about straining at a gnat and swallowing a camel and so on. Burlesquing them with his impressions. Mugging like hell."

"What do you think of his impressions?"

"Whose?"

"Stew's. I think they're amusing but I'm not always any judge. What do your set in general think of them?"

Smackenfelt cleared his throat noisily and sauntered in, wearing gray flannel trousers and a Navy blazer in which he was beginning to look more like an Amsterdam burgomaster than ever. One half expected its middle button to pop off and hit one in the eye, like a shot melon pip. He was neglecting both his diet and his exercise again. Married life seemed to agree with him.

"Hello, Dolly." One of her fondest memories was that of her stepfather taking Ginger's face in both his hands with almost the same affection with which he cradled a brandy snifter in his palms, gently to rock and warm its contents. That was how Smackenfelt kissed her on the cheek now, though acknowledging to himself as he did so a distinct spasm of desire that made it idle to deny the unmistakable: he had the hots for his step-daughter.

Was there no occasion to which Blodgett did not sink? Where would it all end? Again already one began revolving ardor-dampeners. How the daughter would undoubtedly call the shots in any union, sacred *or* profane. How as the clearly dominant partner she would insist on marriage in the end in any case, and then how marriage always decaffeinates sex, leaving us this . . . this Sanka. How that eye liner (around gray-blue eyes however incandescently like Mother's) made her resemble miners whose faces are edged with coal dust permanently ineradicable . . . Too, she *was* married, to somebody named Spontini, and no amount of yen suffered by Blodgett had yet been strong enough to make even the rosebud-gathering Smackenfelt forget his number one lifelong rule: Never smell a flower with a bee in it. (Or had he already forgotten it?)

Sauntering over to twitch a window-blind, he inquired after his son-in-law now, Spontini, and stark, staring mad, was told by the women as they themselves brushed non-existent crumbs from their laps and diddled studiously about with their cups and spoons,

that he was fine and that they had arranged a dinner
foursome at Claude's, a restaurant they all liked.

Claude personally clucked and fussed over them,
while Dolly tried to break the ice with a laughingly
open account of how *she* felt undertaking a second
marriage. She said she felt like the London Bridge,
which had been taken apart and then re-assembled in
Arizona, with the surplus portions of granite, authenti-
cated by engineers, properly labelled and sold for use
as paperweights. Spontini had one in his house, gift of
a house guest, which was what made her think of this
as a metaphor for her condition.

"I try to keep her at work on her new play," Spontini
said, with a glance at the swizzle stick clenched in
Smackenfelt's hand. He held it across the backs of two
middle fingers — now get this — and *under* the small
and index fingers, as though he were trying to snap it
in two with one hand, perhaps inadvertently. Zap
spoke of Dolly's instant success as the Swamp Girl for
one of his most important soap clients, though realizing
her writing came first. A good producer was definitely interested in the new script, but felt it needed work
and to that end was shopping for a collaborator.

"What it comes down to," he said with a laugh, "is
that the producer likes the play and is looking for
someone to adapt it to the stage."

"I take exception to that, Spontini."

"To what?"

"That last remark."

"Why? Dolly doesn't mind."

"I do. I consider it snide."

"She's laughing. Aren't you, Doll?"

"Ye-heh-hes."

"See?"

"I'm not. I'm not laughing."

"Look. What the hell is the matter with you anyway, Smackenfelt?" First names, briefly returned to in the first flush of good feeling, were now again abandoned in the glacial formality that customarily preceded open hostilities between the two.

"There's nothing whatever the matter with me. It's you there seems to be something wrong with. Some basic lack of chivalry that I find it hard to let pass without comment. Know what I mean?"

"Anything more than comment, by any chance — *Sir* Walter Raleigh?"

"If you wish."

"I really don't see what you're racing your motor about. She's my wife."

"Therefore you should be the first to leap to her defense against ungentlemanly slurs."

"Not in here, though?"

"No. Shall we step outside?"

"Don't mind if I do."

"Oh, for God's sweet *sake!*" Dolly's hands came vehemently down on the tabletop. Ginger rolled her eyes with a sigh. "Are we going through all this again?"

"No, I've got a better idea," her mother said. "*We'll* step outside, and leave them to eat the fifty dollars worth of duck and claret we've got coming between them."

The arrival of this food just then proved the financially sobering spectacle she had surmised. Matters were somehow smoothed over, and the meal consumed in relative composure. The rest of the evening passed without incident, save for a brief interval when the two men fought over the check. Claude himself had never seen that ritual more earnestly enacted; it seemed he would have to come over personally to avoid their literally belting one another over the tab, when the women again took hold and determined that they should go Dutch.

"Anyway, it looks as though we're back to normal again," Ginger observed, somewhat ambiguously.

The love feast would in time prove to have borne more fundamental and far-reaching fruit than that. Something Spontini had said was destined radically to alter the shape of all their lives. Something to which the very last note struck at the table happened to bear a quite accidental relevance, though it was doubtful any one of the four ever made the connection in recalling it later. Ginger was summing up all that had been hashed over concerning the ebb and flow of the professional fortunes of the other three.

"People in show business — and we must include television in that now, Zap dear — people in show business always have a lot of irons in the fire, but few of them ever jell."

"Few of them ever jell indeed," said Smackenfelt, as though stepping briskly forward to claim half equity in the metaphor, in that and any future locution of like interest from the same source, conveying also with a glance of smiling regard, as they rose together from the table, that *that* was how a gentleman behaved toward the lady of his bosom.

ten

"I'm not sitting on my buff. I'm sitting on my duff. That's what I'm sitting on, Ginger."

Smackenfelt spoke without heat, yet with a certain measured emphasis very nearly its equivalent.

"Nor am I an old movie duff, or you either. We're old movie buffs. As people are old car buffs, or railroad or ragtime buffs."

She clawed her face, smiling at him through a lattice-work of fingers. "We've loads to talk about."

"You've had the two terms confused, is all," he finished, moderating his tone at the last moment with a smile of his own. "Like flaunt and flout. You flout convention, while flaunting your unconventionality."

"So those weren't vintage me. Oh, well. Live and learn. So anyway. Kitty cat knows what's making Stew edgy, don't you?" she said to Mordecai, employing the old device of hers which through obliquity made it possible to air matters that might prove a shade touchy

for frontal communication. "Someone isn't sitting on
her duff, while he chooses to crawl into his shell like
this. Or maybe that's why he is. Not just the commercials, they don't mean anything, but she has two plays
making the rounds and another hot in the typewriter.
Kitty cat feels that even the commercials are getting
under his skin. I doubt that, but still, you never know.
They make her a walloping financial success, a bread-
winner in her own right. That might take the starch
out of a man. So kitty cat speculates, in his secret
wisdom."

They regularly caught Dolly's television plugs as the
Swamp Tease, not by design, but inevitably along with
the old movies they watched, as buffs. The sight of his
ex-wife slinking about the bayou as she had across the
floor when it had been one of his inspirations for a
bedroom "bit," now holding a cake of Palmleaf Soap as
she extolled its efficacy in even so abysmal a milieu
(the scenes had been photographed on location in the
Louisiana country) was enough to drive him into the
kitchen for another Blodgett and a fresh can of beer —
for he was eating like a horse again as well as neglecting his exercises.

"Eating between snacks again, he is," Ginger remarked to the cat. "Just look at the size of that one.
With that slice of tongue hanging out of it, *like* a
tongue, kitty cat observes. To say nothing of packing
both cheeses and meats into one, thus confusing our
liver by feeding it two kinds of protein. Well, I'll just
have to let these trousers out again, back to the way
they were and maybe a little extra, for future reference."

She was letting out his entire wardrobe, striking

whenever possible thereby an admonitory tableau in their evenings together, in the parlor or in the television room before the boob tube. One in which kitty cat himself played a part by swiping at her thread or toying with her pinking shears. A domestic scene at odds with the traffic in evil spirits Smackenfelt had in his own fancy tried to pin on the beast. So far from stealing out nights to engage in assorted diabolisms, he was a plump purring house pet, a very calendar cat. Smackenfelt was feeling let down by everybody.

"He'll never get any parts if he continues letting himself go," she confided to puss. "Ah, he shudders at the term, it comes as a surprise to him that men can be guilty of that as well as women. A healthy shock maybe. Oh, yes. Not that he ever consults *Variety* any more to see what's cooking, or calls his agent." She put the case more humorously. "He's applying for permanent unemployment benefits. He's filling out his form."

"That tears it," said kitty cat, licking his paw. Or appeared to, to the imaginative observer. Ginger pressed forward, airing what very much needed airing, whatever the risk, whatever the cost.

"Do you know what I think?" Overturning in her lap the britches being altered. "I think he's still married to her. Never quite got her out of his system. Views her as a threat."

"To his own self-respect," Smackenfelt amiably finished, backing toward his chair with his eyes on the television set which he had just turned on for the Million Dollar Movie.

Thus kitty cat fell privy to a lot that was going on around here. He learned how the subject of Dolly's new play remained a closely guarded secret; how Stew was scared stiff it might be about all of them, a triangle involving a male chauvinist pig who divorces his wife to marry her mother, as an attack on contemporary woman; how the drama itself would thus be a scorching counterblast on Broadway, an "equal time" in the continuing sex war. All their dirty linen would be washed in public.

"Is that what's got him paralyzed on dead center, hung up there, do you suppose?" Ginger continued, on his rising to eliminate the sound from a clutch of commercials prefacing *The Little Foxes* (chosen over Blodgett's preference for an old Cagney). While the floor moppers and cereal eaters mouthed their testimonials unheard, she went on: "He won't even go out and socialize. I can understand his not wanting to run into the old friends they had, but why won't he call on these new neighbors of ours, the Stillwells?"

"They have a dog named Talleyrand," Smackenfelt explained, to the cat. "It's the woman mainly. You know the type. They wear leather jewelry and serve runny Brie and have daughters named Erika." Kitty cat flung a hand across his eyes on the chair where he lay. "Deliver me," he was saying in effect. He knew the type well. "They can be seen shovelling snow in their mink coats," Smackenfelt said, "and in summer clipping roses in slacks nobody can really seriously garden in, and they will eventually open yet another cunning boutique where ancient Chinese pressing irons are sold as ashtrays." Kitty cat threw the other paw across his brow, veritably pleading to hear no more. "Like don't!"

Ginger begged to differ with this self-defense. Became quite forensic.

"He has a thing about people," she said, getting in

her licks. "It's got to be said, faced up to. He's developed this thing about them. Doesn't want to dine out, rather put it all together at the ice box and wash it down with another crock of suds in front of the TV." She looked directly at Stew. "Why don't we ever go to the theatre?"

"I never go to the theatre." Thus this actor was like Mozart, who, when asked what kind of music he liked, replied, "No music." But as Mozart may have liked the theatre, he enjoyed the concert hall, and promised Ginger smartly that he would see about getting tickets to an upcoming all-Beethoven concert at Lincoln Center. They both liked Beethoven. They would override Blodgett's wish rather to catch a production of *La Boheem*, hey.

"Swell. I must remember to let out your tuxedo pants, then. Here, see how these are now."

She watched him slip into his trousers, again under his bathrobe, as he had done in another era, when she had taken them in, the same pants, while waiting for their wandering girl to come home. He held the waist out to show the extra play they now had.

"Allowing for further expansion," she said, rather drily, putting her things away in the sewing basket. "It's your health I'm really concerned about, you know, dear. Do you ever read the obituary page, the ages of the men who should be just swinging into their prime? People just don't live the way they used to."

He took a deliberate stance before her, resting his weight on one foot. "People used to eat, in addition to what I tuck away in these, I admit indiscriminately," he said, flourishing the sandwich, "cheese by the carload and eggs by the crate."

"Cholesterol —"

"That's what I'm talking about. They buttered their bread like a bricklayer slapping mortar on his bricks, they breakfasted not only on bacon and ham, but something called fried cracklins, the rind. They slathered pure goose fat on pumpernickel by the inch. They poured gallons of maple syrup on pancakes by the stack, and it would never have occurred to them to trim the fat off the meat."

"They worked it off. And they kept physically active outside of their work. They thought nothing of walking ten miles to visit friends."

"I don't think much of it myself."

"There, you see?" She appealed again to kitty cat. "He does have this thing about people. But the important thing is, we've all simply got to distinguish between hunger and appetite."

"Sounds like Birdie wisdom. Look, has she shown you that thesis — ?"

"There's Dolly!"

Ginger darted forward to turn up the sound, so they could hear as well as see her in a commercial for a new product altogether. Dolly was in this instance the one being proselytized, a young housewife despairing of remaining indefinitely palatable through the use of any unguents known to her, whom a confiding neighbor put next to one which, applied to her person, enabled her to find total security under all circumstances and in all weathers. Dolly was required to thank her on a scale on which, as the Swamp Girl, she had had gratitude showered on her by lifelong converts to Palmleaf.

"Jesus Christ," Smackenfelt said, impatient to get back to the familial horrors of *The Little Foxes*.

"Well!" Ginger heaved a sigh and looked brightly about. "Let's liven this party up, shall we? Get it off the ground? How about a few imitations?"

With that she began to lick her paw and wipe her face with it. Smackenfelt ignored this astonishing development, but it slew kitty cat. Oh, he dug it! Not missing how she did behind the ears either, bending each one over double as she swiped the side of her head with a downward motion, the sly comment on kitty cat's kind. Oh, he dug it all. The parody killed him. So that, as though in response to his choked pleas for more, the whole animal repertory she apparently had had up her sleeve all this time, she let herself be coaxed into doing her bird. Standing on one leg, she put her head under her arm and began to pluck feathers out with her beak. Till kitty cat liked to died. She was a blast, though you couldn't tell it by Smackenfelt who, his face set like flint, even like that One who set his own steadfastly to go to Jerusalem, there to be mocked, spat upon and given a crown of thorns, went on eating the Blodgett and watching the television. It was when, blinking intelligently, hunched over on all fours with her knuckles on the linoleum, she threatened to favor them with her chimpanzee that he smiled wanly and nodded, but made no outcry. That the Scriptures might be fulfilled which said, even in the words of the prophet Isaiah: "He was oppressed and he was afflicted, yet he opened not his mouth, as a sheep before her shearers is dumb."

All this at least drove the thesis clean out of his head, which was what Ginger wanted, though she knew she was only playing for time. That the time would come when she must tell him something of its contents. He professed indifference to what Birdie for her part shrank from showing him, drastically disguised to protect the innocent though it was. Birdie's relations with all of them had now been quite patched up, thanks mainly to Uncle Fats' good offices in tracking her down to the Italian restaurant where she had gorged herself on spaghetti after that terrible scene (rivalling any in the Hellman drama) she had accidentally overheard, there to disabuse her of the ideas she had erroneously gathered from it. With the divorces and remarriages, Birdie came to accept events as now respectably resolved. She visited everyone again, though in separate households, and was bringing a young man of her own around. His first meeting with Smackenfelt left a lot to be desired. This is what happened.

In a brief renaissance of interest in his figure, Smackenfelt had tried jogging, inside the house, as it embarrassed him to be seen steaming along out of doors. Even there he only jogged when home alone, running from room to room and up and down the stairs yelling, "Fire!" or "Stop thief!" as a means of relieving the boredom engendered by this type of locomotion, by lending some imaginary kind of melodramatic context to what was another tediously repetitive discipline at best. Sometimes he would lighten the way by spinning a monologue of one kind or another. "Cure you of your guilt feelings?" he shouted, as a psychiatrist given to telling his patients off in plain language. "What for, I should think you would feel guilty after all the things you've done, you dreadful old bitch! Come here you harridan, you awful old party! Get out of my house!"

Pelting down the stairs in the middle of this particular outcry, he found Birdie standing in the vestibule, with her swain. His exclamations had apparently drowned out the sound of the doorbell.

"I thought you were calling to come in," Birdie said, seeing him standing there in his shorts, heaving noisily, sweat dripping from his brow and running in rivulets under his arms.

"Well, I was. You go sit down, I'll get into something more . . . Ginger will be back from the store any . . ." He turned and pounded back up the stairs.

The youth, named Barton Domby, was at work on a master's thesis of his own, in ecology. His subject was commercial river pollution in the New England States, 1925–1970.

"What will you call your paper, 'The Effluent Society'?" Blodgett cracks, and guffaws like a fool. They all sat drinking coffee together.

Domby and Birdie exchanged looks of solemn thoughtfulness, considering the title. But at last her young man shook his head. "I'm afraid Holstein would think I was being funny," he said, and she agreed with him about this academic superior to whom he was accountable, and his possible reaction.

About a week before the night of *The Little Foxes*, Birdie had met Ginger for tea in a restaurant and let her skim through her thesis there, fetched along for the purpose. A week or so after it, Ginger plucked up the courage to tell Stew what it said, ignoring his wish to hear nothing of the case history for which he had "sat." She owed it to both of them. It was for his own best. We must all have our moment of truth, and this was his.

They were sitting in the parlor reading. Suddenly

she dropped her book in her lap and rattled off at high speed:

"About Birdie's thesis, yes, I read it. Just dipped into it, enough to get the drift. She calls the subject 'M.' She makes him a salesman in the Middle West. The disguise is complete of course. Well, M, she decides, it's her own analysis, M doesn't really want to conquer his eating compulsion and lose weight, because" — she drew a deep breath and plowed blindly on — "because that way he can always blame his professional failure on his appearance."

She wanted to cut her tongue. She sat frozen in her chair as he rose from his and fished a cigar from a humidor, one of the clear Havanas bootlegged by air from the Swiss tobacconist whose address Bert Shaftoe had given him. He licked a lesion in its wrapper till it had been mended to his satisfaction, and set fire to it. It took a good deal of puffing to get it alight, being one of the enormous Churchill model for which he had developed a fancy. At length the coal was going properly.

Shaking in her shoes, Ginger continued with the résumé from which there was now no turning back.

"He never bags his quota, M doesn't, this salesman, and gets fired from one job after another. He could slim down and so make a success of this line of work where appearance is important — *maybe*. That's the ultimate test he's afraid to be put to, you see. He's not sure. He may get down to normal size and still flop. That's the risk he can't bear to take. His ego couldn't stand it. His ego prefers the other. Chooses the other," she jabbered on, hoping to keep a grip on her exegesis until she had finished it, like a recitation. "He breaks these diets he has no intention of staying on, so he can blame his failures on his appearance. There, I've said it. And may God have mercy on us all." She crossed herself, though no more than a backslidden Congregationalist.

Smackenfelt strolled to the piano. There he stood, the cigar clamped in his teeth, picking out *The Messiah* with one finger. When he had finished, he turned around with a smile.

"And is Birdie familiar with Zero Mostel? And with Edward Arnold and Burl Ives?"

"Why, I suppose . . ."

"And Jackie Gleason and Jonathan Winter and Buddy Hackett? And does she attribute their failure in life also to their great size? Is it owing to their excessive bulk that they have not made a mark in their chosen field?"

"I see what you mean. It's no excuse for an actor because there are parts of all kinds. Including fat parts."

He brought both fists down on the piano keyboard and roared, "That's not what the expression means!" No he didn't. Every morning he would awaken and find her body beside him, like a loaf of freshly baked bread. Yes, every bit as warm and aromatic, every morning, freshly baked bread.

"That's right."

"Well, anyway, it worked for the salesman. And the thesis has been accepted," continued Freshly Baked Bread, relieved that it had all gone as smoothly as it had. "So you see, it's just come out a piece of fiction after all — like you said from the beginning. Would you like to read it?"

"Nah." He flung a hand generously into the air and turned away.

"And you're not angry with me for telling you?"

He turned back to her again, clearing his throat ever so slightly, and emanating other of the minute signals by which a skilled actor telegraphs that more is in the wind, something in the way of a diversion. "What do you think, my dear?" he murmured, pursing his lips in a tiny smile as by humorous small degrees he detached his gaze from hers and wandered back to the chair he had vacated, ogling just ever so slightly.

"Orson Welles!"

"Let's go to bed."

Thus they did, but Ginger managed to delay it till something more like their normal retirement time, in order to take advantage of his good humor to bring something else up. Zap. Why did he take him as seriously as he did, fearing to run into him at parties and the like, which she guessed was in part behind his withdrawal into this shell? She spoke of Zap's shortcomings as a husband, measured against Stew Smackenfelt as a yardstick of acceptability in that area.

"Well might Dolly spend all the time she's got at the typewriter, evenings too, never knowing when he'll get home from the city or whether it's really business that's keeping him. I don't mean to insinuate he's swinging there, but he does fancy himself a hot shot. Just the greatest thing since sliced bread. His nickname implies it, that people know he's got this image of himself. That, all in all, he's quite a piston. What's the matter, are you ill?"

Smackenfelt sat bent over forward with his elbows on his knees and his head in his hands, caught in them as in a noose, or locked in them as in a vise — the way

Dolly had when listening to "Motherisms," in what now seemed another era. It was vivid domestic theatre, into which he didn't realize he had again fallen until he was halfway through the struggle of trying to extricate his poor old coco from its steel trap. Having at last done so, he turned it slowly toward Ginger.

"Pistol. Not piston. It's a pistol Zap fancies himself. That's what we call it. A piston is an organ in an internal combustion engine."

"So? It says it just as well, doesn't it?"

"What do you think the expression means? He's a pistol."

"I suppose it has sexual overtones. Originally anyway. Phallic, as we say."

"Precisely. It's an image. So why do you make it piston?"

"What's the difference? It carries the basic meaning just as well one way or the tother. Maybe better. Why make a hassle out of such a small thing? Like the other night I noticed you grinding your teeth when I said Hemingway said love makes the world go round."

"It made the earth move for them. That's what the Hemingway lovers said. About sex, making love."

"What's the difference?"

"Oh, my God." More Gnashville. How explain it? That a hair might separate the false and true, even right from wrong, but a gulf yawned between the O.K. and the *de trop*.

"If you can't see the difference between love makes the world go round and it makes the earth move, then I can't explain it to you, Ginger."

"Oh, you only explain to people what they already know."

He emitted a sigh of one who needs at least a thousand years of sleep — a death rattle really. Oh, the freedom of Blodgett from all this, the rack and strain of subtlety and nuance! "That's right. And the English major the other night wasn't an officer in the British army, he's much too young for that. He's a student at Harvard. And virgins are not defoliated, they're deflowered. But speaking of sex . . ."

After they had made love, she lay wakeful a long time beside his oblivious form, smiling to herself as she thought of him, among other things, broiling a steak outside on the terrace, blowing up the coals by training the exhaust end of the vacuum cleaner on them, wearing a derby so as not to set his hair on fire with the sparks, which flew upward in a furious shower. Then standing there holding the water pistols which the book on barbecue cooking recommended as the best means of dousing flareups from the dripping fat. He would station himself at the grill, firing jets at each such tongue of flame leaping up and threatening to set the meat itself ablaze, producing each time a very satisfactory hiss, and looking like the fastest gun in the West, or a sheriff adroitly handling any such incoming menace. "He's a pickpocket," she whispered to the cat, who had wandered in. "He has taking ways."

She resolved to worm out of Dolly what her new play was about, to get him off the hook if at all possible. She did so the very next day. And it wasn't about any such thing as a triangle involving a male chauvinist pig at all, they should have known better than to think Dolly capable of anything so vindictive, notorious as writers were for pillorying in print people close to them. She hurried home with her good news as fast as her legs could carry her from the tea at Dolly's where she had managed to extract it. Not that she didn't keep Stew in suspense a moment, having the feminine talebearer's natural sense of the theatre herself.

"Well, it's the oddest thing." She stamped the snow from her boots in the vestibule to which he had hurried to hear, the cat capering at his feet. "Remember that spat you and Zap had in the restaurant, when he called you Sir Walter Raleigh for coming to your ex-lady's defense after his own crack about her last play? That's what the new one's about."

"About Spontini and me?"

"No, no. Raleigh. The incident reminded Dolly of a paper she did on him in college — she only stuck it out one year, you know, so she must have been a freshman at the time — and thinking at the time there'd be a good play in his life. She dug it out, did a little more research, and zingo! Off to the races. Where are you going?"

"Library. Maybe I can be of some help to her. We're *all* fascinated with Raleigh, of course."

She eyed him skeptically as he bundled himself into the Immensikoff, which he had plucked from the closet after hanging her own coat up.

"What's the matter? You O.K. or something? You going to do the right thing or something? While you're being a brick, she asked whether you might want to attend an opening of Zap's in town. A gallery there is exhibiting some of his new paintings. A group show, but it's a start." She laughed. "That would really be heaping balls of fire on their heads."

He stooped to rumple the cat. "I suppose while I'm gone you're going to tell her it's coals of fire, not balls. You're such a meddler." And sailed out the door and off to the library.

Dolly had given the marriage two months. Here they

had already been married eight, and the end was not
yet in sight.

eleven

He knew, or thought he knew, the exact moment when Spontini had decided to steal his wife.

The two had had a fight at the Wusdatts'. Zap had made some slur about women as a pressure group, with which Smackenfelt quite agreed. He had even put the matter far more strongly himself. "Woman is the wheel that will always squeak, grease it though we may," he had observed. Which was better than anything anybody else had said on the subject, including Schopenhauer and Freud, going straight to the heart of the matter as it did. But the validity of any truth can never quite be disentangled from the question of who's talking, and hearing his own convictions played back by a sideliner with no right to — a passive spectator and not a player in the thick of the scrimmage — Smackenfelt tended to resist them. In fact they had set his back up. Then it had been the same story; a discussion ending in a quarrel and that in a fight, though willing peacemakers had again managed to separate the combatants before blood was drawn. Smackenfelt's final thrust had been worse than an uppercut. The emotional and intellectual elements were hard to sort out in sober review, but as nearly as he could reconstruct his role in the brouhaha, he had been defending husbands as a category against the charge that they were intrinsically absurd. Now, he personally regarded a husband as intrinsically absurd, but not to be so lampooned, even tangentially, by one whose life style was apparently to be that of the perpetual extra man, an uncommitted escort available alike to hostesses well in advance and unpaired women ringing up at the last minute — in short, as Smackenfelt had finally blurted out, inflamed by the image of Spontini tooling about town in his Ferrari zipped into a blue velours flight suit, "a Platonic stud!"

That did it. A mouse hung on Spontini, or lip laid open, would have healed. Not so that acerbic thrust, which was destined to smart forever, even for Smackenfelt, the one to apologize that time. Too late. He had become a matchmaker. Hindsight could clearly now fix the instant when Zap had resolved to make his rebuttal by stealing Dolly, whom he proceeded to cozen and beguile by offering her a leg up in a career Smackenfelt had only up till then managed to impede, if not bring to a grinding halt.

That, at any rate, was how Smackenfelt sized the whole thing up. Who could say for sure? The theory made as much sense as anything in this rum world. It certainly made dramaturgical sense, as a seed of character motivation sprouting at a critically auspicious juncture. At the lowest, it was a serviceable "fiction," like that of the salesman M into whom he had been sea-changed in Birdie's fat-city monograph of him. But having settled on a working hypothesis for Spontini's motivation, what about his own? Would he retaliate in kind? No. He had had enough of human pettiness and perfidy, including his own. From now on he was going to be the "brick" Ginger had said. He would become the very embodiment of knightly fealty about whom Dolly was writing and whose name Spontini had flung at him by way of a satirical epithet. He would become Sir Walter Raleigh indeed.

So that when "this producer friend of Zap's" conked out, coming through with not a dime of option money in the end, Smackenfelt stepped into the breach. He spread his cloak across the intervening mud pools of the marketplace, sparing Dolly's having to put her own dainty foot into them, by finding her a manager himself. He took the completed draft in to Bah personally on a Friday morning, and by Sunday evening Bah was on the blower to Dolly, expressing his interest in the property though feeling it still needed a lot of work.

Here Smackenfelt continued of further service, as the figure about whom the drama after all principally revolved. He spent hours in the library, or at home poring over books fetched from there. He devoured biographies, histories, Raleigh's own writings; anything having bearing on himself, as re-incarnation of the quixotic role into which he threw himself with a more self-obliterating intensity than any he had ever assumed on the stage. He grew more tautly into focus every day he lived; with every breath he drew, more fully exemplified each apprehended attribute of the great courtier: the starborn *panache* sustained through every change of fortune: the heroic style: the dark dazzle: the vaulting if often rapacious valor. Daily, sometimes hourly, he despatched suggestions to the toiling playwright as to how she might deepen and enrich her dramatic representations of all this, either by special post or sending Ginger trotting round to deliver them by hand, down the street to the great white house beside the chuckling river where his poor lady now lived imprisoned as Mrs. Spontini.

But striking a blow for chivalry was uphill work. Impediments to princely grace lay everywhere, not least of all at home where proliferating Gingerisms often as not had him sitting with his head in his hands. "I do rely on you, as a wife, but don't say 'lean on me a little,' in that regard. That is a gangster term for roughing somebody up. And you keep referring to Mr. Kloosterman down the street as 'eighty-three and just as light on his feet.' "

"Now what?"

" 'Light on his feet' "— and here he contrived at last to get his head out of that vise — "is an expression used for homosexuals. It has definitely that connotation these days, nor does it have any other. It can't be used as you use it, without provoking laughter, and we don't want to provoke that, do we?" he added, a little grimly.

"Well, we could use some of it around here. But getting back to the Kloostermans, he certainly is in much better shape than his wife. She's a couple of years younger, but has the look of one not long for this world."

He tried, too late, to convert a fist brought down on the arm of his chair as simply part of the act of rising from it.

"For God's sake, that refers to people who die

young! Of course the woman's not long for this world if she's in her eighties! How could she be? But you have *to die young* to be 'not long for this world' in the sense in which the phrase is proverbially used, originally in old-fashioned romances relating to girls in fragile health, generally stricken with consumption or some other wasting disease. Now have you got that all straight?"

"Why isn't it just as valid the way I used it? You *know* what I mean."

"That's not enough. So the term refers to those of few summers doomed to be having them drawing to a close. It has nothing whatever to do with people pottering on the brink of the grave. I mean doddering, obviously. Christ, you've got me doing it!" And he flung a book into the chair he had vacated in the course of all this pedagogy.

"Make a list. Keep at me. I know I need help."

"*I* need help." He paused before a wall glass to examine his face, which was managing the feat of becoming simultaneously fleshier and more haggard by the day. Putting out his tongue, he saw that some species of fungus was beginning to grow on it. Or perhaps lichen, which, if memory served, was fungus in symbiotic union with algae. Gray-greenish in hue and rather sinister-looking. Perhaps he was not long for this world.

"I suppose you've married beneath you," she observed, quite objectively.

"Of course I have, in some ways, just as you have in others. It was the same with Dolly and me. Or any two people. We were — are — superior to one another in different ways. These things all even out over the long haul."

"How long?" Then she smiled, assessing him. "In what ways were you different? And vice versa? You and Dolly?"

"I'm not allowed to give out that information. Let's go to bed."

They made love, and afterwards, propped on one elbow with a glutted gaze, he touched a fingertip to her navel, traced it delicately down the firm bubble of her middle to her sweet fleece. "Oh, and don't say 'on all our behalves.' 'All our behalf' is good enough. There's no plural of 'behalf.' So forget about correct English."

Swimming into his bathrobe with the accustomed backstroke, he snuck down the stairs and listened. The two women were again having tea. They conversed in low tones. Ginger was speaking.

". . . don't suppose he's grooming himself for the . . ."

". . . certainly acting as though . . . always did it before whenever he was up for . . ."

"Yes. Steeps himself in . . . right for the part? I mean he's an American."

"Well, it's the point he made so tellingly when he was turned down for the part in *Tawdry Audrey*."

"What part was that?"

"The devil worshipper who lost his faith."

"Oh, yes. What was the point?"

"That you needn't cast a part within a nationality. Vivien Leigh played a southern belle in *Gone with the Wind*, Alec Guinness was a desert sheik in *Lawrence of Arabia* and so on and so on. As for Raleigh, so thick —"

Dolly rose and stole into the vestibule to make sure the coast was clear. By which time Raleigh had popped into the closet, emerging again when it was

clear from his point of view, and the nearby table-talk
had resumed.

"His Devonshire brogue was so thick a London actor
would have to put it on just as much as a New York
one. Well, that's not for me to decide, thank God. It's
Bah's headache."

For Bah had taken an option, and suddenly they
were all having dinner in New York to celebrate the
signing of the contract. The Smackenfelts and the
Spontinis arrived at the appointed fish house early, or
at least enough in advance of the equivalently tardy
Bahs to give Stew a good ten minutes in which to
re-assess his sexual rival and son-in-law. Zap looked
quite prosperous in his midnight-blue velvet jacket and
Twenties-craze bow tie; in other respects, somewhat
toned down under the Dolly administration. His hair
had been given what producers up against scripts running overtime called a little judicious cutting, while
the dots under the long graying sideburns had been
shaved away, terminating their resemblance to exclamation marks. The two had been seeing one another as
members of a Citizens Rezoning Committee back
home, a group agitating for changes which would allow constructions of the first apartment buildings in
town, the end in view being inexpensive houses Ne-
groes could afford. Smackenfelt recalled these meetings
through both the gauze of boredom endured while
sitting in on them, and the haze of his steadily thicken-
ing identity as Sir Walter Raleigh.

He had striven to relieve their tedium by expressing
his opinions, in all conscience radical enough, through
the use of darkey talk, which amused no one but a few
blacks on the committee, notably a minister named
Reverend Maddock who remained in stitches over

Smackenfelt's improvisations. "Our opponents *supposes* dis gwine lower property values. Dey *supposes* dose river sites gwine be useless for anything else anyway 'cept human habitation. Dey *supposes* integration coming no matter what in de long run. What Ah want to know is, how we gwine reconcile all dem suppositories?"

It was now not at all certain Reverend Maddock was not going to suffer an apoplectic seizure there and then, and have to be carried out. The others glared at him no less than at Smackenfelt, who, enormously encouraged, forged ahead.

"Now, 'bout dis new draft of de broadsides we got cheer, a copy of which Ah got cheer before me. It say such a high rise complex out chonder would be a major fortification in de battle for suburban democracy. What is a fortification? Ah spect it's two twentifications."

He was seized at the elbows and drawn to one side by two members, one of whom audibly hoped for his sake he had taken a snootful before arriving, the other emphasizing that they would like to know, as a committee, when this Uncle Remus business was likely to stop. They would all appreciate some reassurance about it. They looked like people making a citizen's arrest, hauling Smackenfelt across the room with only his toes grazing the floor. Others looked on with sympathetic shakes of their heads, as though they were dealing with someone more to be understood than censured. He settled on the dirty work for which he had infinitely more stomach than meetings with groups of liberals, such as stuffing and licking envelopes for the cause. The broadsides all prepared, he bundled them up and took them to the post office himself, hunching through a light snow with his plantation shuffle as he sadly mouthed old wrongs he hoped the work would do a little something toward righting.

"I suppose you don't have the same dedication about it, not being a member of a minority group," Spontini observed with a tolerant smile, as they sat in the fish house with their drinks.

"I suppose not," Smackenfelt said, smiling secretly over his own memory of the street Italians of his Chicago boyhood chanting at him:

> *"Oh, the Irish and the Dutch*
> *Don't amount to very much."*

The thing about minority groups was that they tended to outnumber you.

The event for which they had been waiting now occurred.

A tall woman muffled to the chin in green carpeting entered, trailed by a man supplying by this juxtaposition her identification, he being Bah. He would seem to have smuggled his wife here in some of his own imported merchandise, for reasons not surmised until she had unrolled herself from the rug, like Cleopatra before Caesar, to reveal the rest of her outfit: slacks of which the legs varied in color, the one being solid yellow and the other orange; a man's smoking jacket the shade of the broadloom in which she had arrived swaddled; and a scarf covered with small bells. Strings of tiny brilliants were disposed about the rims of her ears, rather than dangling from the lobes in more platitudinous fashion, and she sported enormous hexagonal rose-tinted glasses, which she kept on at table, as though she were too rich for her own blood. The women bore down on one another with long-pent-up reunion cries. Cordial introduced Bah to Ginger, those two being known to each other only by name and hearsay, then threw her arms around Smackenfelt, with a hearty buss on the cheek he was sure had left a large crimson stain. He tried to correct this later with some discreet use of his napkin.

Bah's dark hair, Smackenfelt noticed as he took the familiar handshake with the usual Spartan determination to suppress an outcry, had been going from a premature gray to a rather sulphurous yellow. Ginger later explained that such a phenomenon was a result of heavy smoking. Whether because the nicotine was soaked internally upward through the scalp or discolored the hair on the outside she didn't know. The theory was credible in the case of Bah, whom clouds of cigarette smoke incessantly wreathed.

"I've been trying to get him to quit but he won't," Cordial said.

"I'm a weak character," he said. "And there it is."

"They make the strongest adversaries. God forbid any of you should be up against anything so weak as Cyrus."

"Let's talk about something pleasant. Let's talk about Dolly's play. Now then — the sixty-four-thousand-dollar question — who can play Raleigh?"

Smackenfelt opened his mouth to make some response to this when something occurred that put to another severe test his ability to live in the style of a Renaissance gallant.

He had assumed this to be Bah's party. Now he was no longer sure what foundation there was for that. Bah had wined and dined the Spontinis before in connection with the play, and may have figured it was somebody else's turn. Zap showed no eagerness to do the honors. He was deep in a discussion of the marine murals garnishing the walls when the captain wafted up to take their dinner orders, posting himself ominously beside Smackenfelt who had given the instructions for drinks. Bah was deflected from his pivotal question about casting the lead by this lecture of Zap's, who, as an executor of puppy messes, must have thought the Dufy-haunted paintings banal to a degree. One other factor contributed to the swiftly brewing mess, insidious for Smackenfelt who had thirty dollars in his pocket and sat face-to-face with a sign reading "We do not honor credit cards." The table hadn't been reserved in anyone's name, as the restaurant also preened itself on booking no reservations.

Gallantly accepting the role foisted upon him by mischance, Smackenfelt asked everyone what they would like first. Orders for turtle soup, coquilles St. Jacques and clams casino ricocheted from himself onto the pad on which the headwaiter scribbled these wishes. The party was soon in full swing, everyone eating and drinking happily. The varieties of fish were the best, and many a full-mouthed mumble of gratitude came his way, not the least from Bah, who seemed to have got the idea into his head that Smackenfelt wanted to invest in the show. The wine was carefully selected — it was white. Bottle after bottle arrived at the table via the headwaiter, who, Smackenfelt suspected, divined the jam he was in and secretly relished contributing to his downfall. He was a rather sinister looking customer, for all his dinner jacket, with a jutting asymmetrical jaw across the lower slopes of which ran a long white scar, as though it had at some time in the past been broken in a brawl and mended with epoxy, or undergone plastic surgery aimed at minimizing a resemblance to Popeye. He kept smiling down at Smackenfelt in an unsettling way, visual reminder of the debacle toward which he seemed to be rushing headlong under circumstances over which he had no control. Smackenfelt laughed several times into his plate as an unstable exhilaration replaced the anxiety with which he had first apprehended his pickle. The size of his financial ruin making no difference since he was to be wiped out anyway — indeed had already been wiped out — he set an example of gay abandon, flourishing his glass as he dispensed among his circle of guests a smile which said to be of good cheer: he had overcome the world.

At last he heard, repeated inevitably as he knew it must be in some pause in the conversation, the question for which his ear had all along remained alertly cocked.

"Getting back to the play," Bah said, fixing them through the Franz Schubert specs possibly worn as a reproachful, even chastising contrast to his wife's preposterous windowpanes, "who can play Raleigh?"

Smackenfelt hurriedly sluiced down a mouthful of trout with a gulp of wine, finger aloft in a sign that he might have some helpful comments in this area.

"Two or three things. First, he was an upstart. Let's never lose sight of that. The entire age saw him as that. No doubt it was what Queen Elizabeth found especially beguiling in him, being herself the daughter of a daughter of a country squire, whose mother was beheaded for an adulteress. He had style, but it was the style of a roughneck. Physically . . ." Smackenfelt shrugged. "We know that all too well from the portraits. Eyes like truffles. Or" — he lowered his gaze modestly to the table — "you might say the color of those Dutch pastilles. Now his speech. That's important. For dramatic effect as well as authenticity, because we must stick to the historical facts here. And the fact was that he was a West Country character, and spoke to the end of his days with a broad Devonshire burr. He never lost that, even at Court."

He paused to clear his throat. In the silence, he gazed vaguely off in the direction of Ginger, who was no fool.

"What does that burr sound like, Stew? Can you do it for us?"

"Well here, for example, is how the most backbitten of Renaissance men sounded when he sounded off on his enemies and detractors: 'If any man accuseth me to my face, I will answer him with my mouth, but my tail is good enough to return an answer to such who traduceth me behind my back.' "

A hearty round of applause and laughter followed, interrupted suddenly by a development that might have been foreseen by anyone watching Cordial at all closely.

She was having mackerel, which if not properly boned is a pincushion. Surgery had not been too skillful in this case, if performed at all. The rim of her plate was a collection of tiny bones that had been worried out between her teeth and transferred there by hand. As Smackenfelt finished his imitation she choked, everyone thought with laughter, and maybe that partially. Amusement was no more than an accessory to the real trouble.

"Here, eat this," he said, quickly taking charge by

handing her a piece of bread. "It's the thing to do when we get a bone in our throat. The bread pushes it down. Go on."

It seemed to do no good here. She swallowed several large wads of it, to no avail, and began to protest the flow of pumpernickel and Parker House rolls as having already set her diet back a week. "Eat!" he insisted, until finally she began choking on the bread. Willing hands broke off further pieces and passed them along, like attendants handing a surgeon swabs of sterilized cotton — an association all too apt as it turned out. Attempts to drink water met with the same failure. She had spluttered half a glassful when Bah stood up.

"This is no good. You can tell when it's stuck there. I'm taking her to a doctor."

"No," Smackenfelt said. "You'll never find one, and a hospital's just around the corner. Been through this same thing myself. Went to an emergency room and had it out in jigtime. Nothing to it, if we don't let something get made of it," he added, glaring around at rubbernecks at adjoining tables. "Everybody sit down. Please. I'll handle it. I *insist*." A nod from the coughing victim registered her own wish that this be done, and before there was time for any more demurrers, he was bundling her into a cab, making a strong effort of will to separate the act of helping a lady in distress from the thought that, integrated with the quixotic good deed, was the near-certainty of somebody else being now stuck with a hundred-dollar tab.

There were no other patients in the emergency ward, luckily, and within five minutes a resident intern had Cordial seated on a stool under a bright light, some winking cutlery in his hand.

Smackenfelt stepped outside for a smoke, sensing she

preferred his not hanging about. He paced slowly along on a gravel walk surrounding a circle of grass and privet. Some chance association reminded him of the leg wound Raleigh had sustained in the naval action at Cadiz, which made him limp for the rest of his life. An actor scrupulous on detail would have to incorporate that, without making a thing of it. He rehearsed a possible limp as he circumnavigated the patch of green. Suddenly his train of thought broke, like a snapped bootlace. How much would one be charged for this minor surgery? Courtesy on the knightly level would require his taking care of a bill the patient could hardly be expected to attend to in her condition. "God's blood," he murmured in his best Elizabethan vernacular, and continued hobbling about the bit of verdure.

That was when the medic appeared in the doorway behind him.

"I can't seem to — What's the matter with your leg?"

"I'll be all right. How is Mrs. Bah?"

"There's no fishbone in there."

"Why not?"

"No. You see, very often it'll leave an abrasion that gives the *feeling* of its being there, the way we think we've got something in our eye when it's only the scratch left on the pupil by the speck of foreign matter that *was* in it."

"Ah, yes."

Smackenfelt's fresh sense of deliverance was again short-lived — terminated by the sight of Cordial, visible through the glass door, doubled over in the hallway in a fit of coughing more prolonged than any yet. The ministrations seemed so far only to have made matters worse.

"Of course there's a bone in there. Good God man, can't you see?"

One remembered that people were sometimes done in by this kind of predicament. Merrily dining one minute, gone the next, to the stupefaction of friends. "Let's go in and win," he said, striving for a less testy tone, so that he sounded like a coach sending a player back to the game after an encouraging half-time pep talk.

None of which set well with the medic, who, with a sigh ill-concealing his vexation, took Cordial back into the treatment room once again. Smackenfelt's limping in his wake did little to repair his spirits, nor did the suggestion now offered.

"I don't want to appear to be telling you your business, but this very same thing happened to me once, and the doctor couldn't find the bone at all at first either. It was buried way down in the soft palate. Have you looked there?"

He stood over the doctor's shoulder, watching. Cordial flirted her eyebrows at him in an expression of gratitude for his interest, and for the aggressive manner in which he had made a suggestion that might prove valuable. There is something unreal about looking down into a human hatch under blinding illumination, to say nothing of magnification. To supplement the light strapped to his forehead, the doctor held up a magnifying glass. The pink orifice into which he gazed gave Smackenfelt an emphatically intimate, even sexual, experience. He could feel his testicles twitch and tighten.

"By God, you're right," the medic said. "There's the little son of a gun, buried way over there in the soft palate. No wonder I didn't see it."

He soon had it out with his tweezers, and after a last bout of tearful coughing a grateful Cordial began to pull herself together.

"Where do we settle up?" Smackenfelt asked.

The resident laughed. "You were the doctor . . . Well, come with me . . ."

He led the way around to the front office, where in the end Smackenfelt was divested of twenty-five dollars, for which Cordial assured him he would be reimbursed by Bah. They strolled back to the Triton, taking their time.

"God, am I glad that's over," Cordial said, gratefully squeezing his arm, through which then her own remained looped. She only dropped her hand to take his own, as they stopped before a shop window filled with music boxes. She seemed loth to rejoin the party awaiting them until she had more completely composed herself. They loitered along from one window to another. Their hands fell away as they turned the corner onto the street where the restaurant was.

There, nearly an hour after they'd left it, they found Bah with every appearance of having supplanted him as host. Looking up from their coffee and brandies, the group broke into smiles at the sight of Cordial's happy face. Bah sprang up to kiss her, and then to express his gratitude gave Smackenfelt's hand an especially painful wrench. The party was reconstituted in a mood of buoyant gaiety, and when the check arrived Bah snatched it from the headwaiter. Smackenfelt put up a half-hearted fight for it, expecting to be repulsed if there was a God in heaven.

"No way," Bah said. "You've done enough. I don't mean just Cora either, though thank God that's over. Your marvelous stuff about Raleigh shows you have

real insight into the part, and clarifies the casting problem enormously. Now I have a much better idea what
kind of actor to look for in England. Because I'm flying
to London in the morning."

twelve

High noon in London. From the Tower window not so much a view, as a sense, of the city, decimated by plague. Thousands of deaths a week. The bells ringing for the victims steadily, all through the fortnight it has taken for Raleigh's self-inflicted wound to heal — some said insincerely dealt his own person. As though he hadn't wounds enough! A scratch in the right breast from a seized table knife, not a hundredth of that suffered at Cadiz, for what? For Essex, the official "hero" of the action, in which he, Raleigh, had rather fallen dead away upon the deck from splinters sent in all directions by cannonshot, reviving to see the Spanish admiral surrender to Essex, before fainting dead away again. While Essex the lunatic leads the land forces to sack the defeated town. Only such a megalomaniac, not so much drunk with power as thirsty for it, would have conspired with James to seize the throne from Elizabeth. They said Raleigh smoked a pipe while

Essex was executed. The fact was he could not bear to see him on the block, and though as Captain of the Guard he should officially have attended the beheading, he was overcome, and had withdrawn from the scene to be alone . . .

He had always totally immersed himself in a part. But his transubstantiation into Raleigh was so complete as to make his auditions for the role a model on which other actors trying out might draw, or against which those out front could measure the competition, or even the author make last-minute enrichments in a script now all but ready for rehearsal. He was a walking encyclopedia, or rather limping encyclopedia, of the era concerned, since he hobbled around the house as well as at the theatre with the disability permanently contracted in the Cadiz action, to say nothing of speaking only in the Devonshire brogue, which grew thick as gruel. These things had all become second nature by the time the date was set for the first rehearsal call.

It was therefore all the more difficult to tell him that in the end an actor named Ian Carter had finally been chosen for the lead. Dolly came to break the news one rainy Saturday afternoon. He was upstairs in the attic where he now spent most of his time, a better place to concentrate and study than his old cellar digs, abandoned for this eyrie. It was accessible through a trapdoor approached by a set of ladder stairs which could be pulled up or down, as required.

The two women were waiting for him in the main parlor when he was summoned down to hear the verdict. They sat tensely watching the stairs down which he could be heard slowly, deliberately, approaching.

Ginger nudged Dolly and pointed. What they saw made their skin creep.

From the middle step on the bottom flight there was a glint, a flash of light. A moment's gaping stare revealed there a pair of buckled shoes elegantly decorated with scores of glittering jewels. The shoes said to have been worth "sixty hundred pieces of gold." The feet they encased continued on down a step, then another, bringing into successive view calves encased in silk, knee breeches, doublet resplendently embroidered and brocaded. A pearled velvet cape fastened with a gold clasp at an immaculately starched white ruff completed the ensemble of "the most gorgeously dressed man of his time." A costly bangle hung from the left ear. The dark hair receded from a lofty brow above eyes like truffles, or pastilles, while the Van Dyke beard was trimmed to a dagger's point.

"Well, Dolly? How do you like it?"

Dolly rose, came a step forward, hesitantly, then turned and rushed from the house in tears.

Bah was delegated to break the news, which he did by telephone. The costume went back to the rental shop and Raleigh to the Tower, there to await execution.

In the uncertain interval thus remaining to him, he worked steadily at his writings, in particular trying to recompose some of the poems strewn to the wind in a lifetime lived to the hilt, and so in danger of being lost to posterity. In his peaceful seclusion he smoked pipe after pipe of the tobacco he had himself brought from the new world, reviled as a foul weed by the monarch who had clapped him here on a false charge of treason. Occasionally he crept downstairs the better to overhear some conversation the woman Ginger was holding over the telephone, or with the local character, Doctor Pathfinder, whose advice she sought. The nearest thing to a family physician in those parts, the croaker pitched in on any level called for.

"He doesn't have to let me at that leg to know. It's completely functional. I'll stake my reputation on it. The limp is hysterical, we call that. Often happens as the result of a trauma. There was a prizefighter years ago, what was his name, from South America. Got a paralysis in his leg because of something emotional."

"And the Devonshire brogue that he has no use for now any more either, but which won't clear up? Is that psychosomatic too?"

"That too."

"I don't understand it. You might as well tell me he's got the Dutch elm blight."

"He does. Pride. That's their national disease. Ego, if you want to put it in psychological terms. Also their national strength, of course, but I know those people. Bullheaded as the day is long, stiff-necked as they come. They don't take defeat very easily. He's not going to take this lying down." Here Doc Pathfinder could be visualized giving his head an upward jerk to indicate the Tower. "He won't come down from there till he's good and ready — if ever." A bag snapped open. "Here. Give him four of these, one after each meal and one at bedtime, and call me in the morning if there's no change."

"Pills for delusions of grandeur?"

"Why not? We're leaning more and more on drugs these days, for everything. And how can I treat him any other way if he won't talk to me? I can't go into this thing in depth if he'll neither come down out of the attic or let me up."

"What will these capsules do?"

"One thing and another. You can see each one is a collection of little tiny beebees of different colors, set to go off at different times of the day. So he'll always be tranquillized, along with being energized. It's a combination we've developed."

"I'd feel silly giving them to somebody who thinks he's Sir Walter Raleigh."

"Then give them to him as though you're Mrs. Raleigh."

"Who do you think *you* are? One of the Menninger brothers?"

"One or both. Take one of these yourself now and again. You look as though you could use a little picking up, Mrs. Truepenny." The good croaker laughed. "There I go calling you by the name you first came to me as, with that terrible cough. I'm sorry, Mrs. Smackenfelt. This is going to be a tough row to hoe, but between us maybe we can see it through. So get all the rest you can, and as I say, call me in the morning if there's no change. Or even if there is. Call me anyway. I like talking to you. Meanwhile, there's going to be a lot of homework to do if we're going to handle this right."

The good croaker certainly did his conscientious share. He made his next house call fortified with an armload of books, histories mostly, from one of which he read aloud to the woman Ginger.

"This is the sentence pronounced. Listen. See how it all ties in. 'The judgment of this Court is, that you shall be had from hence to the place from whence you came —' That's the Tower. '— to the place from whence you came, there to remain until the day of execution; and from thence you shall be drawn upon a hurdle through the open streets to the place of execution, there to be hanged and cut down alive, and your body shall be opened, your heart and bowels plucked out, and your privy members cut off and thrown into the fire before your eyes; then your head to be stricken from your body, and your body shall be divided into four quarters, to be disposed of at the King's pleasure. And may God have mercy on your soul!' "

The book could be heard clapped dramatically shut, with a noise like a pistol shot, followed by a moment of silence.

"But I don't understand."

"It's perfectly simple. What you've got here is your classic castration complex. He identifies himself with Raleigh first by throwing himself into the part. That's O.K. That's just professional thoroughness. But when he doesn't get the part — when he's passed over for somebody else — why, *he's only begun to identify himself with the Knight.* He's been emasculated by a woman who's demoted his male ego in a competition situation aggravated by your contemporary sex war."

"But I don't believe in the sex war."

"Little good that'll do toward shortening it! I'll be glad to issue you hourly communiques on how it's going out there." Doc Pathfinder jerked a thumb over his shoulder to indicate a world in which the hostilities under review were universally rampant. "Would you believe I've got a woman patient who's nauseated from the instant her husband arrives home at night till the moment he leaves the next morning? Between those hours, she knows peace. Fact. The rest of the time, when he's around, it's violent nausea, with intervals of upchucking or the threat thereof. I've examined her with everything we've got and there's nothing organically wrong with her either. No, this is your classic mutilation complex."

The other nodded, looking into her hands with an expression suitable for the receipt of such baleful diagnoses. "How long . . . well, will it go on, do you think? I mean thinking he's Sir Walter Raleigh?"

"That's hard to say. It *is* a plain case of delusions of grandeur now — if you can call thinking you've been castrated grand." He pronounced it "castorate," as though from long years of prescribing castor oil. "You see, he's got to believe not only that he's a better Raleigh than what's-his-name who got the part — and 'part' is an interesting word to have mixed up in all this — he's got to *be* a better Raleigh than his ex-wife (who I understand left him for another man?) could ever *write*. He's got to be *the real thing*. He's just got to pick up the marbles here."

"Even if it means losing his own?"

"Right! Couldn't have put it better myself. His ego needs it. It's the only thing that'll restore his manhood."

"Will such a thing ever come about? Can we have that reassurance?"

Doc Pathfinder frowned as he set the book aside.

"I hate to be this cynical, if that's the word. But my guess is, if the play flops, he'll snap out of it. Then he'll be his old self again, such as that may be. He's not my patient, so I don't know him. In fact I've never laid eyes on the man, as you know. You tell me he has another doctor he won't see, but as your own, Mrs. Smackenfelt, even for so short a time as I have been, let me tell you that I know what it's like living with these artists."

"And if it's a hit?"

He shrugged, choosing not to answer directly. But his expression betrayed his professional opinion clearly enough: that in the event of a Broadway smash, delusion would be permanent, possibly requiring institutionalization, permanent or temporary. At least for the length of the run.

Ginger guessed as much, for she said: "Well, I'd like another opinion."

"Of course. We always allow for that. Who did you have in mind?"

"Birdie."

"I don't believe I know any Doctor Birdie, but call him in by all means if you wish. Local man?"

"No, it's a niece of ours. A student. I was just thinking aloud. She knows a little about the case. In fact she was in on the start of this, from another angle."

"I'll be glad to consult with her. I've got to go now. I'll look in again in a few days. Call me any time if you have any questions, and give him the pills for the megalomania."

Footsteps scurrying up the stairs — as fast at least as the injuries sustained in the naval action at Cadiz permitted — indicated that the passage had been overheard. As were Doc's whispered encouragements at the door. "It's often hard to say whether somebody's really flipped, you know. Hamlet could tell a hawk from a handsaw when the wind was southerly, he was only mad north-northwest he said. Feigning it has got to be crazy enough, God knows, and then when you get to the level of pulling the wool over your *own* — Look, would you like to go to a lecture with me next Sunday afternoon at the library? Milton Hurlbutt, the psychiatrist who wrote that best seller about how to handle members of the family that seem to be going round the bend, is speaking."

"I'd love to, Doctor. Anything to help in handling this."

"Fine. I'll ring you then. Maybe by that time you can coax him down from the Tower. A doctor ought to see his patients, it's really the best arrangement. Meanwhile, don't let some quack get his hands on him. Till Sunday then, Ginger."

From the small circular window in the Tower turret the healer's car could be seen driving off, as it had been glimpsed arriving. Likewise Birdie's appearance later that afternoon. But the woman Ginger had to report to her that her Uncle Fats refused to see her.

"Golly, who does he think he is?"

"Well, he's not himself these days." An odd laugh escaped the older woman as she set a large volume in Birdie's lap. *The Encyclopaedia Britannica*, open to a page on which was a line she wanted her to read. With her two hands she carefully concealed everything else, especially the subject title at the top. The sentence indicated was underlined in pencil:

"Here he made what appears to have been an insincere attempt to stab himself, but only inflicted a small wound."

She removed the book. "Who does that sound like?"

"Why, Uncle Fats."

Ginger again lowered the book, showing her the title of the article.

"Raleigh, Sir Walter. God, is that who he . . . ?"

Ginger nodded. "You see how it all fits?"

She walked to a bookshelf and squeezed the volume

back into its place in the set. She minced no words in putting their dilemma into focus, leading the way to the tea table as she did so.

"They open in New Haven on the twelfth. That's Thursday. So we hope it's a hit for Dolly's sake and a flop for his. That's the situation in a nutshell. How does that grab you?"

"It's one hell of a dilemma to be up against, Aunt Ginger."

"I keep hoping for a miracle. You take lemon, don't you, dear?"

"Doc, I'm now beginning to think I am Lady Raleigh."

"Ouch. I'll be right over."

Deep night in the Tower again. All of London brooded and seethed below. Certainly he would smoke a last pipe before his execution. They seemed all last pipes, this one too. Clouds wreathed him as he sat hunched over the books and papers and maps that had been allowed him, sent or brought by kind friends. They would all appear themselves, each in turn, to say a last goodbye. The most hated man in England before his trial, since its juridical infamies the most revered. Only by being condemned to death had he lived to see himself requited. He had always been "the most" everything, including the most fluent linguist of his time, "except in English." Thus his enemies had mocked his Devon brogue. That knave Bah —

The trap door was swung open behind him and a head appeared.

"Is it time? I'm ready."

"Time for supper."

It was the woman Ginger. She nudged a tray along the floor toward him. On it were some sliced lamb, a dish of succotash, a heel of good crusty bread, and a half-bottle of red wine. He took it to the long table on which were spread out his books and documents and fell hungrily to. Her head and shoulders remained in the opening, her arms spread along its edge, smiling as she watched.

"Up the hatch and then down the hatch."

He nodded, breaking bread. She was to his left and a little behind him.

"I'd like to read you something."

Plenty of illumination was supplied by the single bulb suspended from the ceiling rafters, in whose rays the woman Ginger now produced a book from somewhere on her person and spread it open before her on the attic planks, still perched on the ladder stairs herself.

"Let me say first that this raw deal isn't the work of a woman, but a man. Queen Elizabeth didn't put you here — James did. His are the trumped up charges of conspiracy with Spain, his alone the responsibility for railroading an innocent man with that travesty of a trial leading to that awful, awful sentence — which was *never carried out in full,* of course, just the simple beheading is all. *Not all that other.* Well so. Anyway, here we have what a leading authority of the times" — she consulted the spine and gave the author's name — "says was the condemned man's reaction. His bearing after hearing the worst, which at the time was what he thought the fate in store for him, remember. It says he accompanied the High Sheriff to prison 'with admirable erection.' That interesting? That fine? Those were his exact words in describing how the prisoner took it, his downfall. That was how he showed he had the stuff — that he was a man. Striding right out of there, head high, what did he care what they did with his giblets . . ." She closed the book again. "Well, anyway, I just wanted to read that to you. I just wanted to make sure you knew all that."

She watched him awhile as he ate his supper and drank his wine. Then:

"She still doesn't want us there opening night. Won't hear of it. Adamant. But I just got the dope about the dress rehearsal. Over about half an hour ago, and she called to tell me how that went."

He turned his head and looked over at her.

"Went like a charm. Not a hitch. Isn't that a bad sign in the theatre?"

He gave a vague shrug, cocking his head to one side. He drained his glass of wine and poured himself another.

"I talked to Zap too. He asks after you, and says he still wants to paint us that mural for a wedding present. I think we should let him, to show there are no hard feelings. He really feels bad, after the beautiful wine cooler we gave them. So I think we should let him. There's that piece of wall in the television room, that we always sit with our backs to? An abstract might be nice there." She cleared her throat rather sharply. "Don't sit up all hours writing. Come to bed. This is no place to brood. And you are brooding again. I can tell it. You've got that look on your face that always seems to double the resemblance to your mother, anyway in that picture of her on the piano. She's the melancholy half of your heritage, all right."

"My blue genes."

Ginger sank from view, shaking her head as she

picked her way down the ladder again. She tried, God knew she tried, but what was one to make of answers like that? A rational discussion, two people trying to have a meaningful dialogue, and *wham!* Zowie! Something completely senseless out of left field or right field or wherever it was things came from at you . . . Well, tomorrow was opening night, and maybe there would be good news then — whatever she meant by that. Because the question was getting to be: Will Ginger snap?

The news was that the performance had again gone beautifully, but they would have to wait for the first reviews. Those appeared the following day in New Haven and other newspapers. Adjectives most used were "static," "leaden," "turgid" and "eternity." *Variety* had of course not been heard from yet, but conclusions might be drawn from the behavior of its man, an acquaintance of Bah's, who, seeing Bah try to flag him after the final curtain, was himself seen fleeing through the lobby and into the street, melting into the throngs like a thief who had just held up the box office rather than a member of the critical fraternity. Oral comments from theatre-goers themselves had anticipated the notices. The next time Dolly phoned it was to ask for Stew himself.

"I'm in trouble. Deep trouble. You'll see what it is when you come up tonight. There's so much, well, flesh here, but what it needs is bones. Organization. And Stew? I thought you might even, you know, help me fix the damn thing. You seem steeped deeper in the subject than I've ever been. You know him backwards and forwards." She laughed. "Maybe that's the way to do it." Her hilarity was, he sensed, that of fatigue. It was out-of-town hysteria. He knew it well.

"We'll leave in half an hour. Hang on."

So it was their private history repeating itself. They were back in New Haven as they'd been that time shortly after they'd first met. He'd popped back with her to catch her in — What was it? Some piece of schnitzel the title of which he couldn't even recall. She'd been an actress, then, but the predicament was the same for everyone concerned. They were headed for Boston, hoping for mixed reviews.

thirteen

He hobbled up to the table reserved at Locke-Ober's and greeted them all with a flourish of his stout stick before relinquishing it to an attendant waiter to prop in a corner for him, and in the rich burr of which he had been therapeutically divested no more than he had of the limp, fortunately for the lead, this Ian Carter, who prized its constant out-of-town example as one by means of which he might measure and refine his own grasp of a diction still at best faulty, being himself London-born and bred. The limp was in its way even trickier, since, with the flashback and flashforward techniques introduced by the collaborator, one had to remember which scenes preceded, and which followed, the action at Cadiz where the wound had been sustained. The manner also ever consummately on display was itself the most delicate blend of one who, though a gentleman, was not always a gentle man, and about whose very person hovered and flickered the question to which he alone knew the answer and would carry to his grave, being unresolved then, now, and for all time to come: whether he had in fact been the Queen's lover.

So there they were in Boston, ready to see on its feet for the first time the script as revised in partnership. There were the Bahs. There was Ian Carter, his eyes not quite like truffles but his black beard dagger-sharp enough. There was a man named Eckenrode, an investor with ten thou in the property, a "conglomerateur" as the *New York Times* designated him in guest lists of some of his other cultural participations, such as openings at the Lincoln and Kennedy Centers. There was the durable Ginger, shimmering in an apple-green gown that was sleeveless and low cut. There was Doc Pathfinder, who had tooled up from Connecticut at the last minute, getting his first glimpse of the patient, tickled to death his diagnosis had been on the beam, and his prognosis; tickled to death also to be part of such a group. Weather-beaten at some fifty-odd, he had a nearly completely circular face and eyes of the deepest blue imaginable. They were the blue of pool chalk. A vivid contrast to his black hair, though of that Ginger had said that "his locks were not as raven as they used to be." He was one of those people who can actually be said to have a chuckle, usually delivered in response to something he had himself just said, a witticism made with his head down and in a voice so low it would have to be repeated for the benefit of all except those in his immediate vicinity. "What did he say?" people would ask, at this localized amusement, and someone would oblige. Tonight it was Ginger, seated on his left, who willingly relayed these nuggets. "He said, 'He's always wanted to take unto himself a wife, but could never make up his mind whose.' " Another time: "He said, 'He likes to keep his love life a la carte. He doesn't want the table d'hôte quite yet.' "

The show stank. It seemed to go from bad to worse despite everything done to it, major revisions or details, new lines shoved into the actors' hands as they were going onstage. It had lumps in it, like the porridge in state institutions. It had lumps in it, like an old mattress. It had lumps in it, like a *mousse manquée*. It was an accident looking for some place to happen. That place was the Royale, on Broadway, unless Bah decided to fold in Boston. Still, he stuck with it. So did the authors. Boston behind them, they headed for Philadelphia, riding coaches worse, if possible, than those previously thought to have been the nadir in American transportation. Where did they get them? "These cars are so vintage," Ginger said, denuding a banana, "you half expect to have a train robbery." The fancy amused Smackenfelt, tinkering with the third act on a pad propped on his knee. He toyed with it: the train grinding to a halt as masked marauders, flanking for the last quarter-mile windows opaque with filth, sprang from their mounts and, adjusting their masks, relieved the passengers of their cash and valuables at pistol-point . . . Where was he? Oh, yes. Petitioning King James for release from the Tower in order to go find for the monarch the El Dorado of New World legend.

Suddenly the play began to take life.

From the beginning Smackenfelt had been trying to think of some device similar to that of the Common Man used to such advantage in *A Man for All Seasons*, in bridging the successive scenes and giving the work flow and cohesion. The idea he hit on was equally simple: the Rabble. A gaggle of fishwives and strumpets and tosspots chattering intermittently on street corners about the great man in a way that gave a sense of the ebb and flow of his fortunes, and in a dimension characteristic of it: Gossip. Dramatically "thinner" than the substance of the action itself, the stratagem nevertheless helped smooth out the lumps.

They watched from the back of the Philadelphia theatre the curtain go up on what must be the last try. Improvement was clear from the beginning. The audience laughed at the assortment of snaggle-toothed and clown-nosed types hustled in from New York and whipped into shape overnight, also sitting still for the more solemn scenes within which their appearances were sandwiched. Cordial and Bah periodically nodded to the authors in the gloom, Bah from behind his Franz Schubert specs, Cordial through her pink windowpanes. The reviews, still no raves, were enormously better. "We're taking it in," Bah said, simultaneously wringing Dolly's and Stew's hands with a force that ground their bones.

The authors slaved in their hotel rooms, keeping themselves revved up on hogsheads of coffee. One afternoon they were touching up the last of the new scenes that could possibly be incorporated before the show must be "frozen." It was in Dolly's room this time. Zap, appearing intermittently like the rabble themselves, was momentarily in New York on concerns of his own. Stew walked to the window, rubbing his eyes. He was losing his burr, and the limp showed signs of clearing up as well.

"How are you and Zap getting along?"

"Oh, fine. He's O.K. I mean as a husband. But there

are these periods of — *he* calls them non-verbal communication."

"Ah, yes. Complaining mates used to call them prolonged silences. Thank God for jargon, where would we be without it? Well, the Latins are a demonstrative race. They show their feelings."

"Brute. You're good at sitting around with your mouth full of teeth yourself." Pause. She takes a beat. "And you and Mother?"

"Oh, fine. No complaints there. Like mother like daughter, the apple doesn't fall far from the tree, and all that sort of thing."

"How are the Gingerisms coming?"

"Collecting them like mad. You heard her on the train coming down, when we caught a glimpse of the Sound. She said you could see Long Island clear as a bell. All those tolls on the Turnpike are highway robbery. Betty Friedan's name has become a household word. She never misses. You know that as well as I do."

"Doc Pathfinder has taken a shine to her, you'd better watch out. Come lie down here. You look like death warmed over. Come on, rest for a bit. Lie down, young yeoman." Dolly moved over on the double bed on which she had flung herself, patting the place beside her on the counterpane. "We're both too pooped to constitute menaces to each other, God knows."

He stretched out next to her in his shirtsleeves, exhaling a grateful sigh as he loosened his collar and tie. They lay gazing at the ceiling for some time in silence. Some stray association made him think of Birdie, who had been up twice to see the show, looking quite pretty and fresh, first in a strawberry-colored frock, then in a cool lemon-yellow silk pants suit. He had the hots for his young niece-by-marriage. That much must be admitted.

"Do you know what Zap's doing?"

"Painting that mural for us in our television room, isn't he? Your long-delayed wedding present?"

"Oh, that was supposed to be a surprise."

"It will be. Did you know that our television room is lined with books except for that one wall, now to be covered with the artistic handiwork of a TV producer with an avocation? How's that for a situation comedy?"

"That's not what I meant. He's also sticking around while our burglar alarm system is installed. The breaking and entering rate is getting to be horrible, in the suburbs as well as the city. The house next door to us was robbed twice. Junkies mostly, they say. Don't you think you should have a system put in? Like I mean I hate to think of Mother all alone in there, ever."

"They set up such a godawful racket the burglar is scared away?"

"And they ring at the police station, if you want that feature. People sometimes set them off accidentally themselves, and then, another commentary on our times, you phone the police and tell them it's a mistake, and they turn up anyway. They assume you're making the call with a pistol pointed at your head . . ."

While she rambled on toward sleep, he noted how, with all his simmering desire for the well-remembered Dolly, Blodgett the old sexual anarchist made no move. Once he raised a tender hand toward her cheek, before letting it drop away with a sigh of voluptuous fatigue. Intellectual toils and emotional drains had left the poor animal spent; and sleep, too, is an appetite. Saint Augustine had cried, "God make me chaste, but not yet!" "He has made me omnivorous, but not now," was more the size of it here.

Drowsy fantasies of Dolly, inordinately erotic, shaded swiftly into slumber in which, at some point, he dreamed of her (or some woman) as turning naked on a spit in a rotisserie window in which Spontini, cast as a hatted chef, basted her with melted butter, drawn from a pan by means of a bulbed siphon, as she revolved till golden brown, for the delectation of a sidewalk audience.

They both awoke starved, having slept straight through from five till nearly eight. They bathed in their separate rooms and met again in Dolly's for dinner. The duck sent up by room service was, as Blodgett quipped on his level, no chicken, but it was sluiced down with a bottle of white Burgundy even he recognized as noble — for there were, as he put it, "gaps in his ignorance of wine." Stew sat back in his chair, glutted, with a sigh of satisfaction.

"Well, that's the first time I ever slept with another man's wife."

"That's our boy. Munching the dry crust of rectitude."

They caught the last two scenes at the theatre. Friends coming to bid Raleigh goodbye in the Tower the evening before his execution, with Lady Raleigh's tearful farewell, and then the famous last words on the scaffold the next morning. That speech, and lines like "All the world is a prison, from which some are selected for execution each day," had always been sure-fire, and Ian delivered them with noble feeling, always apt-

235

ly short of grandiloquence. The significant thing was that the house was still packed. No one any longer ever walked out.

Then at last their draining labors were done. It was three weeks later in New York. They stood at the back again. It was that thrilling, terrifying, bright axe-blade of a moment: the house lights to half, the house dark, the curtain going up. They shook hands all around, Bah with even more than his customary vigor, so that an audible moan of pain did this time escape Smackenfelt's lips. Dolly exchanged smiles with him: it had become an intramural joke. Suddenly she turned and bolted through the door into the lobby, laughing hysterically. She had truly given way now. She stood with her hands to her face, her shoulders shaking. He managed finally to steady her. He drew her hands down, and they faced each other, there in the cold foyer.

"Well, this is it, baby."

"This is it." She began to cry in his arms. She was pale. Her raggedly lipsticked mouth especially wrung him. She was quite convulsed. "I think I'll go back to the hotel and stay."

"Right. You've had too many of these. I'll walk you."

The Algonquin was only a few blocks away. As they made their way along the grimily garish Broadway district, she said, shaking not from cold, as he now knew, "Whatever happens, I wouldn't have missed it for the world. I've never had this two-against-the-world feeling. Not even with love and marriage. Every couple should write a play together at least once. No second thoughts about your name on as co-author? I gave you the chance to take it off, remember."

"Wouldn't for the world. It's sink or swim together."

"What will we do if the play flops?"

"Inhale and exhale."

They parted at the door of the hotel.

"Sure you want to go back?"

He answered with Raleigh's own last words. His head on the block, Raleigh noticed the executioner's hesitation. "Think of a batter checking his swing!" had been Bah's bawled direction to the actor. Anxiety that the condemned man could see him was the executioner's motive. But the prisoner cried: "Strike, man! Should I fear the shadow of the axe who do not fear the axe?"

fourteen

We had an opening night party at Act I, in the Allied Chemical Building on Times Square — if I may once more circle back into my own story, to relate developments now clearer than those just put behind us, of which my recollection is necessarily hazy, even as a principal in the little drama concerned, which I have therefore tried to reconstruct objectively, as though it involved someone else, relying as often on my imagination as my memory. There was nothing imaginary about my sensations as Dolly and I together entered the restaurant, where we were given a seated ovation. I had some scraggly hopes as we awaited the reviews, though of the eternally springing human kind — few illusions, despite shining performances from everybody in the cast. What troubled me was a certain increasing queasiness, different in degree and kind from the stomach butterflies normal to such an occasion, which I had experienced a hundred times before in one way or another. We weren't far along into the night when I began to suspect what the trouble was.

We had packed in our luggage some packets of soap for use in washing linen and other incidentals in a hotel room. They were samples Spontini was passing out to everybody, a new product being test-marketed by his client, the Palmleaf Soap people. What was new about them was the fact that they came in capsule form, convenient for travel — Handi-Kapsels they were called. You just dropped one in a basin of warm water and they dissolved instantly into rich, penetrating suds. By chance they bore some resemblance to the capsules I was taking as a tranquillizer, and in my haste I must have gobbled one of them instead of the medication, just now when I had briefly popped into my room at the Algonquin after the curtain came down, and before setting out for the party. My suspicions to that effect were confirmed — I should say were simultaneously roused and confirmed — when, having entered the restaurant with Dolly and begun to mingle with the guests, I gave a sort of burp, or hiccup, and saw a bubble float out of my mouth and sail over a few heads before bursting in midair.

Luckily no one else seemed to have noticed, and I continued my round of greetings, as kind of co-host with Bah, though moving about somewhat warily, and trying to remain more or less on the edge of things, to the extent compatible with this social chore. It was a crowd buzzing with the blend of anxiety and expectation common to an opening-night vigil. People milled, paced, hopped from table to table, smiling, frowning, trading speculations. At one of these Doc Pathfinder was once more on deck, getting off pleasantries in the snickering undertone that again required Ginger's having to repeat them for the benefit of hungry consumers who had heard but not understood the latest mot. It was part of his style — theatrical in itself. "What did he say?" was the familiar buzz of enquiry. "He says he's bisexual. He likes both women and girls." Doc smiled at this relay from Ginger, looking into his plate. The response was cut short by a shout from the television set before which one group was keeping watch on the late news reports, switching back and forth from channel to channel for the network critics. They had caught the first of these couriers. In the hush that followed, Dolly stepped quickly over to where I was standing and clutched my hand.

"*Sir Walter Raleigh*," the reviewer began, "is a most moving drama — for the last twenty minutes. The previous hour and three quarters are, unfortunately, much too often much too static, heavy, and — the main objection in this opinion — episodic. A kind of wooden portentousness characterized the whole, which a brilliant and finely shaded performance by that excellent actor, Ian Carter, fails in the end to offset . . ."

"Poor girl. I'm afraid I haven't done you much good.".

"Shh! They've got another."

A snap of the dial had caught the newscaster on a rival channel just as he was saying, ". . . has attended the latest Broadway opening. Here he is with his reaction."

A man with a broad face and black horn-rimmed glasses began to read:

"*Sir Walter Raleigh* just misses. Unable to make up its mind whether it is a play or a pageant, it falls between these two. Individual scenes of great power are not enough to . . ."

"There's still the papers, baby."

"They'll be worse."

Just then another low eructation inside of me propelled a second bubble into the air. This one was longer lived than its predecessor. It floated iridescently over the tiaraed head of a woman standing just in front of me, sailing away above two or three of the festively decorated tables before breaking gently against a wall. Again, no one noticed it but myself, whose wondering eyes followed its course to the delicately bursting end. But I knew, from my churning middle, that there would be more, lots more, projected as from a bubble pipe inside me, drifting through the room in a dreamy fantasy at odds with the inclement reality it was now clear we had all congregated to endure. The prospect was phantasmagoric enough to get my mind off both the notices and the fact that I was getting decidedly sick to my stomach. I stood transfixed, feeling Dolly knead my hand and seeing Bah stare at me from the side of the room. I thought first he was mutely reproaching me for these lousy notices, but then instantly realized he had been flabbergasted by the sight of one or two more bubbles emitted by myself, and after following their course across the room, was glaring at their source as if to make clear what he thought of that kind of jape at a time like this. Dolly became aware of something unusual at about the same time.

"What. In God's name. Is going on? What are you doing?"

"Blowing bubbles."

"I can see that. But what is this, some kind of gag or something?"

"I swallowed one of those travel soap capsules by mistake. Those samples Zap's been handing out? Now I feel as though I may be going to . . . I have to . . ."

I had unfortunately drunk a glass of water a few moments before — or fortunately, depending on how you look at it. A head of lather was by now definitely building up inside me that was bound to bring matters themselves to a head, and in very short order if all the signs could be believed. I asked a passing waiter the way to the men's room, and without further ado bolted in the direction indicated. But it was too late. A series of volcanic belches filled the room with dense clouds of suds as I shot toward the washroom. The faces of people between ranks of whom I sped, parting to form a path for me, were something to behold, to put it mildly. Their jaws fell open and their eyes popped as I had never before seen jaws open and eyes pop, and probably never will again, for we were doubtless witnessing a "first" to which it seems hardly likely there will ever be a second. I was literally throwing *up*, in the genre so named. Bubbles of all sizes floated gaily toward the ceiling, when they did not disintegrate by colliding with the wall or with one another, or with my awed observers for that matter. Some people sportively swiped at them as they drifted by, as at balloons momentarily released at a gathering otherwise lacking in any such note of merriment (and probably destined to decline even further from the dispiriting point already reached).

I learned most of this from descriptions later vouchsafed me by participants or bystanders, of course, since I was charging along at a speed too great for even tentative impressions of the overall scene being lived through. Not that one couldn't fairly accurately recon-

struct it from imagination even as one did, so copious
were the eruptions — and conclusive. For by the time I
had reached the haven for which I was headed, all but
knocking over an emerging party, leaving his ruffled
shirt-front whiter than white with a closing blast, it
was all over. Relief was as complete as it had been
sudden. There was little to do but stand before the
mirror over the washstands and tidy up. I was "foam
flecked," like the hard-pressed steeds of old romances.
Some work with paper towels and my own handkerchief soon had me presentable once again and ready
for the return to the party. The celebrants were, as
intimated, on the whole grateful for the *divertissement*
briefly relieving a night funereal enough. For fresh
precincts were being heard from, contributing little
change in the way the tide was running. Explanations
to the curious as to how I had managed what they had
just seen were soon made, and I joined Dolly at our
table. Everyone settled down to await the newspapers.

Falling to my shrimp cocktail, I began to have a
sixth-sense awareness of something else disturbing.
Looking up, I saw Spontini standing a little distance
off, watching us with the most oddly intense expression
on his face. He looked pained. I thought at first he was
still unhappy about the havoc wrought by his Handi-
Kapsel — if havoc it was — but that must really be
thought of as behind us. I finally divined what was
troubling him. The two hands missing from the table,
mine and Dolly's, must be locked together under it.
That was the case. Dolly had refused to let go from the
moment the first notices had come in. She clung to me
for dear life. There was certainly nothing amorous
about it. But when I sensed Spontini circling the room
in a wide arc calculated to fetch him up behind us,

obviously for a more advantageous check of the scene disturbing him, I disentwined my fingers from hers, but she snatched them back again as a fresh commentator appeared on the screen.

We were like canoers shooting the rapids only to hear the roar of another in our ears just as we had settled down to catch our breath. The new judgment was no softer than its predecessors. Nor had it quite ended when Ted Wiley, the company manager who had friends advantageously placed on the newspapers, returned from a few minutes spent on the telephone. He shook his head. The *News* and *Times* were both adverse.

"Well, at least it's over," someone said. "More champagne!"

That was how everyone felt, or appeared to. Commiserations by word, glance and embrace were soon complete, and the good food and drink heartily resorted to. Dolly began to get a little tipsy, laughing and crying by turns, and even simultaneously, as the long months of toil and tension were at last dispelled. She touched her glass to mine innumerable times, and once popped to her feet to make a speech. Some sensed possible embarrassment in the offing. At least only a few heard her beyond the range of our own table.

"I want to toast a guy I like very much. He did his best to adapt my play to the stage." I smiled in Spontini's direction, in acknowledgement of him as the source of the witticism. "I think he knew all along it was a sinking ship, but he elected to go down with me."

"Oh, for God's sake, Dolly." I pulled at her dress. She was not to be stopped.

"Or to put it another way, he spread his cloak across a very muddy puddle so a lady wouldn't soil her feet."

As she sat down, to a round of applause and appreciative exclamation, also taking a peck on the cheek from me, Spontini's face took on a definitely harried air. He frowned, and his mouth was a tight seam. Also he made repeated checks of the tablecloth, keeping count of the hands visible on it. At last he set his glass down and came around, wedging a chair in between me and Cordial, who was on my other side. I was expressing for the hundredth time my regret at Bah's misfortune with the play. She had on a long sleeveless orange gown, and was otherwise also more rationally dressed than usual, except for a gold bracelet on her upper left arm, around the biceps. She said Bah had just decided to close the play Saturday, the advance sale beyond that being all but non-existent. We looked over at him as he stood nodding in conference with Wiley, no doubt about that measure. He had a strained aspect. His characteristic wasp-waisted suit and pinned shirt collar gave him a constricted, rather than a natty, look. Some accident of the light made his face, behind the wire glasses, look lined and gray. He resembled a steel engraving of himself. I experienced a pang of sympathy, quickly dissipated by the reminder that he had tried to make both Ginger and Dolly, though on separate occasions.

Cordial turned to someone else, and then suddenly Spontini said to me in a rapid whisper: "How would you like to write a play for television? Hear me out. It's a dramatization of a novel. *The Cool Country.* I've heard you say you admired it. I think it's your dish of tea. It would pay . . . oh, five thousand. An hour and a half, for the Hampton Hall Greeting Card Company. One of their specials."

"What about Dolly?" I lowered my own voice, speaking out of the side of my mouth. We looked like two gangsters consulting on some base chore, such as the elimination of an enemy, or even a troublesome colleague. Now Zap seemed taken by surprise. Even displeased.

"Well . . . if you want, fine, Stew. These collaborations are tricky, as you now know. It's always sort of sticky being a producer to somebody in the family."

"You produce her commercials."

"Oh, come now, for God's sake. That's different. Well, think about it."

"All right, I'll do it. One way or another."

"Great."

Our huddle was concluded just in time. A buzz of gaiety signaled another aphorism by Doc Pathfinder, again apparently muttered to himself, so that Ginger had to repeat it as the one alone privileged to have caught it. "What did he say?" we all pressed.

She cleared her throat, glancing at Doc, who was smirking into his plate.

"He said, 'A critic is like a eunuch. He can't do it himself but he can tell others how it's done.' "

A tall waiter had been respectfully standing by, waiting for the exchange to end. When the sounds of appreciation had died away, he bent down to whisper in my ear that I was wanted on the telephone. I excused myself, to return almost instantly.

"What was that?" Ginger asked, noting my expression.

"That was our hometown police. The house has been

vandalized. I think we'd better start back immediately."

The effect on the entire party was instantaneous and tonic. It was the best news they had heard tonight. A ripple of excitement spread through the company. Everyone shared vicariously the relief experienced by the Smackenfelts in suddenly taking flight. Some openly envied us. We had intended to stay one more night, but now we hurried to the Algonquin only to pack our bags and check out for the drive home. Doc Pathfinder had driven in himself, and also went back. It was by now scarcely one-thirty, and our car was in a garage only a block or two away. As we were firing clothes into our grips, there was a knock on the door. It was Dolly.

"I'm going with you. Do you mind? I just have to get away from here."

"What about Zap?"

"He's got to be here tomorrow first thing on business, he says. But I'll go crazy if I stay. I mean I couldn't face tomorrow morning here alone. Or even tonight, lying there in bed wondering what you're going to find. What did the cops say, Stew, is it pretty bad?"

"Well, I don't guess we'll find the place exactly strewn with flowers. Hell, sure, come on along. The night's still young."

fifteen

It was a brilliant night. White clouds flew wildly across a full moon. Stars appeared, glittering fiercely, once the lights of the city were left behind. I drove, as the soberest; indeed, quite stark awake. Dolly sat beside me. Ginger rode in the back with all the luggage stacked beside her, against which she leaned with a yawn, though denying she was in the least tired. In fact she professed to be greatly keyed up, having observed elements in the evening put at last behind us which might have seemed incidental to the casual eye, but which were fraught with undercurrents significant to the informed watcher. The potentialities glimpsed in them had honed her faculties to razor-sharpness, and left her mind fairly roaring with speculation. Dolly, who had huddled down into her fur coat in a determination to relax, maybe even catch forty winks, now began to prick up her ears at these remarks, as having undercurrents enough of their own.

"What the devil are you chattering about back there, Mother?"

"Things I noticed. This television offer makes them all fit. Zap had eyes only for you two. A success with *Raleigh* he might have been able to fight. Hold his own against. But not its failure. Being in a crisis sort of — melted you two together. Welded, I guess I mean. Emotionally. He's afraid you're going to get together again. This collaboration has cemented your relations."

"That's nonsense — apart from Zap's always talking about human relations being broken and cemented, as though they're some kind of crockery. If he was afraid of a reconciliation why would he go out of his way to throw us together again in another collaboration?"

I turned to look at Dolly. "He asked you that?"

"Just now. A while ago, while I was packing."

"He asked me at the restaurant to do the adaptation alone. He didn't have you in mind then. I suggested it. Teamwork I mean."

"Hm," Dolly mused, following my train of thought. "Well, it was nice of you."

Ginger straightened in the back seat, like a puppet pulled erect. I could glimpse her in the rear-view mirror.

"You see! It all fits. His game was to get Stew *away* from you, back to work alone, before you could get to teaming up on another try. Then when Stew spoke up for you there was nothing he could do but agree. In fact he figured he'd better ask you himself, and pronto, or it would make him look like a louserino."

"You're becoming quite a student of human motives, Ginger. That Doc Pathfinder's influence?" I called over my shoulder with a laugh. "How is Doc doing?"

"Doc's all right," she answered, defensively. "He's one of those doctors that think ninety percent of their patients are quacks, except that those are the kind he likes. Can get his teeth into them. He prefers hypochondriacs and neurotics to simple appendectomies that come right out and offer no challenge."

"I mean how's he getting along with you? Is he still uttering mating cries?"

"Oh, get out of town. I think when we get home we'd better all put our cards on the table."

"There may not be any tables, if these hoods have done a proper job. We'd better do it here."

"The trouble with most of us is, we're not satisfied with the hand life dealt us because we don't just want a hand. We want the whole deck."

"*What?*" With that last gasp of response Dolly retired once again into the depths of her coat collar, huddling down against her door. I reached across her to snap the lock fast.

"This will teach you to listen to Zap and me about burglar alarms," she murmured sleepily. "Leaving your name at the station for the police to make nightly house checks while you're away means nothing. They always turn up after the damage is done."

"At least it's good to know our cops make their rounds," Ginger said. "What did they say? Is it really bad?"

"Christ, I told you ten times, Ginger. Plus you heard yourself what the desk clerk said. The police called the hotel number we left them, and the message was promptly relayed to the restaurant number I'd left with the desk clerk. That's all I know. Of course it'll be bad. Often it's because they fly into a rage because they can't find anything worth stealing. Unless it's the kind high on something. That happened to the Wusdatts. And Poodle Slater had his entire French clock collection smashed. I mean why wouldn't they take them instead of break them? One would almost prefer that."

"Maybe because they don't know fences who can dispose of objets d'art. But poor Poodle. Though I don't know why I say that, he's such a vixen. At least we don't have anything valuable in that sense. Those vandals," Ginger continued, with a despairing cluck. "There was a house down the street from, you should excuse the expression, Art Buckett and me, that was broken into for the plain unadulterated hell of it. It was *empty*. There wasn't a lick of furniture in it."

"Stick."

"What?"

"Stick of furniture. It's licks of work people do. Or rather don't do. They hadn't a stick of furniture because he never did a lick of work."

"So are you going to do this script Zap wants you to?"

"Yes, one way or another."

She leaned forward, and lowered her voice to a whisper.

"She asleep?"

I glanced at Dolly.

"I guess so."

"You think you two maybe belong together, after all?"

"You like Doc Pathfinder that well, do you?"

The house was only a quarter of a mile off the Turnpike. Dolly was instantly wide awake as we turned off it, if, in fact, she had ever been really sound asleep. A sudden tension gripped us all as we reached the street where the house was. I slowed to a stop before it. I turned off the ignition and then the lights. We sat looking at the white frame two-story Colonial, as though really seeing it for the first time. It was illuminated at the windows where I had set up metered "Away Lights," staggered to go off and on at different times, so as not to appear to have a fixed pattern to anyone casing the place with evil intent. The upstairs bedroom window blacked out as we watched, communicating a quite eerie sense of someone's actually being inside up there.

"That's me turning off my reading lamp," I said.

"Then how come downstairs is still lit up? I mean I'm a crook watching it," Ginger said. "I suppose somebody else could still be up, or stole down for a late snack?"

"That would probably be it."

"It gives you the creeps, something like this." She sat forward on the edge of the seat, bending to peer upward through the car window. "At least there's no damage in front. Nothing broken, and the door looks closed. They must have broken in the back or side."

"What's that poem of Frost's about house fear? Going into an empty one alone even under normal circumstances."

"I suppose it wouldn't make sense to call the police before we do, or hope they might have been here to greet us?" Dolly said.

"Of course not. Why do we need the police? There's nobody in there now." I had my hand on the door handle. Still I hesitated a moment longer, making yet another observation. "What's creepy about it is the very fact that everything looks so normal. Why didn't they smash the lights? Of course, maybe they did, some of them."

"Maybe they did it during the day."

"Ah, yes. So it may have been just kids, rather than burglars. I mean just — just vandalism."

"I suppose it isn't terror we feel, or even fear," Dolly said. "I mean *of* anything. Just dread of what we're going to find inside. I feel as though it's as much my house as yours, again."

"Yes, well, here goes." I opened the door and climbed out. "I'll go have a look around the back first. You two wait here."

I disappeared into the shadows beside the house, materializing again after a moment or two.

"Nothing broken in back there. Oh, hell, I forgot the cellar door. Oh, hell, let's go in." I put my head inside the car long enough to withdraw my ring of keys from the ignition. Then I helped the women out, leading the way to the front porch. They waited on the walk while I went up and tried the door. I turned with a shrug. Locked. I selected my house key from the ring, fitted it into the door, opened it, and stepped gingerly inside.

The vestibule lit up as I snapped the chandelier switch there. I turned and walked slowly into the parlor. The women could see my shadow cross the middle front bay window, behind the lace curtains, then vanish. To reappear a few seconds later. I stood in the doorway. My face must have been pale, but apart from that there couldn't have been anything unusual about my expression. It was certainly not that of a man who has looked on horror or chaos, or, certainly, seen a ghost.

"I can't find anything out of the way. Come on in."

"Could it be a mistake?" asked Ginger, timidly entering.

I shrugged. "Maybe they got us mixed up with some

other house. The police I mean. Or phoned the wrong
number on their list. I mean, say there was a place
broken into but they reported another. They must have
lists a yard long to check every night."

We all wandered slowly through the downstairs
rooms. Everything seemed in order. There was a chair
overturned, and some books on the floor, but they
represented a start Ginger had made on house-cleaning
the shelves. "God. There's still upstairs," I said. I turned and dashed up the stairs two at a time, galloping
back down immediately. "Nothing there either."

"Then it must have been a mistake." Ginger sank
onto a chair. Dolly followed suit.

"Wait a minute."

I had only poked my head into the television room,
the book-lined one off the main parlor, which was
dark. Now I returned to it, switching a light on. I stood
in the doorway viewing for the first time our wedding
present from the Spontinis, the epithalamium painted
on the back wall in our absence.

Across its white expanse were disposed at random
intervals splashes and splotches of naked color, looking
as though they might have been administered with a
spray gun, or some other instrument for catapulting
pigments at a short distance. These were loosely connected with fine spiralling tangles of brushwork, not
unlike the snarls on a fishing-line that has backlashed.
Here a spot of upchuck, there a little egg left on a
plate. To the left and lower part of the wall was the
large initial S. The monogram was executed in the
"loose," or "free," manner of the whole. Lines dripped,
or dribbled, from it, as though it were the work of an
iconoclast accustomed to hurrying from one public
wall or fence to another, defacing them with revolu-

tionary legends slapped on the surfaces in question with a broad brush dipped in a bucket of black paint, always in danger of being detected by constituted authority, always a step ahead of it.

"Zap's mural."

Dolly came over to view the opus with me. I moved aside to make room for her, then for Mrs. "S." The three of us stood silently before it.

"Like it?" Dolly said. "I saw a sketch he did for it — which this actually outdoes. He didn't want to show you that. He wanted it to be a complete surprise."

"It is. It's — stunning," Ginger said, at last.

"As you see, he didn't really paint the wall. It's on a canvas that's fixed *to* the wall. In case you ever move or something."

"That was very thoughtful of him."

"Stew?"

"Just a minute."

I went out to the porch, where, pressing my nose to the window and shading my eyes, I bent to peer inside. I waved the two women away from the doorway where they stood. They moved aside into the parlor. I nodded, as though satisfied with something I had gone out to check. I returned.

"Just as I suspected. One of the timed lights is in that room — on the table there. When it's on, it sort of floods that wall. Which a cop looking in the window could see. He noticed the mural and took it for the work of vandals."

We all sank into chairs now. We had had enough criticism for one night, whether of the theatre or the graphic arts. We deserved our rest. That was what our combined attitudes said. We were beat. We'd had it.

Dolly's head went down on a tabletop, coming to rest on her arms. Mine followed suit. Ginger sat with her elbows on her parted knees, her hands dangling between them, staring at the floor. There was a sigh from Dolly, then another, more like a sob. I was soon convulsed myself. Paroxysm after uncontrollable paroxysm racked me. Tears streamed down my cheeks. "I'm sorry, I —" I began, and choked. One couldn't go on. It was too much. Still, even this was destined not to be the end.

The telephone shrilled, making us all jump. Ginger answered it.

It was Spontini. He had decided to leave too. The thought of Dolly home there alone, even with a maid under the same roof, on that night of all nights, had in the end been too much. He had gotten into his Ferrari and sped for home in our wake, half hoping to overtake us. He had paused at a booth on the Turnpike to call, guessing Dolly might have stopped to look in at our place, which was on the way to the Spontinis'. "How is it — bad?" he had asked, and Ginger without thinking had answered, "Yes." She couldn't tell him the truth, obviously. Now he would be here in five minutes.

I sprang to my feet.

"Jesus, this is terrible. What'll he think when he finds everything in apple-pie order. We can't tell him the truth. But he'll guess."

"Oh, no. That would be too awful," Dolly said. "What can we do?"

I paced, thinking hard.

"There's only one thing we can do. I mean if we want to spare his feelings."

"Oh, we must! It would kill him. I mean to be the laughingstock of — well, of everywhere. The cops have probably got a report to follow up on, they'd talk, it might get in the papers, avant garde artist's work mistaken for that of, oh God, the Associated Press would get it, the United . . ." She was babbling hysterically. She turned to me. "Do you mean . . . ?"

I nodded. "We'll have to rough the place up a bit ourselves."

I started pulling a few books from the shelves and letting them drop to the floor. The effect was hardly convincing. I jerked several more down, then some more, also overturning a couple of chairs. I got into the spirit of the thing. There must have been an odd grin on my face. The women watched me, transfixed. I was clearly enjoying myself.

"Come on, pitch in."

Something now happened to all of us. A sort of mob hysteria gripped us, if three people can be considered a mob. We found ourselves caught up in an irresistible urge of destruction. We became vandals.

"We've got to make it look good," Ginger said, yanking a Spanish shawl from the piano, in the process toppling a vase to the floor, where it crashed in smithereens.

"It's got to be convincing," Dolly echoed. She hurled a souvenir glass ball into a corner, a memento carrying disagreeable schoolday associations which she had never liked and had left behind here.

I had by now turned my attention to the pictures. Some I contented myself with merely knocking askew, but one or two I plucked from their hangers and flung to the floor. They were either the tastes of other people that I had too long put up with, or those of myself, now outgrown. There was one from a period when I had collected "primitives," in particular an oil of a horse in a barn, really so badly drawn that I had decided it must be a self-portrait. I paused in my frenzy to gaze into the adjacent dining room. It had the scenes-from-Williamsburg wallpaper that had been Ginger's selection when she had been the mother-in-law. She herself noted the gleam in my eye.

"Go ahead. I never really liked it either. I just thought you and Dolly liked it."

"You did? Word of honor?"

"Cross my heart."

"And we're going to have it changed anyway?"

"Whoever 'we' is."

"That does it."

I rushed into the kitchen, where I could be heard pulling things out of the refrigerator. I returned with my arms loaded with eggs, tomatoes, oranges, bottles and jars of jelly and condiments. "Here," I said, passing the ammunition around. "If we're going to save Zap's face we might as well do it up brown."

I continued to set the tone, and the pace. Standing off, I cocked back a hand with a bottle of ketchup in it, like a grenade I was looking for a spot to throw at. I took aim at a wagon wheel and let fly. The result was a very satisfying crimson blotch glittering with tiny fragments of shattered glass. The women began pelting the wall with objects of their own. The result was soon an astonishing free-form improvisation in its own right. We talked as we heaved away, though by now laughing a great deal as well.

"So you and Dolly think you'd like a rematch?" Ginger asked, flinging a tomato.

"And you and Doc?"

"We rap each other."

"Dig. Dig, rap with. And we don't stick to our *p*'s

and q's. We watch them. It's our knitting we stick to. Nor can anyone have two strikes in his favor."

"Of course. I shall miss you."

"And I you, Ginger."

It was like a drawing-room comedy, were we not in the dining room, and plastering that with all manner of refuse.

"He's in his fifties, Doc."

"As much older than you as you are than me, and I than Dolly. What do you think, Dolly?"

Quickly! Things must be tidied up before Zap got here.

"Well, I feel he's betrayed me. I mean with this sneaky business about the new adaptation," she said, pitching an orange with all her might. "Almost better if he hadn't tried to cover up his tracks with that last-minute switch, ringing me in because you already had. Shows he knew it was shabby. I mean it's worse than a sexual betrayal."

"Not that you haven't had those?" Hurry! Loose ends still to be tucked in.

"He's attractive to women."

"It's all settled then."

Empty-handed, I dashed into the kitchen for replenishment, pausing midway to snatch up a bottle of ink from a nearby desk and throw that. In the kitchen, I stumbled on a bonanza. It was a bag of bananas, forgotten on a corner shelf, well past their prime. In fact quite rotten. I rushed back in with these, plucking them loose from the bunch and passing them around. These were particularly gratifying to hurl, making a loud, thick *splat* as well as leaving a mess. We ran up and retrieved them where they fell, to throw them again, and again, till all the pulp had been mashed out of them, leaving nothing but the limp, mottled skins. We continued to fling even those.

I want to say that it was here, in this climactic moment, that my daemon and I were at last one. Blodgett and I, those disparate, desperate halves of the precariously housing Self, were finally fused, like two circles that, long blindly shuffled this way and that, now perfectly coincided. Not that our motives were the same. Far from it! His was a candid pleasure in at last liquidating Spontini; mine a moral satisfaction in sparing him even while this was being done. Flooding me was a sense of the extension of Christian charity toward a rival whom Blodgett — seen, say, as an overly dapper mobster given familiarly to calling me Smacky — was, for his part, successfully despatching. It was a finally and completely integrated man whom we see hurling rotten fruit at that wall, flanked by two hard-breathing women doing the same thing. Perhaps we were *all* being pulled together. And this a man who had once been so schizoid as to split a wishbone with himself. Blodgett grasping one prong of course.

In our transport, we had not heard a car stop outside or the front door open, or Spontini enter — the object and beneficiary of this sacrificial purge. He must have seen us at the height of our frenzy, as travellers say of savages in their tribal hysterias, slinging our depleted peels. He stood a moment, open-mouthed. I reconstruct this with absolute confidence, being able to see him as vividly in my imagination as you can. Then he took a step forward, and halted again, his jaw hanging loose. He looked from us to the wall, now dripping with abominations, and back again.

"What. In the name of Christ. Are you doing?"

We spun around as one at the sound of his voice.

Our own jaws dropped. The women turned to me, by their gaze appointing me spokesman. I started to speak, but my voice broke in an inarticulate squeal.

"Hello, Zap," I brought out at last.

"What the hell is going on here anyway? Have you all taken leave of your senses?"

"That's right, Zap." I pulled out a handkerchief and wiped my stained hands, also dabbing my beaded brow with it before passing it along to the women. "Well, it's kind of hard to explain. No, it isn't. It isn't, not really." I swallowed, with difficulty, my throat being bone dry. "When we got here and found the place ransacked, funnily enough we weren't too upset. Too upset. A lot of the pieces were a few we had co-co-come to hate. And as for this wallpaper. We thought — well, something seized us. Call it an impulse, but we all pitched in to finish the job. Nothing was lost, you see, by our taking advantage of the situation to get something off our chest. It would have to be cleaned from stem to stern anyway, this would have to come down, that —"

Spontini rushed to the doorway of the television room, to see if any harm had befallen his handiwork. Relieved to find it had not, he turned back to hear the rest of my story, now deteriorated into utter incoherence. It, too, had become more in the nature of a surrealist improvisation, on a par with the graphic creation just checked and the one at our backs.

"— once in an ice storm. You may remember it. Year or so ago. Hearing the trees crash all around me, the power lines coming down till the whole town was spaghetti, a sort of insane rapture seized me. *I was glad.* It was ecstasy hearing the boom and crash of destruction all around me. I snatched up chunks of ice myself and hurled them every which way, like piles of shattered glass. An orgy of demolition . . ."

Something in our demeanor, as much as what was being babbled, made Spontini suspicious. His instincts were telling him better. His intuition took him straight to the truth.

"There was nothing wrong at all, was there?"

"Why, Zap —"

Zap jerked his head in the direction of the mural.

"The cops saw that and took it to be the work of vandals. That's it, isn't it?"

"No way, man."

"It'll make a great story, won't it? Fuzz is art critic. Artist laughingstock. A real yack. The boff heard round the world."

"Man . . ." I shook my head, smiling at the floor as I wiped my hands on my trousers. Ginger cut through it all.

"No one need ever know, Zap dear. Yes, you're right, we wanted to spare your feelings, and the only way to do that was to become vandals. We had to do the job ourselves. We're all in this together. If you'd walked in that door two minutes later, we'd all be home and dry. Now . . . But it'll go no farther than this room. If you can call it that now. But anyway, no one will ever know."

"I'll know. And I'll know you know, and what you're secretly thinking. This cat especially. He'll be laughing on the inside for the rest of his —"

"Zap. Zap fella," I said. "Let's once and for all stop lacerating ourselves and each other. We're not Dostoievsky characters."

"Maybe we are." Zap gave a nod, as if to add, "So there," or "What do you know about it?" A gesture at the shambles asked what further proof was needed that we were souls in torment. He continued, "I don't need your sympathy. I know you don't like my stuff, Smackenfelt. You never have. So if you want to make something of it —"

"Oh, my God, not again!" Dolly beat the wall with her fists, not the one befouled, another. Against which Ginger simply rested her arms, her head on those, for all the world like a child playing hide-and-seek. Spontini seemed unaware of either. His eyes were dangerously glazed.

"Or maybe I'll just relieve you of something intended as a . . . somehow failing of its intended . . . no one's fault . . . just one of those things, a damned misunderstanding —"

He darted past me, like a football carrier eluding a potential tackler, into the television room and straight for the mooted mural, which he began to tear from the wall. He had made a beginning in one corner, ripping the removable canvas away from the nails securing it there, by the time I made after him and leaped onto his back. There were elements in the moment that reminded me of another in the past, or were at least registered on my brain for tranquil reconsideration and comprehension later. Clawing at his handiwork, as Spontini now did, perhaps represented an impulse to destroy as well as recover it, of a piece with the fit of passion in which I had tried to take my life even while in my furor selecting for the act an implement as fully calculated to save it: to wit, the famous can opener. Piggyback, at any rate, we two crashed together to the floor, where we began rolling around in the real dogfight for which we had all along been spoiling.

"It's mine. You gave it to me."

"I will not cast my pearls before —"

I never heard what it was my adversary refused to cast his pearls before. A floorlamp came down on both our heads, as Ginger rushed to the telephone to call the police. A squad car, cruising in the neighborhood on empty-house checks, and due here in a few minutes in any case, arrived before we had torn our clothes altogether from one another's backs.

"Let's go down to headquarters, shall we, boys?" said the officer patrolling in it.

We were booked on a charge of disturbing the peace, then almost immediately let off with a warning. Before the couples parted, diverging toward their separate homes, Dolly had a chance to whisper something to me, after drawing me to one side.

"I can't leave him now, of course. You understand that."

"Of course. Good luck. And I'll see you around."

Poor Blodgett. Would he always be balked by the claims of the soul? Must he forever stand aside to let the spirit pass?

sixteen

Dusk. Of a late winter afternoon. You walk beside the tidal river, Smackenfelt, bundled into your Immensikoff. Your chin well down in the great fur collar, your shoulders sagging a little under the weight of the bearskin, so that at intervals you pause to prod yourself erect with your walking stick. You have been ill. Your cheeks, clean-shaven once again, are pale, though winter may restore to them the roses summer could not. To those gliding by in warm automobiles you must resemble in the gloom some species of woolly animal learning to walk upright, rather than the diamond merchant from Amsterdam of which you fancy yourself the tintype, to the magnetized watcher, swinging your gnarled blackthorn and drawing on your "Churchill," the chair-splat-size cigar to which you've become addicted now.

Pausing, you gaze across the Sound till you have coaxed from it some resemblance to the burning sea-

scapes of Petoskey and Charlevoix and Escanaba, those
Lake Michigan cities where you spent the summers of
your youth. (Where are you now, Amelia!) You fling
yourself back in time, trying by an effort of the most
intense concentration to recapture those leaps of ecstasy common to early manhood, the raptures of illimit-
able hope, of a vista opened — that vista which you
yourself now, woefully, occupy. Thus you experience
for a fleeting moment that most haunting of all human
memories: the memory of expectation. In Charlevoix
was a restaurant with a ceiling of patterned tin panels,
stamped out by a drop-forge no less indelibly than the
ceiling itself is imprinted on your memory. (Where are
you now, Lucille!) Your cry pierces the twilight, star-
tling even yourself. You dart a glance over your shoulder to see whether you may have been overheard. Only
a boy and a girl, with a romping dog, distantly share
the scene with you. Storing up memories like yours of
Lake Michigan, perhaps . . .

You leap with astonishing agility across the three
rocks by which you ford the stream there, just where it
boils into the Sound and back out again, day after day,
as it has for hundreds of years. Pitching away your
cigar stub, you smile as another fancy comes to mind.
Dolly in her lean months, between jobs as an actress,
would sometimes take on ushering in the theatres.
Those working the steep heights of the upper balconies
were called Rocky Mountain goats. You remember her
telling you that on your first date, grinning also at the
memory of your "demanding satisfaction" of the
waiter.

You would probably have been dead by now in
another century, one in which you would long ago
have "called Spontini out," or he you. There are the

two of you, with your seconds, arriving to pace it off, pistol in hand, along the very stretch of beach across which you now strike out, phantom figures in the half-light of dawn. Two physicians standing ready with their black satchels, one Doc Pathfinder (even now perhaps discoursing on the yanked pitcher as symbolic scapegoat). Your women pacing in anguish elsewhere, wringing their hands as they wait for news — or the one woman being fought over.

The wind has died down, but you still have gas on your stomach.

You have leisure and occasion now to pursue those notions of Freudianity that prefaced the entanglements from which you have lately emerged, those that find us as much riven as ever in conflict between flesh and spirit, as the old order had it. Blodgett would be the "old Adam" of Christianity, or "old man" as the Apostle Paul kept terming it — and your own old man too, for that matter, tanning your hide when you cut catechism, back there in Chicago. "Knowing this, that our old man was crucified with him, that the body of sin might be done away, so that we should no longer be in bondage to sin." Romans six six. Then let's see. "That ye put away, as concerning your former manner of life, the old man, that waxeth corrupt after the deceits . . ." No, "after the lusts of deceit." Ephesians four twenty-two. And "lie not one to another, seeing that ye have put off the old man with his doings." Colossians three nine. Jesus Christ, you still know chapter and verse! That's just it. One liberates himself intellectually to find his morality in his very guts. Well, you've lived on the whole as decently as you have fully. You never missed a trick — but you never tricked a miss. We all seem to be coming out of this honorably in the end, though it has been a near thing. But think of the incomprehensible cellular components which, proliferating in the primordial beers, gave birth to Blodgett, then yourself. Going now through you to produce — what? God only knows and he isn't saying. (Note: one must apparently read Pierre Teilhard de Chardin on all this.)

He tramped along the stony sand, dreaming and musing, in the bracing cold, his course set toward the west where a golden moon sank slowly toward the horizon.

Ginger he had set free, to marry her good Doc Pathfinder (who pronounced Smackenfelt dead upon the field of honor). Salt of the earth, both of them, who deserved each other. "Did you hear what he just said? Did you hear what Doc said, everybody?" "No, what did he say? Tell us." General laughter when she does, Doc smirking into his hands. One sensed a lasting bond there, from the very beginning. Smackenfelt approved the match.

Birdie was marrying her Barton Domby, the ecologist, who, his own thesis finished, was, like her, teaching at a Western state university. Smackenfelt had just got an announcement. They had discovered what many young people intellectually opposed to the bourgeois institution of marriage, on the ground that it was basically materialistic in motivation, have discovered: that they could use the wedding booty to feather their nest with. Radically slimmed down herself now, Birdie elicited from Blodgett the comment that she was "the pertest and prettiest package ever to come down the pike" — which was typical of his elementary, and rather obvious, taste in alliteration.

Blodgett would remain to the end one of those people who tap the salt cellar with their finger when seasoning their food.

The house was still Smackenfelt's though precariously. He didn't see how he could go on meeting the mortgage payments very much longer, or why he should. He had a part in a rattletrap sex farce about a famous artist, hanging by its teeth downtown on a share of the season's middling business. *Nude Dressing* would close soon. The adaptation for Spontini had fallen through.

He had now reached a point on the waterside where a road running parallel to it curved out of sight along a high stone wall overgrown with ramblers. A car shot into view around that bend, slowing as it neared him. A blue station wagon he seemed to recognize. The driver parked alongside the road and sprang out. It was a young woman in a camel's hair coat with a long muffler of alternate red and white blocks flung over one shoulder, the other length dangling down her front. She seemed familiar too, the cute trick. A red-mittened hand waved at him in greeting was an aid to identification. Dolly was unmistakable, even at this distance in the fading light.

She climbed over a low wall and ran toward him, stumbling once over a rock and nearly turning an ankle. She laughed, her breath pluming the cold air.

"Who is this I see?"

"I'm the devil worshipper who's lost his faith. Remember? I now go to church, pitch in at benefit car washes, collect Tennessee Ernie Ford's records. By studying Revelations against population-growth projections, I have it doped out that the end of the world will come when the thirty-five years environmentalists

give us on this planet are used up. Simple. That's what
the Bible's been teaching. All right. Now. Distributing
my leaflets about this door to door as I trundle people's
waste paper away to the dump in the local drive, I
come to you, a landlady with eleven children all of
whom have left you to become ecologists. Thanks to
the likes of them we may yet attain zero population
growth. All right. You take me in, clasp me to your
evacuated bosom, and, making love as though we're an
endangered species —"

"What's the title of this one?"

"*Point of No Deposit No Return.* Now —"

"Speaking of all that, do you know how I knew I'd
find you here? Your Sunday constitutional. You're getting to be an old man. Sot in your ways."

"Yes. We become more creatures of habit with every
passing year. But I ran across a line in Pushkin the
other day that offers solace there. *Eugene Onegin*:

> *Habit is Heaven's own redress;*
> *It takes the place of happiness.*"

"God, you are in bad shape. Must you ossify like
this? I see you here quite often when I drive by."

"My father once sensed himself falling into a pattern, and do you know what he did? Made a point of
breaking one habit every day. Pick it up again later, of
course, we don't have that many to spare, but he'd do
one thing different every day. Adhered to it rigidly till
the day he died. That was what he called not getting
too sot in your ways. How are you, Dolly? You look
great. All lit up. More than just the winter in your
cheeks I mean. What is it?"

She declined to answer the question for the moment,

joining him in his tramp along the water's edge. They struck out toward a causeway, a jumble of quarry rocks that marked the border of the town's beach. It reminded him again of her Rocky Mountain goat days, over which they now shared a laugh — his first, he said, in fifty-six hours. They exchanged gossip, stooped to pick up an occasional stone to throw into the water. All at once she blurted her news.

"Zap and I are packing it in. It's he who's really left me, not that there's much point in a distinction. It's been brewing for some time, as you know. At least I stuck with him when I thought he needed me, but he didn't, really. He says he can't live with me any longer. Not me as me, but as a woman he suspects is always secretly laughing at him, the artist polished off by a cop."

"The one inside whom there was a critic struggling to get out? That cop?"

"Yes. I don't know how the story ever got out. None of us told. Maybe the police in general got wise to what happened. Anyway, it's now folklore around here. Not just something to dine out on. Poodle Slater blabbed it all around. It's too priceless, and all that sort of thing. Zap says he can't go to parties around here any more. All those straight faces are worse than outright laughs. So that's the way it is."

"I'm sorry."

"I was hoping you might be glad. I mean I'm free again, back where we were the night of the Great Disaster."

"I meant I was sorry for Zap. Being the butt of something like that. I'm glad about the other. Of course I want you back."

He said it quite simply, and quite simply they

stopped there and kissed. The embrace took some little doing, bundled as they were in thick impeding layers of clothing. They could hardly get their arms around each other. They broke apart, laughing at the spectacle they made.

"So . . . I mean do you believe in miracles?" Dolly asked, drawing back a little to search his face.

"Yes, Santa Claus, there is a Virginia." Then: "Does Zap have somebody else?"

"A girl in town. Nobody whose name he's going to put in lights or any of that. Somebody in his office. I know her."

"Is she good-looking?"

"Very. She looks like Henry Fonda."

They resumed their walk, though back in the direction they had come, the stony promontory having been reached as an objective. It was getting darker as the moon dipped lower; ready to sink from sight below the water that for the present it briefly illumined.

"At least you know what you're getting in me," he said, "because you've had it before. No illusions. I can never decide whether that's good or bad."

"A little of each, probably."

"Will you go on working?"

"Sure, commercials, for a while anyhow. I'm in demand elsewhere than in Zap's office by now, you know. Though the Swamp Tease is his. Or yours. That's at least one plus he got from you!"

"Maybe we can embark on a return voyage in better shape for having run aground once before. I think I've learned a lot from that shipwreck. A lot of the stormy weather is self-created. I mean we expect it. I'm not now talking about sex in our time. I'm talking about the sexes in our time. That stuff. We've been sold this bill of goods that there's a war going on between us, and, accepting it, we expect hostilities, and so partly produce them. Those self-fulfilling prophecies. But take my life. Running parallel to my troubles with you has been, as well, an obligato of troubles with Zap. A man. Do you understand what I'm driving at?"

"Yes, but explain it for the cheap seats."

"All right. *Who's Afraid of Virginia Woolf* sets down the pitched battle between husband and wife. But you've got to take *The Odd Couple* alongside that to get a balanced view. Which is one that cancels the whole point out. *People* get on each other's nerves, not just men and women. *Human beings* get in each other's hair at any close quarters, not just males and females." He spread his arms as at the simplicity of it.

She looked at him blankly. They had more or less slowed to a halt to facilitate the delivery of his thesis, and make possible her closer attention to it, so that they now faced one another again. She continued to stare at him.

"But that's what my mother has been chattering for years. It's one of her notions. She even babbles it to the cat!"

"It struck me all of a heap, a sort of Road-to-Damascus revelation." He paused to emphasize the point by tapping a gloved palm with a forefinger. "You can't pin on the sexual relations what isn't true of human relations in general. Ergo there is no sex war. It's all a myth. A bill of goods we've been sold. In a sense it's the moral of my life."

Dolly simply shook her head once, with a faint shrug, as they resumed their walk. Their pace quickened, for it was growing colder. He continued after a bit, striking a cautionary note he felt he owed her:

"You know what I am. I'm me. Spots on the leopard and all that."

"I've had practice being a good wife on more than just you, you know. I seem always to be shuttling among male egos. I've learned a lot about myself in the process too. I know I take some doing, for a man. But for my part, if I'm supposed to be answering your question — if it was a question — there are worse things to live with than a man who . . ."

Did he sense her bridling at a word? Might it be the word "ham"? Whatever the term at which she'd shied, a substitution was brought out after some moments of careful reconsideration.

"Well, a man who does tend to dramatize himself."

He nodded, frowning as he chewed his lip in thought. His face, when she turned to scrutinize it, suggested no question of rejecting the stricture, certainly of any resentment toward it. He merely seemed to be revolving her judgment. To reassure him, she added, rather playfully:

"It must be tough being Stew Smackenfelt."

"Yes." He sighed, and she knew that was only a preface to his response; what is called in the theatre a "handle," telegraphing to the audience that more is to come. She was on the waterside, and now averted her face toward the Sound, in case she should smile, while at the same time clutching his arm in both of her own. "Yes," he repeated, "and I sometimes wonder whether I'm right for the part."

She was a long time gazing out across the wintering sea.